Rock Island Public Library
401 - 19th Street
Rock Island, IL 61201-8143

FEB - - 2017

W9-ABQ-758

ROAD TO
PERDITION

DISCARD

ROAD TO PERDITION

A NOVEL BY MAX ALLAN COLLINS

BASED ON THE GRAPHIC NOVEL
WRITTEN BY MAX ALLAN COLLINS AND
ILLUSTRATED BY RICHARD PIERS RAYNER

SCREENPLAY BY DAVID SELF

DIRECTED BY SAM MENDES

The characters and events portrayed in this book are fictitious. Any similarity to real persons, living or dead, is coincidental and not intended by the author.

©2016 DW Studios, LLC.
All rights reserved.

No part of this book may be reproduced, or stored in a retrieval system, or transmitted in any form or by any means, electronic, mechanical, photocopying, recording, or otherwise, without express written permission of the publisher.

ISBN: 1941298966
ISBN 13: 9781941298961

Published by Brash Books, LLC
12120 State Line #253,
Leawood, Kansas 66209

www.brash-books.com

Also By Max Allan Collins from Brash Books

The Perdition Saga
Road to Purgatory
Road to Paradise

Black Hats
Red Sky in Morning

AUTHOR'S NOTE

This is the full-length version of my 2002 novelization of the film *Road to Perdition*, the script for which was based on my graphic novel. It was originally published in much shorter form (under protest from me), including only material directly from the film; this version draws equally upon the graphic novel.

It's long been my wish to see the complete novel published, and Brash Books—with a nod of thanks to Steven Spielberg—has made that possible.

As my two prose sequels, *Road to Purgatory* (2004) and *Road to Paradise* (2005), are also being reprinted by Brash Books, I have made certain cosmetic changes for the sake of consistency: the film's "Michael Sullivan" is once again the graphic novel's "Michael O'Sullivan"; and "John Rooney" reverts to the historically accurate "John Looney."

Two major plot points, however, remain as changed for the film, though my two sequels reflect the graphic novel's "real" version. Not wanting to tamper with what I originally wrote here— which satisfied me then and now—no major rewriting has been done.

M.A.C.
February 2016

For Richard and Dean Zanuck—
another father and son
who shared the road

"You must choose a road for yourself."
Kazuo Koike

ONE

This Angel of Death you've heard so much about was my father, Michael O'Sullivan, born in Ireland in 1887.

The family nearly lost its "O" at Ellis Island, but my grandfather insisted it stay, and the family of three stayed too, right there in New York. For a time my grandfather toiled in a railroad switch yard, until the promise of better work drew the O'Sullivans to Rock Island, Illinois, with its John Deere and Harvester plants, and government arsenal, where guns and tanks were manufactured.

Immigrants in America—whether Irish or Italian or Jewish— quickly learned that local government ignored them; the only real government was what the Black Hand-type gangs provided. Little criminal kingdoms—subgovernments—grew up in cities all around America, thriving further with the onset of Prohibition. The Tri-Cities—Rock Island and Moline, on the Illinois banks of the Mississippi River, Davenport over on the Iowa side—were no exception. And the ruler of the Tri-Cities was John Looney.

The Irish Looneys had an unlikely but nonetheless abiding affiliation with the powerful Italian/Sicilian Capone gang in Chicago. John Looney himself was a self-trained lawyer, and considered by most micks in the Cities to be a benign presence, a benevolent despot. He and his son, Connor—a glorified chauffeur for his father, and widely considered a pale, rather unstable shadow of the old man—had the politicians and police in their pocket.

John Looney controlled everything in the Cities—brothels, bootlegging, gambling; but the most outrageous of Looney's enterprises undoubtedly was his newspaper—the Rock Island News,

1

which boasted of being the area's only publication brave enough to print "all the facts." In reality the News was strictly a shakedown operation.

Headlines would scream scandal at the rare politician who wouldn't play ball—MAYOR SCHRIVER IN SANITARIUM FOR SYPHILIS TREATMENT—and typical front pages would announce "Acts of Shame Dishonor Prominent Citizens and Elected Officials," and LOCAL BANKER SEEN WITH PROSTITUTE. In some cases these were adversaries and even enemies Looney was settling scores with; but mostly such tactics were bald-faced blackmail.

A victim would be approached with a scandalous story— sometimes containing a germ of truth, more often not—and be given the opportunity to pay for said story to disappear. Farmers from the surrounding rural area made easy targets: one of Looney's prostitutes would throw her arms around some poor bumpkin and a photographer would just happen to be there to capture the moment for posterity...unless, of course, the rube chose to pay the price.

In retrospect, it's hard to picture my father being any part of such sleazy underhanded racketeering. Michael O'Sullivan, Sr., was what they used to call a family man—quiet, dependable, honorable; he didn't drink to excess, he didn't whore around. Maybe you think he did those things and just didn't tell me, or hid such acts from me—but I know he didn't, just as I know with soul-deep certainty that he loved my mother...his Annie.

Yet, there was indeed another, darker side to my father. Though he never spoke of it to us, he was a proud veteran of the Great War. After all those years, he had returned to Europe, where he had learned to use a gun to kill other men, a sin in God's eyes that Uncle Sam saw fit to reward him for, sending my father home with decorations for bravery...and a terrible new skill.

And so Michael O'Sullivan went to work for John Looney, and served him well, still a loyal soldier.

Whatever bad things the Looneys were involved in, the micks of the Tri-Cities knew only that—despite Hard Times—Old Man Looney got jobs for our people, at his newspapers, his restaurants, and, using his publication for blackmail leverage, at the factories and even the government arsenal. Of course for my father, and many of his peers, John Looney was the government.

I never knew exactly what Papa did for the Looneys. What I did know was that we lived in the nicest house in town (except for Mr. Looney's) and that John Looney treated my father like a second son, and my younger brother Peter and me like cherished grandkids. We loved Mr. Looney—though we sensed our mother did not share that affection—and knew only that Papa did something dangerous for him...something involving a gun. Like Tom Mix, or the Lone Ranger.

Usually that gun was a Colt .45 automatic. We had seen him with that weapon, Peter and I, on many occasions—spying on him with pride and wonder as our father slipped the pistol into a leather holster under his coat, tucked under his shoulder. Once, however, we saw Papa with an even more formidable firearm, and the sight had fueled our kid conversations deep into the night.

On that one occasion, we had spied him with his shiny black case; this hard-shell valise-type affair we had seen many times, but only once did our wide eyes observe its contents; only once did we (unseen by Papa) observe that case actually being opened.

The shiny black case might have protected a musical instrument—a horn, say, or a violin; however, the parts broken down within, in their plush little compartments, were those of a Thompson submachine gun. These pieces my father could assemble quickly, efficiently, into a single frightful unit; and last would come the drum-like canister of ammunition, which he snapped onto the assembled weapon, closing the lid, flicking the latches until the shiny black case seemed harmless again.

Funny. When I look back now at those days and nights, after all these years, I can see little Michael O'Sullivan, Jr., and it's from a distance wider than time—as if I were no longer that eleven-year-old boy who, for six weeks in the winter of 1931, went on the road with the killer called the Angel of Death.

As his accomplice.

On his bike, peddling furiously, Michael O'Sullivan, Jr.—hands warmly mittened, face obscured by a long woolen scarf, a satchel of newspapers slung over his shoulder—crested a hill and flew down a street whose gray cement was a solitary ribbon in a vast landscape of snowy white. Leaving the residential area behind, he was soon speeding along an endless stretch of closed factories—even Mr. Looney's beneficence could not entirely wipe out this Depression—summoned by the whistle of one of the few remaining, thriving industries.

Before long Michael—a slender pale kid with a thatch of brown hair, small for his age—was standing out in front of the gates of the John Deere plant, whose smokestacks billowed black, as workers poured out to hear the paperboy's cry: *"Man dies in factory accident! Man dies!"*

The Deere factory was not one of the boy's usual corners to peddle his papers, but Mr. McGowan at Rock Island Drugs & Sundries—where Michael picked up his daily supply of the *Rock Island News*—had recommended he go there. White-haired bespectacled Mr. McGowan—the proprietor of the drugstore (though of course Mr. Looney owned it)—had said the working men at the plant would find this story of particular interest.

"People like to read about their own kind dyin'," Mr. McGowan said, with the same twinkle in his eye that accompanied his serving up an ice-cream soda.

And the toil-haggard men outside John Deere did in fact reach into their pockets for nickels and dimes to read the story of how Danny McGovern had fallen into the machinery at Mr. Looney's soft-drink bottling plant.

UNAVOIDABLE ACCIDENT A TRAGEDY, a smaller headline said; and Michael had glimpsed in the write-up how Mr. Looney was generously bequeathing the dead man's family a full two year's salary, though "nothing but the goodness of John Looney's heart required it." The family couldn't afford a funeral home, so Mr. Looney ("the embodiment of generosity") was providing his own mansion for the wake.

But the eleven-year-old boy was wise enough in the ways of the local press to know that the *Rock Island Argus*, Looney's chief competition in the newspaper business, would present this story in an entirely different light. The *Argus* called Mr. Looney "a gangster," among other equally unflattering things, and the editorials in the two papers were like the salvos of opposing battleships.

In under ten minutes, Michael had made a real haul, and he was grinning—despite the bitter cold—when he hopped back on his bike, pockets jingling with change. He pulled on his mittens, threw the scarf over his face, and streaked out of the industrial area to the *klik-klik-klik* of the baseball card clothespinned to his bike's back wheel, the card playing the spokes like a brittle harp. He peddled past the Harvester plant (not enough papers left to bother with, darn it!), gliding by one of the soup kitchens where Mr. Looney saw to it that hungry out-of-work men at least got something warm to eat, then ducked down an alleyway between two huge warehouses, the chimneys of industry receding behind him.

Before long he was sailing past St. Peter's Church, its ominous gothic shape and spires looming behind the iron fence; then he cycled straight down the middle of Main Street's two lanes, drivers frowning and even cursing at him as, going in either direction, they narrowly missed the boy. This dangerous game of auto tag Michael had played for as long as he'd been hawking papers; he liked the exhilarating feeling it gave him.

Some of the stores were boarded up, even on Main Street—often he had heard his father tell his mother, "We are lucky to have it so soft in such hard times"—but not the drugstore...or any of Mr. Looney's shops or restaurants, for that matter.

Michael parked his bike out front, and sauntered in, dropping his newspaper bag on the counter. Mr. McGowan acknowledged the boy with a nod but immediately began counting out the few remaining papers. Unwrapping his scarf, Michael dug into his pocket for the change and deposited the coins on the counter, where they danced and rang. White face exposed, the boy drank in the scents of penny candy and pulp paper and tobacco—what a wonderful place a drugstore was.

The druggist quickly counted the coins, then glanced up, an unruly eyebrow raised, signaling to Michael that the books were not balanced. And, with a sigh, the boy again dug into his pocket, found the missing nickel and slammed it onto the counter.

With a humorless smile, Mr. McGowan nodded, and returned to his calculating. While the druggist was counting out the meager coinage that would be the boy's commission, Michael surreptitiously—so careful even the faces on advertising signs posed around wouldn't see him—sneaked a pouch of Bugler Tobacco from the shelf below and up under his coat, into the waistband of his trousers.

Pocket jingling with the nickels he'd earned (as opposed to pilfered), Michael strode out of the drugstore, onto the sidewalk, where he wheeled his bike around the corner into an alleyway. Ripping open the pouch of tobacco, he removed the baseball card from its paper wrapper—Rogers Hornsby of the Cubs—and bent down, affixing the card to the back wheel.

Then, glancing around, he withdrew from a coat pocket a battered-looking brown briar pipe with a bit of a Sherlock Holmes shape to it, a smoking instrument that his father had thrown out a few weeks ago. Michael filled the bowl with tobacco, tamped it down, and fished a book of matches from another pocket, lighting up like an old pro.

Two cards clicking at his rear spokes now, puffing the pipe as if that were powering him, Michael cycled out of the downtown, into the nearby residential district, flush with that satisfying feeling known only by a kid who is putting one over on the grownups of the world.

When he finally coasted into the long, tree-lined driveway of the two-story stucco structure that was the O'Sullivan home, Michael grew suddenly cautious. He should put the pipe away, he knew, before getting in range of the windows of the large house, set against an idyllic background of the snowy woods. If his father saw the boy puffing away, Papa would just kill him...

As Michael slowed, contemplating that, an assassin took advantage of this momentary caution on the boy's part, and a projectile hurled with deadly precision knocked Michael off-balance—and off his bike, onto a pile of white, the glowing pipe flying, dying a sizzling death in a snowbank.

Stepping from behind a tree, in mittens and snowsuit, Peter O'Sullivan, age 10, also small for his age, laughed mercilessly, delighted that his snowball had done such a spectacular job of it.

But Michael had survived many such onslaughts, and was already fashioning a snowball of his own, so deftly, so quickly, that Peter had no time to run: he was doomed to take Michael's shot in the forehead. The younger boy pitched into the snow and rolled to a stunned stop, staring upward, breath pluming.

Michael too was on his back, also "dead"—the smoke of his breath outdoing the dying embers of the pipe.

Neither boy noticed the woman in the kitchen window, their mother, Annie O'Sullivan, smiling. From this distance, she had not discerned the pipe—or else her smile might have curved into a smirk—and knew only that these daily attacks by the younger boy against his big brother represented affection.

Annie—approaching forty, a petite, quietly pretty peaches-and-cream-complected woman in a quietly pretty blue house-dress—was pleased that the two boys got along so famously. Often brothers could be rivals, even adversaries, and since her husband seemed to favor the youngest boy (who had almost died in childbirth), young Michael might easily have resented Peter.

Right now the rumble of her husband's Ford sedan was making minor thunder, announcing the imminent arrival of the head of the house. What was Michael, Jr., doing out there? Making a snow angel?

In fact, the boy—still sprawled in mock death—was trying with his foot to bury the pipe in the snow, hiding it (he hoped) from his father, whose face turned rather blankly to the two boys as the big dark green Ford headed toward the freestanding garage at the end of the long driveway.

Peter, of course, chased after his father. Michael just watched. If he were to tag after his younger brother, all that would happen was that Papa would ruffle the younger boy's hair and smile at him and maybe, maybe if Michael was lucky, he'd get a nod. That he could live without.

In the kitchen, before the table had been set for supper, while their mother was still at the stove, Michael and Peter sat together and did their homework.

Michael envied his brother, who was something of a whiz at school; right now the kid was writing in his notebook like the pencil was doing its own thinking. Criminey, how did he do that? Michael, on the other hand, was slogging through his math problems like he was trying to run in a snowdrift.

The older boy sensed his mother beside him—the fresh-scrubbed smell of her—and when he turned she was at his shoulder, smiling at him like the Madonna, whispering, "Don't worry—I'll help you with it later."

He grinned at her and she touched his cheek, then lifted away, saying, "Peter, clear these school books and help me set the table...Michael, fetch your father. Tell him supper's ready."

The house was pale plaster, greens and yellows, against dark woodwork; his footsteps echoed off the hardwood floors. Not exactly a rich person's house, but Michael knew he lived better than any of his friends. He loved the smooth feel of the banister as he ran up the stairs, palm gliding over sculpted wood.

On the second floor, at the end of the hallway, the half-open door of his parents' bedroom gave Michael a view of his father at the mirrored dresser. Even without Mama's summons, Papa was preparing for dinner—removing his cufflinks and placing them in a small carved wooden box with other personal items; taking off his striped necktie and turning to lay it on the bed as if placing a baby in its cradle; finally slipping out of his jacket, revealing the dark leather holster and the weapon under his arm.

The boy didn't know it, but this was a Colt .45, army issue, a weapon that his father—Michael O'Sullivan, Sr.—had brought home from the Great War.

Gun—holster and all—was soon on the bed as well, and it wasn't until O'Sullivan was removing his vest that he sensed his son, and flipped the vest on top of the weapon, concealing it.

Without looking at the boy, O'Sullivan said, "Michael, have you seen that pipe I threw out?"

Michael, startled, had already hopped back a foot at the first sound of his father's voice. "No! No, sir."

"Perhaps you didn't hear me. I said, have you seen the pipe I threw out, Michael?"

"...Yes, sir."

"Did I see you with it? Smoking it?"

"No, sir."

Silence throbbed in the big house, the tick of the grandfather clock downstairs deafening; Michael felt like a bug, out in the hallway, hoping his father wouldn't step on him and squash him.

His father's voice, from within the bedroom, did not rise in volume as he asked again: "Did I see you with that pipe?"

"Yes, sir...Dinner's ready."

"Thank you."

The boy scrambled away, down the hallway.

And in the bedroom, Michael O'Sullivan, Sr.—a tall, muscular man, pale, blue-eyed, with dark hair and regular features touched by a pencil-line mustache—looked at his own reflection. The man in the mirror—or was it three men, in the three panes of glass?—seemed to know that the boy required punishment; but the father did not like administering punishment...not to his son.

At the kitchen table, in a scene typically formal for this little family, the boys sat silent and scrubbed, Papa in his white shirt, Mama in her blue dress.

Michael was wondering why his father hadn't said anything about the pipe yet; he hoped nothing would be said to his mother about it...

"Michael," Papa said.

Just the faintest edge in his father's voice.

Michael looked up sharply, and with his eyes begged his father for mercy.

"Will you say grace, please?"

Smiling, relieved, the boy bowed his head, folded his hands, and said, "Bless-us-oh-lord-for-these-thy-gifts-which-we-are-about-to-receive-through-the-bounty-of-our-Lord-Jesus-Christ-amen."

They all said "Amen," and as Mama began passing the food around, Papa said, "Michael, next time..."

Alarmed, Michael looked up.

"...next time, speak more slowly. There is meaning to those words—it's not 'giftswhich,' like a sandwich."

Peter giggled, and Mama smiled.

Father continued. "And His name is Jesus Christ—not Jesus Christ Amen."

"Yes, sir."

And they began to eat.

Later, the boys were listening to the *Lone Ranger* on the radio in the parlor, and their parents were washing dishes in the kitchen—actually, Annie was washing, O'Sullivan drying.

"You're a little hard on Michael," she said, her brogue-touched lilt softening the words.

"I worry about him."

"Do you?"

"He's a little too much like me."

She laughed. "Well, Peter's not the baby anymore. They're both growing up into young men. They both need a father's affection."

"And they have it." O'Sullivan had not revealed to his wife the pipe-smoking transgression of her oldest son.

"Ouch!" she said.

"What is it?"

"Cut myself..." She'd been washing cutlery, a carving knife.

O'Sullivan ran cold water and put her finger under it. Then he examined the wound, carefully.

"It's not deep," he said, fetching a scrap of cloth and wrapping it around her finger. He gazed into her china-blue eyes and kissed her hand, in a courtly manner, a knight and his maiden.

"All better?"

"The best," she said, and nodded, and smiled.

They returned to their dishes, while in the living room, the parlor echoed with the radio's gunfire.

TWO

John Looney's mansion was on 20th Street in the area known in those days as the Longview Loop—so-called because this bluff area had been made accessible by, first, horse-drawn trolleys and, later, electric streetcars. This was Rock Island's Knob Hill—doctors, lawyers, and old money. Looney must have been considered an outsider, where some of these high-society types were concerned, though I certainly wasn't aware of it.

My brother and I went to a private Catholic school—the Villa de Chantal—not far from the Looney mansion. My legs start to ache when I think of peddling my bike up that hill—and back then the streets were brick. At 16th Avenue and 20th Street stood the building where carriers would pick up their copies of Looney's Rock Island News—Looney's Roost, we called it. Several locations around town, including Looney's drugstore, were sort of substations.

Wealthy though he was, Mr. Looney was a man of the people— a Catholic. Most of Rock Island's wealthy Irish were Orangemen, Protestants, while most Irish Catholics were laborers, skilled and unskilled. My father was working-class poor and had grown up in the area known as Greenbush. He'd been in a gang in that rough part of town, though thanks to Sacred Heart Church there had also been a baseball team and other more wholesome recreational activities.

Still, looking back, I can see that my father—when he was my age—must have been a young roughneck. And when Mr. Looney took my father under his wing, he gave our family a life my real grandparents could never have provided.

The next afternoon, a Saturday, the overcast sky suggested the imminent arrival of an overanxious night. Young Michael could think of better ways to spend any part of a Saturday than at a funeral; but he knew not to object—particularly since Papa had said nothing more about the infamous briar pipe...and had obviously not shared his son's dire misdeed with Mama.

Papa had gone out to pull the car around close to the house and get the engine going, to provide his family with a warm car on this cold day. And Michael was the first to join his father, scrambling into the backseat. Papa's eyes probed him in the rearview mirror.

"Michael," his father said.

"Yes, sir?"

"This is a solemn occasion. I don't want to see those dice... all right?"

"Yes, sir. No, sir."

"I don't care if your godfather instigates it. No gambling."

Papa meant Mr. Looney.

"Yes, sir," the boy said, nodding. "Because it's a funeral."

"It's a wake—that's a little different. But I don't want gambling because gambling is wrong."

"How is a wake different from a funeral, Papa?"

"It's a kind of...celebration."

"Why would anybody celebrate someone dying?"

His father's eyes in the rearview mirror grew thoughtful. Then he said, "It's a celebration of the dead person's life—a sort of a send-off."

"An 'old country' thing, right?"

"Right."

Soon Papa was driving, Mama next to him, Michael and Peter in back, everyone in their church-going finery. The boys, like their father, wore suits with ties and vests. Papa was all in black, even his tie, and Mama's navy-blue dress was so dark it too was almost black.

"Papa?" Peter said.

"Yes," Papa said, his eyes on the road.

"Did you know the man who died?"

"Not very well."

"…How did he die?"

"An accident."

"In a car?"

"At work."

This was no surprise to Michael; he knew this was the dead man in the headlines yesterday, whose family Mr. Looney was helping out by holding the wake at his mansion.

But Michael was also aware that the paper he sold—the Looney-owned *News*—was often at odds with the *Argus* and other papers in the Cities. Who was telling the truth? Papa would know…

"What happened to the man, Papa?" Michael asked.

His father's eyes went from the road back to the rearview mirror. "He choked to death smoking a pipe."

Michael almost laughed, Peter, too, but then both stifled it, as his mother glanced first at Papa, then at her eldest son, with her brow knit in curiosity. The boy felt lucky, at that moment, that his mother so seldom asked his father what he meant by the sometimes puzzling things he said.

Though Mr. Looney was their godfather, the boys had seldom been to the mansion. They would see their surrogate grandfather at their own home (when he came by to see Papa), or one of his restaurants (he liked to buy them pancake breakfasts), or Water Tower Park (with its carnival-type rides) for Looney employee picnics. Michael had even been to the newspaper offices, and had been given a tour of the printing facility by Mr. Looney himself.

For the first time, however, as their automobile rolled up the winding driveway, Michael viewed the Looney mansion as not just impressive, but ominous. Probably the dark sky, and the funereal occasion, were giving him this impression, the boy knew...but the massive castle-like structure, with its sand-color brick and reddish tile roof and fat formidable twin towers bookending the main building, loomed like a gothic haunted house. Maybe it was the vaguely Arabic archways mixed in with the otherwise medieval look of the place. Whatever the case, Michael shuddered, a chill running through him that had nothing to do with winter.

Out in front of the mansion were a number of cars and, oddly, several trucks. Mourners of every social station—rich and poor alike bedecked in their finest apparel—were trooping up into the house with the weary inevitability of the occasion.

Mama was carrying a covered dish, the crock containing a corned beef casserole that was something of a specialty of hers. The boys had taken the lead, heading up the cement steps to the landing where massive doors waited. Michael's younger brother was limping.

"What's wrong with Peter?" Annie asked her husband. "He doesn't need new shoes, does he?"

"He might," O'Sullivan said. But he was eyeing his sons suspiciously.

The boys waited on the stoop until their father opened the door for them; their mother, crock in hand, went in first, followed by Peter and Michael, then Papa, filing into a long wide hallway that set the tone for the mansion. They had entered into a high-ceilinged world of walnut paneling and mahogany trim, of parquet floors and oriental rugs, Tiffany lamps and velvet upholstery, ornate mirrors and shimmering chandeliers.

Despite the Sunday finery, it was clear even to an eleven-year-old like Michael that many of the mourners in this entryway contrasted sharply with the lavish surroundings. These were grizzled working men and their careworn wives and their scruffy children, sometimes grandparents, too, ancient-looking with sunken eyes and wrinkled-paper skin and Sunday clothing that dated to the turn of the century.

Hat in hand, their father was guiding them through this chattering, sometimes laughing throng, toward a sitting room.

Peter whispered to his mother: "If the man died, why are they laughing?"

"It's better to be happy than sad," she said, "because the man is with God now."

"But there's nothing wrong with respectful silence," their father put in, his eyes tight in an otherwise blank face.

In the sitting room, a respectful silence, even an anguished one, was indeed on hand, draping the proceedings like a shroud. Relatives and friends were gathered here, seated on all sides. A parlor to the left, its doors folded open wide, served as the visitation area, elaborate flower arrangements surrounding the open coffin, which rested on a bed of ice, buckets catching dripping water.

Michael was wondering what the ice was for when his father leaned over to him and said, "Preserves the body."

"Oh," the boy said.

He and his father were walking in lockstep toward the coffin, but his brother Peter and Mama lagged behind.

Wide-eyed, horrified Peter came to a stop and tugged his mother's sleeve. She looked down at him as he said softly, "I don't want to go up there."

"It's all right, honey," she said gently. "Come on…"

But Peter held his ground, and Mama gave in. They stood just inside the room as Michael and his father went to the coffin and knelt before it and prayed.

Michael was still praying when he peeked over the casket rim at the body. The dead man looked strange: his skin was waxy, pale as spilt milk, his lips and cheeks touched with clownish red; and weirdest yet, pennies covered the corpse's eyes.

Sneaking a sideways glance, Michael saw his father was still praying—something intense in his face.

"Amen," O'Sullivan said, finally.

Then the father noticed his son staring at him and said, "The pennies?"

The boy nodded.

"He has to pay the toll to get into heaven."

They got to their feet, and turned away from the casket. Michael, still mulling that over, asked, "Does that work?"

"I don't know. What do you say we light a candle for him at St. Pete's, just to make sure?"

The boy nodded again.

That was when a husky, unmistakable brogue-touched voice boomed through the room: "Who's got a hug for a lonely old man?"

The attention of all four O'Sullivans flew to the commanding presence standing just inside the room, in vest and shirtsleeves, his arms thrust wide: John Looney.

The two boys ran to their substitute grandfather, filling his outstretched arms.

Annie O'Sullivan watched, fighting feelings of contempt for the man who had done so much for them. The lanky, almost tall, white-haired, white-mustached paterfamilias had been a rakishly handsome young man—Looney had harbored theatrical ambitions prior to politics and law (and crime)—and even now, in his seventies, his powder-blue eyes, Apache cheekbones and strong chin gave him the sort of distinctive good looks many a lady (not Annie) still sighed over.

But of late Annie noted a certain shambling gait, and a wearied, even haunted expression, that indicated John Looney might feel some small burden, anyway, carrying so many sins on his shoulders. She sometimes felt a hypocrite, knowing she and her family thrived thanks to this devious devil; and she tried not to think of what deeds her husband might be carrying out for the godfather of their sons.

She seldom raised the issue with her husband, who would say, "We don't question how Mr. Looney makes his money. It's not our place. We won't speak of it."

And the boys did so love this old man.

Looney was playing a game with them that was almost a ritual by now. "Now which is which?" he said, gazing down at the boys, a pointing finger traveling from Michael to Peter and from Peter to Michael.

Peter began, "I'm—"

"Don't help me!" A fingertip touched one nose. "Michael…" And then another nose. "…and Peter."

The boys groaned and laughed at this purposeful misidentification.

An arm around either boy, Mr. Looney looked across the room where Papa and Mama stood side by side now, the casket just behind them.

"Annie," he said quietly, with a nod, "Mike…Thank you for coming. You brighten a dark day."

Papa twitched a small smile, shrugged a little.

Mr. Looney's eyes widened and his head went back. "Is that heaven I smell?"

Michael didn't smell heaven, not in this room, but Mr. Looney apparently referred to his mother's fabled casserole dish.

She smiled awkwardly by way of response, and then, turning to Papa, said, "I should take this out to the kitchen. If you'll excuse me…?"

Mr. Looney gestured with an open hand. "Only if you'll promise me a dance, later."

She smiled again, just as awkwardly, and that might have been a nod; then she eased away from Papa, through a side door into the kitchen.

Mr. Looney looked down in mock confusion at the boys. "Who *is* that woman?"

Michael and Peter giggled at this jest; their father didn't—his eyes were going past them, to the mourners in the sitting room.

Mr. Looney knelt. To Michael he whispered, "Did you bring the necessary equipment?"

Michael nodded, but eager Peter said, "Yes!"

Mr. Looney stood, still with his arms around his godsons, and said to Papa, "I have urgent business with these gentlemen. Please excuse us."

O'Sullivan watched as Looney led the boys away, in a conspiratorial huddle, and knew exactly what they were up to, and could only smile about it. A little.

Moving into the sitting room, various mourners and Looney minions nodding to him respectfully, O'Sullivan made his way to a table piled with food and drink—appetizers, sandwiches, punch, hard liquor. He helped himself to a glass of whiskey: he needed it.

When he raised the glass for a sip, O'Sullivan noticed brawny Fin McGovern, in his best suit, standing nearby—a bottle of bourbon in one hand, like a Molotov cocktail he was about to throw.

McGovern—in his forties, the oldest of the brothers who had just lost their youngest, Daniel, the man in the casket—seemed to be studying O'Sullivan. His eyes might have glared had they not been slightly bleary.

"Fin," O'Sullivan said with a nod, and a toast-like gesture of the whiskey glass. "My condolences. Danny was a good boy."

McGovern's unblinking gaze held on O'Sullivan for several long moments; then the dead man's brother said, "I'm sure that would warm the cockles of his heart."

And with a disgusted grunt that was almost a laugh, McGovern strode away.

O'Sullivan watched him go, hoping he'd just experienced the worst of it, convinced that was just the beginning.

In the basement of the mansion, O'Sullivan's youngest son had removed a shoe, tilting it to allow a pair of dice to roll from the toe into the heel. The boy plucked out the dice and passed them to Mr. Looney, who said solemnly to his godsons, "Gentlemen—let's play craps."

Michael watched with delight as the old man shook the dice in his cupped hands, then shook them some more; the old man kissed his clasped hands, tossed the dice in the air, caught them deftly, before lifting his left leg and firing them at the far cement wall, from which the dice bounced and rolled to a stop to the tune of the boys' laughter.

Mr. Looney had a grace to him, and a sense of fun, that gave Michael a warm glow.

His mother upstairs, however, was feeling a chill. When she had entered the spacious, up-to-date kitchen, filled with wives busy preparing the evening's buffet, the room was alive with feminine chitter-chatter. But upon her greeting ("Hello, Rose... how are you, Helen?"), all bantering had come to a halt.

Feeling like a leper but not knowing why, Annie looked for a place to set down her covered dish. The chattering did not resume—the silence quickly became oppressive.

She found a place for her casserole on one of the tables, several of which were already laid out with scores of dishes, and went to a counter, helping herself to a cup of coffee. Gradually conversations resumed, none involving Annie, as the women drank coffee and/or liquor, smoking, relaxing, sampling one another's cooking.

Annie found a chair at a table, and though the others were all around her, she sat alone, with her cup of coffee.

Finally heavy-set Mrs. Begley (her husband worked in Looney's soda-pop bottling plant) settled herself down in a chair next to Annie. Dirty looks flew their way, but Mrs. Begley—who'd always been friendly to Annie—seemed to pay no heed.

"You look like you could use a little company," Mrs. Begley said, some Irish musicality in her voice.

"It's nice to see a friendly face," Annie said softly.

"What do you mean, dear?"

She leaned forward, whispered. "When I walked in here, everybody looked daggers at me."

Mrs. Begley smiled and shrugged. "Oh, well, this has been such a shock, dear. Times like this, everyone's under a terrible strain. Nerves ajangle."

"I suppose."

"You probably came in, all somber and respectful, them babbling like magpies—you just embarrassed them."

"Oh. I see. I'm sure you're right...I feel foolish, now..."

The heavy-set woman raised a gesturing finger; the volume of her brogue-inflected voice heightened a notch. "And I want you to know, Annie O'Sullivan, I myself have said to more than one person, I think it's a brave and honorable thing, you coming to pay your respects like this."

Annie frowned. "What do you mean?"

Another shrug. "Well, dear, frankly—Danny McGovern's wake? Even I didn't think you'd have the nerve to show your face."

And Mrs. Begley's smile froze into something that wasn't a smile at all; then the woman rose and left Annie alone again.

Confused yet embarrassed, Annie got up and left the kitchen, aware suddenly that this wake had implications that went beyond what little her husband had told her.

In the basement, the boys were doing much better than their mother. Mr. Looney sat on the floor, his back to the wall, apparently devastated, mopping his brow with a handkerchief. He'd been wiped out by the boys of an astonishing sum: one dollar.

"The chief of police is upstairs, you know," Mr. Looney said. "There are laws against highway robbery!"

"We won fair and square," Peter said, hands on his hips.

"I know hustlers when I see 'em," the old man growled.

"No hustle, old-timer!" Michael said gleefully.

"Pay up!" Peter said.

Mr. Looney held out his hands and the boys each took one, to help him up, but their godfather was the one hustling: he pulled them down to him, drawing them close, arms around them as he kissed their foreheads. The boys hugged the old man back.

"Michael," Mr. Looney said. "Fetch your dollar—jacket pocket in my study—before I come to my senses and call the cops."

Michael got up, headed toward the stairs, then turned and said, "When I'm gone, don't go gypping my kid brother!"

The old man's eyes flared with mock indignation. "That's slander!"

"You'll have me to answer to, you sidewinder!" Michael enjoyed using the word he'd heard the Lone Ranger use on the radio.

Mr. Looney called out after him. "I'm quakin' in me boots!"

Michael ran up the steps and then wove through the throng of mourners and took the big winding stairway up to the second floor, where most of the lights were out. Though night had not yet fallen, the overcast day added to the general gloominess of the big house with its dark woodwork and Victorian furnishings, and the boy's giddy mood shifted straightaway into apprehension.

This uneasy frame of mind was heightened when, as he started down the second-floor hallway, a man and woman emerged from a bedroom, kissing each other. The boy knew they were drunk—what his mother called "tipsy." In their twenties, the man wore a nice dark suit that was strangely rumpled, the woman in a thin, almost flapperish dress; they didn't seem to know they were at a sad occasion.

Ducking into a doorway, watching as if this were a car accident, Michael couldn't believe his father would have found appropriate, even for the "celebration" of a wake, this kind of behavior: the man was pressing the woman against the wall, fondling her, touching her in all sorts of places. The couple's expression of affection—blatantly sexual—was beyond the boy, and certainly bore no resemblance to the kind of affection he'd observed between his parents.

When the couple stopped their smooching, and laughingly, unsteadily passed by his hiding place, they didn't see him, and Michael was relieved. He felt odd—vaguely dirty, as if he were the one who'd done something wrong.

Mr. Looney's study was at the end of the corridor—Michael had sat with his godfather in the book-lined room several times (they'd even played craps up there before). So he knew his way and went in, but the darkness of the room—the curtains were drawn—and the smell of cigar smoke turned his uneasiness to fear.

On the leather couch to one side of the chamber, Connor Looney had stretched out, in his vest and shirtsleeves, a glass of dark liquid balanced on his stomach; he was smoking a cigar and the scent of it hung in the air, rich, masculine, nasty. Lanky, hooded-eyed Connor was in his thirties, a dark-blond handsome fellow who resembled his late mother.

Connor looked right at Michael, his face blank in that way Papa sometimes had. "Hiya, kid."

"Hello."

"Come on in—shut the door. Light hurts my eyes."

Michael let the door close behind him. He and his godfather's only son were alone, Connor's cigar glowing orange in the darkness.

"Which little O'Sullivan are you? Remind me."

"Michael, sir."

"'Sir?'" Glass of dark liquid in hand now, Connor leaned up on his elbow and his grin looked weird. "You don't have to call me 'sir.' I'm not your old man."

Michael, wondering what Connor was doing off alone with the house full of guests, said, "No, Mr. Looney."

"Call me Connor. Hell, make it Uncle Connor. After all, doesn't my old man treat you like grandkids?...since he doesn't have any of his own. Suppose that's my fucking fault."

Michael said nothing, alarmed at hearing this legendary swear word (the only other time he'd heard it, a schoolyard bully had been expelled for its utterance). Feeling very nervous, he eyed his godfather's jacket, slung over the back of the desk chair.

"You want something, kid?"

"No, Uncle Connor."

With a shrug, Connor looked away from the boy, stretching back out, resting the drink on his stomach again, puffing the cigar, making smoke rings, whose floating ascent and ultimate demise he studied with those weird half-shut eyes of his.

Michael looked at the jacket over the back of the chair, where the dollar his godfather owed him awaited; but it seemed miles away, and he was scared. Connor Looney frightened him and he wanted to get out of there, right now.

So he did.

THREE

John Looney's mansion provided an unrivaled view of the Mississippi River Valley, including the mansions below his on the bluff, which of course allowed him to look down on high society. In those days, only one bridge joined the Illinois and Iowa sides of the river—the government bridge, giving access to Arsenal Island from both shores—and most folks invested a nickel and crossed the Mississippi by ferry. The ferry—a riverboat called the Quinlan—included (after sundown) gambling and music.

Research tells me that Bix Beiderbecke and Louis Armstrong frequently played on the Quinlan, but the only time I heard the Quinlan's jazz band was at Danny McGovern's wake. Maybe Bix was there, but not Louis. As distinct as my memories are of that afternoon and evening at the Looney mansion, I would remember a black man—"colored," we said back then—among the musicians assembled in the grand parlor.

Michael O'Sullivan, Sr., sat along the wall in a corner of the grand parlor, in a comfortable armchair, a softly glowing lamp on an end table between him and John Looney, sunk down in his own, rather more throne-like chair; the two men listened as the band played a ragtime tune. Night had come, and such liveliness was to be expected at a wake; the jazz boys from the Quinlan ferryboat were throwing in an Irish tune now and then, a reel here, a jig there—a tenor singing "Danny Boy" had elicited sobs, and Looney himself had instructed the musicians to avoid the number for the rest of the evening.

"Where's Fin?" Looney—hands on his knees, rocking gently—asked O'Sullivan. It was almost a whisper.

O'Sullivan nodded in Fin McGovern's direction—the brawny Irishman was sitting alone on the other side of the room, keeping a bottle of bourbon company. Said bottle was no doubt near empty, O'Sullivan reckoned.

"Has the boyo spoken to you?" Looney asked.

"Yes."

"Any trouble?"

"Not yet."

"Keep watch."

"I am."

His black suitcoat unbuttoned, Connor Looney—just enough weave in his walk to indicate he, too, had had his share of some bottle or other—leaned in on one side of his father, slipping an arm around the old man.

"Well, isn't this swell," Connor said, nodding toward the dancing and drinking. "You put on a hell of a show, Pa. Hell of a show."

Looney touched his son's arm—an affectionate gesture that put a warm look in Connor's eyes, surprising O'Sullivan a little. "Show some respect, my boy," the old man said, lightly. "All eyes are on us."

"As in 'Irish eyes are smiling'?"

"They're not all smiling, son."

The band was playing a peppy version of "Ain't Misbehavin'."

"Got a speech prepared, Pa?" Connor asked. "Nice and pretty?"

"Words from right here," his father, patting his heart.

Looney leaned on Connor, bracing himself as he stood. "This tune seems to be winding down...best I catch them between songs." He ambled away from them, toward where the band played on the little stage, leaving his chair to his son—the real son who now sat beside the surrogate.

Looking out at the reveling mourners, Connor etched half a smile. "Danny sure had a lot of friends."

O'Sullivan couldn't find any sarcasm in Connor's words.

So he gave the man a serious response: "He did indeed."

Now Connor looked at O'Sullivan, his handsome face twisted in its usual wiseguy fashion. "Think your wake'll be this big?"

"No idea."

Connor hitched his shoulders, looked toward his father, who was standing out in front of the band, now. "Guys like us, Mike, we don't get no wake. We're lucky to get buried on church soil."

Somebody tapped a glass with a spoon, silence settled in, and all eyes—including O'Sullivan's and Connor's—were on the stage, where John Looney stood, withdrawing a folded sheet of paper from his inside coat pocket.

Looney looked out on the crowd, his sky-blue eyes moving from face to face, making each of them feel he spoke directly to them.

"I welcome you to my home," he said.

Looney's brogue seemed thicker when he spoke in public, O'Sullivan thought.

"It's good to have so many friends in this house again. Since Mary's death, it's just been me and my boy, walking around these big empty rooms..."

He opened up the speech, looked at it for several long moments, then folded it back up.

"I had a speech, but...truth to tell, it would be dishonest if I pretended I knew Danny well. But lose one of us, it hurts us all."

Around the parlor, murmurs of approval.

"I'll tell you what I do remember—and Fin, I know you'll recall this, too—when Danny was on the high school football team? He'd done us proud all year. Then came state championship: six points behind, ten seconds left on the clock...and Danny threw the block of his lifetime...and took down his own quarterback!"

Gentle laughter rippled across the room.

"Mistakes—sweet Jesus knows, we all make 'em...wouldn't be human, otherwise. Wouldn't need a God, a savior, such case... Give me that bottle would you, son?"

The band leader handed the bottle to the patriarch.

"Great country we live in," the old man said, without irony. "But it does have its quirks, doesn't it? Against the law to a have friendly drink..." He leaned forward, bottle in one hand, raising a forefinger of the other, issuing a mock whisper. "Don't tell the chief, now..."

Rather bawdy laughter erupted as the portly chief of police made a show of turning his back, so as not to see this law being broken.

Looney stood tall; his voice turned somber. "We drink today in our late compatriot's honor."

Around the room glasses and bottles appeared, held high in the fashion of a toast, saluting the dead man. Watching this carefully, Michael O'Sullivan—on his feet now, as was everyone in the room but the musicians behind their stands—casually removed a small silver flask from a jacket pocket. He was not aware that his wife Annie—standing between their two boys, a protective arm around either—watched him closely, studying him as he listened to his "father" speak.

His voice strong, loud, Looney said, "Let us wake Danny to God." Then his voice grew even louder, and wry humor touched it now: "And may he be in heaven half an hour before the devil knows he's dead."

Standing in back with his mother, young Michael—who had never before heard this traditional Irish commemoration—found the words fascinating, and disturbing. Why would a good person need to fool the devil? Had the man with the pennies on his eyes been a sinner?

On the stage, Mr. Looney was introducing the brother of the dead man, "our good friend, Fin McGovern."

Michael O'Sullivan, Sr., was observing this tableau carefully.

"Fin will now honor us with a few words," Looney was saying, somehow managing to be light and serious at the same time, "words that I'm sure will have far more poetry than my own... Fin."

The burly brother of the deceased took the stage, and Looney gave him a fatherly hug. McGovern accepted the gesture, though stiffly...

"Thank you, Mr. Looney...John." Then the roughneck in his Sunday best turned toward the assembled mourners. "My brother Danny was not a wise man, nor was he a gentle man. Like many of us here, he worked with his hands...the sweat of his back, not his brow."

Smiles and nods blossomed around the room.

"And it would be a shameful oversight," McGovern said with a smile, though the moisture in his eyes glistened enough for O'Sullivan to see, halfway back in the crowd, "not to admit that—with a snootful of liquor in him—he was a royal pain in the patoot."

Now a gentle wave of laughter rolled across the assemblage. O'Sullivan, however, was not smiling. Neither was his wife Annie, who—leaving the boys for a moment—slipped up beside her husband.

"Why didn't you warn me?" she whispered.

O'Sullivan glanced at her, almost startled by her presence— and her question. He just shook his head.

"This was not a natural thing, was it?" she asked, an edge in her voice, despite the softness of it.

"Not the place," O'Sullivan whispered back. "Not the time."

She returned to her children, while on the stage, McGovern continued his tribute.

"For whatever his failings," the burly brother was saying, "and Mr. Looney is right, Danny, like all of us, was human...He was a brave boy. A loyal boy. And he spoke the truth...sometimes to a fault."

An uncomfortable silence was settling over the crowd.

"Oh, he'd have enjoyed this party, he would," McGovern continued, rocking a bit, his unsteadiness showing. "Me and the family, we want to say thank you, to all of you...and most of all to our generous host."

These words seemed to relieve the mourners, the sarcasm not registering on many of them—though O'Sullivan knew. And Annie.

"Where would this town be without Mr. John Looney, God love him," McGovern said, voice trembling.

A murmur of approval undulated over the room, Looney bowing his head, humble, grateful for such kind words.

On wavering feet, McGovern turned to Looney, studying him. "I have worked for you many years now, sir...nearly half my life. And we have never had a disagreement..."

Few in the room could have noted the shift in John Looney's expression—the steel coming into his eyes. O'Sullivan did. He was already slowly working his way forward in the crowd.

"But I have come to realize a hard thing," McGovern said, voice quavering...Was it anger? Sadness? Both? "Looney rules his roost, much as God rules the earth. Looney giveth...Looney taketh away..."

And O'Sullivan was on stage, now, making sure his expression seemed friendly as he took Fin McGovern's arm—gentle but firm in his grasp—and walked him off the stage, as the mourners watched, uneasy, not certain what they had just witnessed.

"Strike up the band!" Looney said, buoyantly, and the musicians began a bouncy reel, as the host turned to the assembled guests with a smile and another raise of his glass. O'Sullivan had already hustled the grieving, drunken brother out the front door, two of McGovern's friends emerging from the crowd to follow.

At the back of the room, protective arms again around the shoulders of her boys, Annie watched—trying not let alarm show in her face—as Connor Looney stepped from the sidelines to follow after her husband and Fin McGovern...and two of Fin's tough roughneck chums.

"What's going on?" young Michael asked, looking up at his mother.

"Nothing," she said, cheerfully. "Nothing at all. These parties can get a little out of hand...Let's have some food."

"I'm not hungry," Peter said, not whining, just honest. "I can't eat with that dead guy in there."

Michael said, "There's cake."

Peter thought about it, then shrugged. "All right."

And the three of them headed for the buffet table, though Annie glanced back several times, not showing her worry, while her older boy sensed it, anyway. As his mother helped Peter maneuver a piece of cake onto a small plate, Michael slipped away.

The boy went to the front door, which was ajar. He peeked out and saw Mr. Looney from behind, standing in darkness, looking out on the driveway and front lawn, at a small commotion.

Michael's father was helping the deceased's brother, the one called Fin McGovern, walking the big man toward a truck, where two more big men had gone on ahead, waiting, their nasty expressions at odds with their funereal fineries. Connor Looney was bringing up the rear, trotting alongside Fin McGovern, who was almost falling down, he was so drunk.

His father didn't drink much—he'd never seen his father drunk, rarely seen him take a drink—but one of their neighbors, a man named McFate, was a sloppy, loud "lush" (that was the word Papa had used, speaking to Mama). So Michael could recognize Fin McGovern's condition as drunkenness; and he even understood that the man had gotten this way out of his sorrow.

What surprised Michael was the vehemence, the savagery with which Fin McGovern refused Connor Looney's help, shoving the man away, yelling, "First I bury m'brother! Then I deal with you, m'fine boyo..."

But Papa, on the other side of the drunken man, didn't seem to take this very seriously, just saying, "Yeah, yeah, Fin...You'll deal with all of us. But first get a good night's sleep."

Papa kept walking Fin McGovern toward that truck, where the two other big men were milling and grousing amongst themselves, as they waited. As Papa helped Mr. McGovern up into the vehicle, the other men quieted down and lent a hand, then got in themselves, one behind the wheel, steadying Fin between them.

But Connor Looney—once he'd been shoved—had stayed behind; and when he turned away from them, his face looked white and strange in the moonlight. Michael saw no expression in Connor's face, and yet he knew that the man was furious. What Papa had taken as a drunken remark, "Uncle" Connor seemed to consider a direct threat.

As the truck rumbled off down the driveway, its headlights cutting through the night like swords, Mr. Looney stepped out of the darkness and went down the steps to join his son and Papa, who were heading back to the mansion. They met at the bottom of the porch steps.

"Is Fin all right?" Mr. Looney asked.

"Needs to sleep it off," Papa said.

Shrugging, Connor said, "Yeah, he's fine. Mike's right. Lug just drank himself cockeyed, is all...I'll have a little talk with him."

But Michael knew Connor's casual words didn't match up with that awful expression the man had worn, just moments before.

Mr. Looney said, "Talk to him, but take Mike along."

"That's not necessary, Pa—why waste both our time? I'll be fine."

"Take Mike with you, I said." Mr. Looney shook a finger at his son, as if Connor were a child, not a man. "And you just talk to the lad. Nothing more...We've had enough rough stuff, for a while."

What did that mean? Michael wondered. He glanced back to see if his mother had noticed his absence, and when he returned to his spying, Mr. Looney was coming through the door!

But all his godfather did was tousle Michael's hair and smile down at him, before moving back into where the mourners were having their party. Connor ignored Michael, but Papa seemed surprised, and not happy, about seeing him. When his father's eyes meet his, Michael wondered if Papa knew he'd been spying.

And Michael O'Sullivan, Sr., wondered what his son may have seen and heard—and, if so, what the boy had understood.

While young Michael did not really understand why these supposedly sad people were having a party, he did enjoy himself, as the festivities got more lively. Plenty more people were at least as tipsy as Mr. McGovern had been, dancing to the band, which played lots of different kinds of music.

The mourners seemed to like the reels best of all, and Mr. Looney, charming host that he was, would shuffle across the room, nodding to people, sometimes chatting with them, a glass of whiskey in hand—sometimes two glasses.

Their mother danced with several of Mr. Looney's men— oddly, never with Papa, who sat on the sidelines mostly, just watching—and she would whirl around, her hair flying, looking as pretty as the young unmarried girls. Several times Michael found himself wondering if Mama was drunk, too—but that seemed impossible. Still, he'd seen her pouring something from a silver thing into her coffee cup...

Connor Looney, strangely enough, turned out to be a really good dancer. Much as he didn't care for his so-called uncle, the boy enjoyed watching the man dance—he was really good, slick and smooth, like one of those dark handsome dancers in tuxedos in the picture shows. What was the name of that one actor? George Raft?

Michael wasn't the only one who enjoyed watching Connor dance—everybody kept an eye on him, and he got a lot of applause. The young woman he was dancing with was good, too; she had on more makeup than some of the other girls, and when she looked at Connor, she had a funny expression—like she was hungry or something.

Probably Connor's biggest fan was Mr. Looney, and Michael could tell Uncle Connor liked that—maybe it made up for being treated like a kid, outside. When Connor finished up the latest reel, he executed a deft dip that didn't hide how drunk he was, or how pleased that Mr. Looney was laughing and clapping and proud.

Michael had never seen a grown-up act like a child before—except maybe for drunken Mr. McFate next door (although their neighbor hadn't been causing trouble since Papa "talked" to him).

Even Mama was acting, if not like a kid, kind of…young. His mother, after dancing with another of Mr. Looney's men, flounced over to Papa, on the sidelines, and she was out of breath and smiling and laughing. The boy didn't hear their exchange.

"Kiss me," Annie said to her husband, slipping an arm around him.

He just looked at her. "You've had too much to drink."

She arched an eyebrow. "Maybe I need it."

"The children."

"…Do you really think this is a good time to play holier than thou?"

"Annie. Please."

"Can I get you something, darlin'?"

"No."

A bit of a weave was in her walk as she headed to the table where she could get coffee and something to spike it with. She was just doing that when, from the stage, came a gentle rainfall of piano notes—the opening chords of an Irish air.

As "aaahs" issued forth from the crowd, all eyes were turning toward the piano, along one side of the room, where John Looney sat, playing. The room had gone otherwise silent when Looney looked up, caught O'Sullivan's eye, and with a bob of the head, motioned him over. Moments later, O'Sullivan was sliding in next to the old man on the piano bench.

Annie, cup of coffee in hand, swiveled to watch. So did Michael, off to one side, eating a slice of cake, finally. Peter somehow wound up standing next to Connor Looney, and the two drank in the sight of their respective fathers melding musically, as O'Sullivan played along with Looney, hesitant at first, but gradually catching up.

The beautiful melody had people swaying, eyes tearing; but then—with a leprechaun twinkle—the old man shifted gears, starting in on a jig. O'Sullivan stopped, then joined back in, keeping up easily now. Looney would play an improvised variation on a phrase, as a sort of challenge, and O'Sullivan would play it back at him.

The crowd loved it, laughing, clapping along. To Michael, this was as amazing a sight as it was a sound. His father, who usually seemed so austere, was having a good time! Something moved the boy, seeing his Papa next to Mr. Looney, who was so much like a father to Papa, just as he was like a grandfather to Michael and Peter. To see Papa playing so freely, beside Mr. Looney, made Michael happy...though, oddly, his eyes were tearing up, as if he were sad.

Annie O'Sullivan could only smile and shake her head a bit, knowing that her husband would do anything that terrible wonderful old man might ask. And soon she too was caught up in it, as the music built in tempo—phrase and answer, phrase and answer.

Michael noticed his brother standing next to the scary Connor, who was also clapping along, grinning, watching—but something about the man's expression reminded Michael of

Connor's face earlier, in the moonlight. The man's mouth was smiling, but his eyes sure weren't.

After the piano duet had built to a big, improvised, train wreck of an ending—which had the mourners laughing and applauding, wildly—Looney turned to O'Sullivan, held open his arms, and the two men embraced.

Peter, next to Connor Looney, looked at the grown-up next to him; the slender, dark-haired man was an odd duck, the boy thought—something really strange about his eyes. They were always sort of half-closed, like any second he could fall sleep.

But most of all, the really weird thing, was how the man smiled all the time. Peter wondered about that, and being a child, he decided to ask.

"Why are you always smiling?"

And Connor Looney looked down at him, the smile still going. "'Cause it's all just a goddamn joke."

The boy stood frozen for a few moments, then scurried off, disturbed, terrified, and yet strangely exhilarated, at hearing the lord's name taken so carelessly in vain.

Several hours later, at home, in his pajamas, Michael was in the hallway, padding back from the bathroom, when he heard muffled voices. Pausing by his parents' bedroom door, he could make out both his mother and his father, talking...more Mama than Papa, maybe. Were they...arguing?

Desperate to know, and yet not wanting to, he headed quickly back to the bedroom he shared with Peter. The lights had been officially out for some time, and Peter had been asleep for maybe half an hour; but Michael—as was his habit—was up late, reading.

Crawling back under the covers, he picked up the flashlight and held it over the book he was reading—*The Lone Ranger Rides*, a Big Little Book. He loved the fat little books, which were about four inches wide and four inches tall and two or three inches thick—on each page at left was text, and on each page at right a full-page picture.

Most of the Big Little Books (ten cents each at the dime store) featured comic-strip characters, like Dick Tracy and Little Orphan Annie; Michael's favorites, though, were the western heroes, like Tom Mix from the movies and the Lone Ranger from radio. He flew through the thick books, gulping down the words, inhaling the pictures, each of which had a caption: "Moonlight streamed into the room." Unless he was in the middle of a sentence, he would always look at the picture first, and then read the caption, and finally the page of text. He flipped a page, revealing a shadowy figure climbing in a window: "A man climbed in the window."

The captions always told you what your eyes had already seen, yet somehow the repetition made everything seem more important, more suspenseful...

"Michael?"

He jumped, even though it was just Peter's voice.

"What?"

"I had a bad dream."

"Go back to sleep."

"...It was about Mr. Looney's house."

"Peter, it's just a house."

"The house was scary in my dream."

"It was scary when we were over there—there was a dead body in it."

"...Is that why I had a bad dream?"

Michael wanted to get back to his reading. "Gee, I wonder. It's a big old house, with a dead body and a bunch of drunk people. But it's still just a house. Go back to sleep."

Silence.

Then Peter asked, "Is Mr. Looney rich?"

"What do you think?"

"Richer than Babe Ruth?"

Interested suddenly, Michael leaned on his elbow, thinking about his little brother's question. "Sure—richer than the Babe, even...and the Babe is richer than the president."

"Wow...How about us?"

"What do you mean, 'how about us'?"

"Are we rich, Michael?"

"No, stupid...but we're richer than some people, I guess."

Michael heard Peter getting settled in his bed, again; relieved, the older boy returned to his reading. The first part of the story was about the bad things the outlaws did; later would be the good part, when the Lone Ranger got even.

"Michael?"

"What!"

"You don't have to be mad."

"...What?"

"What does Papa do?"

"What do you mean, what does he do?"

"What's his job?"

Looking at the Lone Ranger's picture—he was on his horse, next to Tonto, his Indian friend—Michael said, "He works for Mr. Looney. You know that."

"Why?"

"Well, you know. Our grandpa died before we were born, and Mr. Looney sort of...stepped in. Looked after Papa."

"I know all that. That's not what I mean."

"What do you mean?"

"What does Papa *do* for him, Michael? What's his job?"

Michael turned the page. The picture was of Beasley, the rancher, in his bed at night, sitting up to turn toward the sound *KLIK*! And the caption said, "Beasley heard the click of a gun."

Peter said, tauntingly, "You're not telling me, 'cause you don't know."

"Do so."

"Do not."

Michael said nothing, studying the picture of the frightened rancher.

Peter was saying, "You don't know any more than I do…and I'm younger than you."

Michael, not wanting to admit that Peter was right, said, "Papa goes on missions for Mr. Looney…They're very danger-ous—that's why he takes his gun along…" Michael turned the page. "Sometimes the president sends Papa on missions, too—because Papa was a hero in the war and all."

Peter, sitting up now, covers in his lap, thought that over. Finally the younger boy said, "You're just making that up."

"I am not!"

Peter rolled over in bed, with a sigh, facing the wall as he said, "It's all just a goddamn joke…"

Alarmed, Michael sat up. "Peter—Peter, don't ever say that word."

The younger boy, without turning, said, "I heard Uncle Connor say it."

"Well, he's a grown-up, and not a very nice grown-up, either."

"He's Mr. Looney's son, isn't he?"

"Why don't you use that word in front of Papa and see what he thinks?"

Now Peter sat up, in alarm. "Don't tell him I said it!"

"I won't, I won't. Just don't say it again."

"…Okay." Peter curled back up in bed.

Michael read a few pages, then he said, "Peter? You still awake?"

"Yes."

"I heard Uncle Connor use the *other* bad word…the *really* bad one."

Peter rolled over and faced Michael again. "The one that Billy used that time?"

"Yes—the word Sister Mary Teresa used the soap to wash his mouth out with because of."

Even in the near-darkness, Michael could see Peter's eyes were wide, whites showing all around. "He must really be a bad man...I don't care if he's Mr. Looney's son, I think he's scary. Scarier than that house, even."

"I think you're right. Go to sleep."

"Turn off the flashlight and I will."

"...Okay."

Michael put the Big Little Book, folded open to his place, on his nightstand. The boys said goodnight to each other, and Michael hoped he wouldn't have any nightmares. If he did, he figured it wouldn't be that house or even the dead body that gave them to him, or even the Frankenstein monster.

Most likely it would be the boogeyman that was Uncle Connor.

FOUR

M y brother Peter and I attended a private Catholic school
called the Villa de Chantal, a sprawling Gothic affair of
spires and stained glass peeking through trees on the bluff—not far
from the Looney mansion, actually.

None of those stories you hear about rulers on the knuckles
and other severe forms of corporal punishment pertain to the
Villa—the nuns were charming and gracious, and wonderful
teachers ("It's in a nutshell," Sister Aloysius would say, meaning
we were supposed to get all the aspects of a subject tied together).

The Villa went from second grade all the way through high
school, so it became a little world a child would live in. Not everyone was from the Tri Cities—the girl students, who outnum-
bered us boys, were from almost everywhere, though mostly from
Chicago. Dorms were strictly for the girls—even most of the local
girls stayed there—and only they could eat in the beautiful dining
room. Peter and I always packed a lunch, and ate it out in the
courtyard, around which the complex of buildings was built, where
we played games and sports and generally horsed around, under
the nuns' wary supervision.

I do remember some of the other kids whispered about Peter
and me, because our father worked for John Looney. I remember
my confusion that the gentle man who was my godfather was also
the stuff of grisly local legend. Most kids would never cross 20th
Street, not wanting to go near the looming Looney house. You see,
older children told the younger ones that Looney was hiding in his

mansion, waiting to capture little children and take them inside and grind them up into sausages.

Peter and I used to laugh about that, but sometimes the laughter would catch in our throats. Even then I think I knew that we had led a sheltered existence, to which the Villa had only added; and the inklings that our life was somehow a lie had begun to take shape in my youthful consciousness.

On the Monday morning after the Danny McGovern wake, the O'Sullivan family sat in their kitchen, having breakfast—or at least, the men in the family sat: Annie O'Sullivan was at the counter, preparing sack lunches for the boys. Sun, made brighter reflecting off snow, lanced through the windows, dust motes floating like pixie dust.

Peter was chomping at his last piece of crisp bacon, and Michael was slathering honey from a honeycomb on a piece of almost-burnt toast (the way he liked it), when their father put down his empty coffee cup, saying, "Peter, I'm afraid I have to let you down."

The younger boy frowned. "What do you mean, Papa?"

Papa's eyebrows climbed his forehead. "Can't come to hear your choir tonight, at the Villa. I have to work."

A meaningful glance flicked between the two boys, and Peter asked innocently, "Work at what?"

From behind them, at the counter where she was wrapping sandwiches in wax paper, their mother snapped, "Work at putting food on your plate, young man."

She always sounded more Irish when she scolded.

Their father had a somber look, but with a twinkle in his eyes, he asked the younger boy, "Am I forgiven?"

Peter thought about it, took another bite of bacon, chewed, said, "Well, okay. Just see it doesn't happen again."

And Papa laughed, and so did Peter. Michael smiled, but he had a funny pang—it made him sort of...jealous, or envious or something, to see how Papa and Peter got along, so free and easy. Almost like they were friends.

"Michael," Papa said, turning his attention to his older son, the laughter over, "you and Peter help your mother...There's time enough, before you have to head to school. Clear off those plates."

Then the man of the house was on his feet, heading out, pausing only to pat Peter's head, saying, "Good boy," and then was gone.

Michael's feelings weren't hurt. He knew younger brothers always got more attention—they were the babies. But when the boy returned to the honeycomb for more sweetness, he made a nasty little discovery in one of the tiny holes: a dead bee.

Peter was already up and using his fork to clean the remnants of his breakfast off his plate and into the waste basket; but Michael sat there frozen, hypnotized by the dead insect. Something about it...something about it...

"Michael?" his mother prompted. "Your plate?"

"Huh? Oh...yes. Sorry."

And he got up and cleared his plate into the trash—and threw his toast away, too.

At the Villa, in history class, Michael sat at his desk toward the back, gazing out the window at the gray trees clumped with snow, a few brown leaves clinging desperately to skeletal branches. He was thinking about the dead man with the pennies on his eyes, and the dead bee, and the dead leaves...and it seemed to him suddenly that death was everywhere.

Being a child, he wasn't depressed by this realization; more, disappointed...

After school, after his paper route, Michael glided into the driveway on his bike, surprised not to be greeted by his brother's usual snowball assault; he looked at the garage and thought about his father and how Papa'd said he had to work, tonight. Would he take his gun? Was this another mission? The boy went into the house, looking for his brother, but didn't find him.

"He's out in back," his mother told him.

Michael found Peter sitting in one of the swing-set swings, gently swaying, lost in thought. The older boy sat next to his brother, the chains screaking, snow getting shaken off just from the gentle motion.

"You know what I wish?" Peter said.

"No. What do you wish?"

"I wish we could go on one of Papa's missions with him. That would be keen, really keen."

Michael didn't admit he'd been having the same thought; instead he just said, "He'd never let us."

Peter gave his older brother a sharp look. "He's going on one tonight."

"Maybe. Maybe it's just, you know, 'work' work."

"You said he did missions for Mr. Looney…"

"It's not always missions. Some of it's just…work like a job."

Peter summoned up a taunting little smile. "Are you chicken?"

"No! And don't you puck-puck at me! I'll hold your face down in the snow if you puck-puck at me."

"I'm not puck-puckin'…puck-puckin'."

"Watch it! Watch it…Anyway, you know he wouldn't take us."

"We don't *ask*! We just…tag after."

"That's crazy."

"I *dare* you to do it!"

Despite the hurling down of that ultimate kid gauntlet, Michael shook his head. "You got a screw loose, sonny boy! Anyway, you have your choir concert tonight, at the Villa."

Peter thought about that. "*You* don't have a concert."

"No…but I have to go. Mom said."

Peter thought about that, too. Then, excited by his own inge-
nuity, the boy suggested, "Tell her you have to study for the big
math test."

"What big math test?"

"The big math test you're gonna pretend you got! Gee whiz,
Michael, sometimes you're so stupid..."

The older boy bristled. "I'm not stupid. And I'm not chicken,
either...Will you cover for me?"

"You bet!"

"Like Tonto for the Lone Ranger?"

Peter was nodding. "Like Tonto."

And the two boys shook hands—like men.

Night had fallen—and a light rain had begun to fall, as well—by
the time O'Sullivan left the dry warmth of his home for the wet
chill outside. The Clemens family—who had a girl Peter's age,
also in the choir—had already picked up Annie and Peter to take
them to the Villa for the concert. Michael was staying behind, up
in his room, getting ready for some test or other.

In his dark topcoat and fedora, O'Sullivan strode through
the drizzle to the garage, stepped inside, and moved to the rear
of the building, to the cupboard, which he kept locked. Using a
small key on his chain, he opened the doors and revealed boxes
of ammunition, several handguns, and a black hard-shell case
that might have, but did not, house a musical instrument. With
the weapon within the case in mind, he also selected, from back
on the upper shelf, two circular magazines—each drum containing one-hundred .45 caliber cartridges, the same as he used in
his handgun of choice, the Colt he'd brought back from the Great
War.

Carrying case in hand, cartridge drums stuffed under an
arm, O'Sullivan shut the cupboard up, relocked it, walked to the
garage doors, which he swung open; he got into the front seat,

behind the wheel, reaching back to place the black case on the floor next to the rear seat, setting the drum-style magazines atop it. Then he started up the vehicle and the green Ford sedan rolled out into the light rain. He paused only to get out and close the garage doors again, unaware that—in the back of the car, inside the compartment under the rear seat—his son Michael, Jr., had stowed himself away.

The rain began to gather intensity, at first tap-dancing on the roof of the Ford, then drumming on it. O'Sullivan drove slowly—the streets were wet and slick, their surface a black mirror throwing streetlamp glow and the headlights of other cars back at him. Still, it took less than ten minutes to guide the Ford from the O'Sullivans' residential neighborhood to the downtown of Rock Island.

When O'Sullivan pulled up in front of the Florence Hotel, Connor Looney was waiting, watching, just inside the lobby doors. The lanky Connor—in a black raincoat, his fedora snug—ran to the car, as if he could beat the rain there; and practically threw himself into the front seat.

"You're late," he said.

"I'm early," O'Sullivan said.

As the car pulled away from the curb, Connor checked his watch. "Damn thing must be running fast...Or maybe it's just me."

O'Sullivan glanced at Connor, who added, "I live for this."

They were less than five minutes away from the warehouse district, even in this weather.

"Hell of a night," Connor said.

O'Sullivan threw him a hard look. "We're just going to talk, remember?"

Connor glanced in back. "Is that why you brought your violin?"

O'Sullivan said nothing.

"You just like to be prepared," Connor said. "Like all Boy Scouts."

For a minute or so, the only sound was the wheels on wet pavement, the patter of raindrops on the roof, and the sloshing of gathered water in gutters.

"Man lost his brother," O'Sullivan said. "We settle him down. Tell him what he wants to hear. And move on."

"'Course. But let's not talk his ear off, drag this out all night—I got to get myself back downtown. There's some skirts need liftin'." The sleepy-eyed Connor plucked a flask from inside his dark topcoat. "Want a snort?"

O'Sullivan shook his head. The last thing Connor needed was a snort—O'Sullivan could tell this one wasn't the man's first of the night. But at least the volatile younger Looney appeared to be in an even temper. Right now he was singing, "T'aint Nobody's Business If I Do," which even made O'Sullivan smile, a little.

As the Ford jostled over the slick streets, the lid of the rear seat lifted, slightly, and the boy hidden away in the compartment got an inadvertent glimpse of the hard black carrying case resting on the floor, stuffed between the seats. The boy had only seen the inside of that case once, when—spying with Peter on their father—he'd watched Papa open it and assemble the parts within into a fearsome weapon.

He knew it was what the G-men on the radio and at the movies and in the funnies called a "tommy" gun—why its name was Tommy, the boy had no idea. Stuffy inside the cubbyhole, he pushed the lid up, just enough to let in some air—but also to have another look at that hard-shell case before him…knowing what lay within.

Up in the front seat, Papa was driving and Uncle Connor was riding—Michael had recognized the unpleasant man's voice all too readily. They weren't talking anymore, though Uncle Connor was singing a jazz song; he seemed in a good mood.

Sitting on top of the hard-shell case were two round metal canisters—each about the size of a can of tuna fish, maybe a little bigger, bouncing a little as the car rolled over the pavement and its occasional potholes. The canister had something to do with the tommy gun—that time he and Peter had seen Papa assembling the weapon, the drum had been the last puzzle piece to get locked in place.

Michael was pretty sure the canister had something to do with bullets. He lifted the seat lid a few more inches; the canisters, jostling gently with the rhythm of the car, were easily within his reach…he could take one and look at it for a second and put it back, no one the wiser…

That was when his father took a corner a shade sharp, and one of the canisters slipped off the black case, hitting the floor with a metallic *klunk*. With one hand on the wheel, and both eyes on his driving, Papa reached his other hand back, and Michael let the lid softly shut, not seeing his father fishing for the case, finding it, steadying it.

Connor asked, "Want me to get that…?"

"No," Papa said. "It's all right."

Again the boy lifted the lid slightly, peeked out, and saw the tommy gun canister balancing on end, like a little wheel, on the floor next to the case. His father's hand found the other canister, atop the case, and was now feeling around for the other one.

Michael reached for the canister, to put it back where his father would expect to find it, only the drum began to roll, with every bump of the road. Finally, as his father took another corner, the canister glided into Michael's grasp!

The thing was heavy, much heavier than Michael had ever imagined, but he managed to put it back on top of the hard-shell case.

But as he drew his hand away, ready to slip back down into the darkness of his hideaway, Michael noticed a slot in the circular can: a bullet was showing! He'd been right—it *was* bullets,

bullets for the tommy gun...and reaching out tentatively with a forefinger, like every child who ever touched a hot stove, the boy put his fingertip against the cold metal of the bullet...

...and the bullet popped out!

He caught it, watching as another bullet jumped into the slot. With his shoulder, he kept the lid up an inch or so, to let in enough light to see his prize. The bullet in his palm was two shades of metal; the Lone Ranger used silver bullets, but this bullet was made of something else.

Its lights doused, the Ford pulled down a narrow alley between brick buildings in an industrial area, though the boy— tucked away in his dark box under the backseat, his father's bullet tight and cold in his clenched hand—didn't know that. All he knew were sounds, like the hammering of rain on the Ford's metal roof, and the slice of sight he gave himself by lifting that lid a crack.

Then the car rolled to a stop, and Michael heard first Connor's door opening and closing, then his Papa's, footsteps slapping at water-pooled pavement. And the back door opened, his father leaning in.

Michael eased the lid shut, returned to the womb of darkness, shivering, not just with the cold of the night.

The boy could hear that hard-shell case snapping open, followed by mechanical clicks and scrapes and clacks of machine-made parts fastening into other metal parts. That last metallic crack, Michael just knew, was that canister of bullets snapping on, like a terrible, wonderful period on the end of a sentence.

Then that was followed by another sharp closure—the back door shutting—making Michael flinch in his cubbyhole. The boy knew he shouldn't be here—even sensed, to some small degree at least, the foolhardy dangerousness of his own mission. But he was nonetheless as thrilled as he was frightened. What brave thing was his father doing on this dark rainy night? What injustice was he righting?

Michael waited forever—perhaps as long as a minute—and pushed up the seat lid and pulled himself out from the seat, staying low. The sound of raindrops assailing the Ford was louder out here, like God had his own tommy gun. Peeking over the front seats, the boy looked out the rain-streaked windshield into the night.

Blurry as his view was, Michael could tell he was in an alley, a wall of brick on his either side. But where was his father, and Uncle Connor?

There they were! Down standing under a yellowish lamp over a back entrance to the building. Was it a warehouse? Uncle Connor was knocking on the door; Papa was standing just behind him, with something at his side—*the tommy gun?* To get a better look, Michael crawled carefully up and over into the front seat, trying not to make noise, though the pounding rain would have covered most anything. He got too close to the windshield, though, his breath fogging it, and when he wiped his own haze away with a jacket cuff, Papa and Uncle Connor were gone, the yellow lamp glowing alone in the night, like a drenched firefly.

As would most any kid, even in a situation like this one, Michael got quickly bored. First he got into the driver's seat, and pretended to steer the car, making his feet reach down for the pedals, fooling with the gear shift stick. When he tired of that, he was back to being just another kid stuck in a car waiting for a parent.

He had come to watch his father "work"—to observe the dangerous, unfathomable things Papa, the war hero, did for Mr. Looney. And inside the brick building, Papa was on one of those missions Michael and Peter had speculated about, deep into so many nights, sometimes till after ten.

So, decision made, jaw firmly set—he was his father's son, after all—the boy stepped out into the pelting rain and sought to do what he'd done so often: spy on his mysterious old man.

He tiptoed through the puddles, making little splashes, hugging the nearer brick wall, staying in the shadows, in case Papa and Uncle Connor came back out, unexpectedly. He wasn't afraid of being left behind—the boy knew Rock Island well, from his paper route, and he could find his way home, though in this rain he might catch his death. But a cold was a risk worth taking...

At the door, he could hear voices within, muffled, faint. No good. He needed to *see* inside, and looked around for a window to peek in, or...*ah!* Just down the alley a ways, was another door, a smaller one, the bottom of it not snug, the wood rotted away, allowing light to spill out into the wet alley like glowing, glistening liquid.

He knelt there, as if at an altar, and peered under the generous gap, which gave him a view inside a huge, gloomy warehouse, a mostly empty expanse but for stacked crates and boxes and two men, out in the middle of the big room with its brick walls and concrete floor.

One of the men was sitting in a chair, arms in his lap, in a brown topcoat and no hat; the other was Uncle Connor, in his drenched raincoat, standing in front of the seated fellow, walking back and forth a little, getting water on the floor, talking while the man in the chair—*was that Mr. McGovern from the wake? Fin McGovern, the dead man's brother?*—just listened, though he was looking at the floor, not at Connor.

Michael could not see his father, unaware that O'Sullivan was standing to one side of the door under which the boy peeked. And of course O'Sullivan—cradling his Thompson submachine gun in his arms like a baby—knew nothing of the boy's presence, though he had noted the two figures in the darkness of the warehouse, undoubtedly two of McGovern's cronies, who would be well armed, themselves.

Both father and son, from their similar vantage points, listened and watched while Connor Looney talked to Fin McGovern, voice loud and hollow and ringing in the big room.

"Don't think I don't feel for you," Connor was saying. "We've all suffered losses in our lives—it's been over a year since Ma died, and yet, still I hurt. We're more than flesh and blood, us people—we're feelings, we're family...So don't get me wrong, Fin—I know what you're goin' through."

McGovern said nothing, just sat in his chair and stared at the floor.

Connor was pacing. "But a little sorrow, and too much booze, can cause misjudgment. What you're suffering don't give you the right to shoot your mouth off like that—embarrassing, disrespecting the man who makes everything in your life, in this town, possible."

McGovern remained silent.

"My Pa is willing to let that pass, however—you and he go back many a year, after all...your father and his father, back in the old country, they shared their share of pints. John Looney is, if nothing else, a fair man...a just man. He asks no apology. All he seeks is an end to this foolish talk."

McGovern shifted in his chair.

"A few ill-chosen words at your brother's wake, we can forgive. But no more mouthing off, Fin—it must end now." Connor wasn't pacing, now—he planted himself before the seated man. "What do you say?"

And now the man in the chair seemed to be looking right at Michael! The boy backed up, an inch, but didn't go scurrying—he was frozen with fear—and interest.

Of course McGovern had not been looking at the boy, whose presence remained unknown; rather he was seeking a more sympathetic court from O'Sullivan.

"Be reasonable, Fin," O'Sullivan said, stepping in front of the door. "Come on, now."

The boy—hearing his father's voice just beyond that door, his view now partially obscured by Papa's feet—knew he should flee. But he couldn't help himself; he was fascinated by the tense tableau before him...

"Fin?" Connor said.

McGovern spoke, but the boy couldn't hear him; the rain drowned out what was clearly a whisper.

Apparently Connor couldn't hear the man, either, because he said, "Speak up, Fin!"

"All right," McGovern said tightly.

Connor sighed and smiled. "Good. Thank you, Fin—thank you for a civil meeting, thank so much for being a reasonable fella. And I am sorry for your loss, and for this misunderstanding...but mostly I'm sorry your brother was a goddamn liar and a thief."

And with a self-satisfied smile, Connor headed away from the seated man, moving toward the door, where O'Sullivan waited.

O'Sullivan—appalled by that last unnecessary twist of the knife—knew trouble could well follow, and his hands tightened around the machine gun.

And indeed—though the spying boy couldn't see them, from his gap-at-the-bottom-of-the-door vantage point—those two men of McGovern's—looking like the workers they were in caps and woolen jackets—stepped from the shadows with their rifles in their hands.

McGovern stood, holding up a hand, cautioning his men. O'Sullivan could tell that the man had been wrestling with himself, going along with these indignities for the good of the cause; but Connor had gone too far.

"My brother was not a thief," McGovern said, loud and unafraid. "My brother was not a liar."

Connor stopped, glanced at O'Sullivan with a slight smile. The man was enjoying himself, O'Sullivan knew, and it sickened him.

Turning to McGovern, apparently unimpressed by the two armed men (who the spying boy could not yet see), Connor said coolly, "Excuse me?"

McGovern stepped forward, chin high. "To protect my family, and for the sake of my livelihood, I'll look the other way…I'll say nothing…for the present. But don't think I don't know something shady's going on, something I can't believe John Looney knows about."

Connor seemed tense now, his voice threatening. "Careful what you say, Fin."

"Something's going on, boyo, and don't think I won't find out."

The men behind McGovern hoisted their rifles.

And McGovern raised a hand, first to O'Sullivan, then to his own men, saying, "Easy, buckos. We're just talking. Friendly conversation…right, Connor?"

"Sure."

McGovern raised a lecturing finger. "You tell Father Looney that my brother never stole from him—I've gone over the books with a fine-tooth comb, and Danny never sold no booze to no one. Every single barrel—accounted for."

"On paper, maybe."

"Danny was not that clever—not with numbers, not with nothing. And besides, where's the money, if he was selling your father's booze?"

Suddenly defensiveness colored Connor's voice. "How the hell should I know? Check his fucking mattress, why don't you?"

"Perhaps," McGovern said, with a nasty smile, "you should check yours."

Hands stuffed in his topcoat pockets, Connor began to pace again; his voice took on an edge that reminded O'Sullivan why the man had been nicked named "Crazy Connor" since his childhood.

"You know, this is downright immoral," he was saying, and he turned toward O'Sullivan, saying, "Don't you think so, Mike?" Then to McGovern he ranted: "My old man, foolish, sentimental soul that he is, throws your little brother the wake of a lifetime—even if the undeserving little son of a bitch had been robbing us blind—and *this* is your goddamn thank you? What a terrible world this is."

O'Sullivan's spirits had fallen, even as his hackles rose: had he been in charge of this "talk," both sides would have shaken hands and gone about their business. Now violence was in the air...

McGovern stepped forward, shaking his finger like a scolding parent. "You think you're so damn clever, but don't mistake me for my brother—I *know* what's going on! You've been spending so much time in Chicago, it's—"

Connor's hand flew from his pocket and the pistol in his fist bucked twice, putting two bullets into McGovern, one in the chest, another the head—stunned, surprised at his own death but without time to come to terms with it, the big man, a red kiss on his forehead and another blossom of red on his chest, flopped face-first on the cement floor.

That was still happening when the two men behind McGovern raised their rifles and Michael O'Sullivan opened fire with the Thompson, round after round chewing the men up and spitting them out, shaking them like naughty children, dropping them to the floor like the meat they'd become, unfired rifles clanking impotently on the cement, streaming blood seeking drains.

It happened so fast Michael wasn't sure what he was seeing, such a blur of activity the boy didn't even rear away, such a thunder of gunfire his ears seemed to explode, as he froze in wide-eyed horror and fascination, viewing the scene of carnage between his father's feet, shell casings falling like brittle rain.

Where one of the men had fallen was directly in Michael's view, a bloodied face with unseeing eyes, and the boy tried to move, tried to run, but he couldn't. His body seemed stalled, as if its engine wouldn't start.

And then he began to cry. He had seen death, and it hadn't been like Tom Mix at all, and his father was no Lone Ranger; the Lone Ranger shot guns out of bad men's hands—his father had gone another way. He lay in a fetal ball and wept and the sky joined in, crying down on him.

Within the warehouse, Mike O'Sullivan was furious. "What the hell was *that* about?"

Connor, as exhilarated as he was frightened, was breathing hard. "Let's take our leave, shall we?"

"That's your idea of talk? You jackass."

Connor glared at him. "Watch what you say to me."

"Jesus, Connor!"

But John Looney's son was moving quickly toward the door, leaving the scattered trio of bleeding corpses behind like so much refuse.

"Hey!" O'Sullivan said. "Don't walk away from me…"

Connor stopped, but not at O'Sullivan's bidding; the man held up a hand, cocked his head. "Quiet—don't you hear that?"

The sound of weeping issued from the doorway, barely audible under the rain.

Connor looked sharply at O'Sullivan. "We got a witness!" He pointed—a small hand was visible just under the ragged, rotted-away lower edge of the door.

Michael O'Sullivan, Sr., knew. He didn't know how he knew, but he knew: that small white hand, that snuffling sob…both belonged to his son, Michael, Jr.

And he ran to the doorway. "Michael!"

The hand disappeared, and O'Sullivan pushed open the door, barging into the alleyway, where—in the darkness and the rain—Michael stood, sobbing, slump-shouldered. Seeing his father, with the tommy gun at his side, its snout still curling smoke, the boy recoiled, but he did not run.

Once his father had seen him, that was that, and he just stood there, letting the rain and his father have him. Stern as he could be, Papa was a kind father—he had never hit either of the boys. Though he had just seen his father killing people, Michael felt not afraid, rather ashamed for what *he'd* done, for the line *he'd* crossed...

His father approached, slowly, quietly. "Are you hurt, son?"

Michael said nothing at first, then shook his head. Uncle Connor filled the doorway—the man had that same terrible expression as in the moonlight; the door framed him, making an awful portrait.

O'Sullivan turned, called to Connor. "It's just my boy... Michael, Jr. Must've have tagged along."

Connor said nothing.

Thompson still clutched in one hand, O'Sullivan knelt before his son, rain streaming down the boy's face like a thousand tears. "You saw everything?"

"...Yes, sir."

O'Sullivan glanced back at Connor, who was approaching from the doorway, slowly. His mind reeled as he calculated a new host of dangers. *Jesus*, he thought, then he looked at his boy, shivering in the rain.

"You must never speak of this to anyone but me."

Michael managed a nod. "Y-yes, sir."

Connor ambled up beside O'Sullivan, who stood again.

To the boy these were two nightmarish figures before him, not his father and "uncle." They were both looking at him, strangely, like the boy was a painting in a museum they couldn't figure out.

Finally, Connor smiled but it was a ghastly thing. "Can you keep a secret, kid?"

O'Sullivan answered for his son: "He's given me his word he'll never speak of this."

Connor touched O'Sullivan's sleeve. "You're sayin' this brat knows enough not to squeal?"

O'Sullivan shook off Connor's hand. "He's not a brat, Connor—he's my son. A man of honor. You do understand the idea?"

The two men looked at each other, rain pummeling them, the brim of Connor's hat collecting the water, his father's fedora funneling the moisture. Even the boy, shaken as he was, could sense the tension.

Then Connor lifted his shoulders in a shrug. "Good enough for you, Mike me boy, good enough for me." He nodded toward the Ford, blocking one end of the alley. "Why don't you take your kid home. I know a speak, couple blocks from here—I'll find somethin' to do." He turned his collars up. "Nice night for a stroll, anyway."

And Connor Looney walked the other way, footsteps splashing, as he headed out into the pouring rain and a dark night, leaving behind three corpses, one father, and one son.

FIVE

Before that dreadful night, I hadn't known who or what my father was. All I'd had to guide me were my childish enthusiasm, an imagination fueled by radio, comics, and the movies, and the natural hero worship my brother and I shared for Papa.

In the intervening years, I learned more. Numerous books about Michael O'Sullivan have been written, some well researched, others far more speculative; and, as I write this, a movie is being made. This narrative, however, is the first time an insider's view of these events and people has been presented; but my very participation in these events, and my closeness to some of the people, limits my perspective.

For example, I never heard my father referred to as the "Angel of Death," and whether that phrase was ever actually applied to him—or was merely some journalist's contrivance—I can only guess. I suspect there's at least a grain of truth in it, because I did on occasion hear him called "Angel," by men we met on the road.

According to one writer, John Looney stood before my father, in the study of the mansion on the bluff, and raised a hand as if in benediction, saying, "In the Great War you made me proud—now you will be my soldier of soldiers. But I will never ask you to employ your terrible talents upon the innocent, only the disloyal...or other soldiers. Soldiers of my enemies, who will be visited by my Michael—my archangel of death."

This may have been spun out of melodramatic whole cloth, but my research indicates some underlying truth, anyway. Certainly my father's reputation extended beyond the Tri-Cities. This

substantiates the claims that Papa was often loaned out by Looney
to affiliated gangs around the country, including that of Al Capone
and his associate Frank Nitti.

By all accounts, Michael O'Sullivan was efficient, unflappable,
deadly. "Was it his somber, almost regretful expression that made
them call him the Angel?" one writer wondered.

That question, which implies its own answer, I fully under-
stand: I saw that somber, sorrowful expression many times, on the
road. The first time was that night, that awful night.

The rain turned to snow, the windshield wipers icing up. His
father drove slowly, carefully, watching the road unwind before
him, lost in thought, troubled but trying not to show it. Young
Michael shivered, staring at the man next to him, his eyes accus-
ing him, but also studying this hero turned monster.

Only the scraping of the wipers, the blowing of snow, and
the jostling of wheels on pavement created any sound; otherwise,
silence shrouded the car.

Finally his father glanced at him and said, quietly, "What
you did was wrong."

Michael reacted as if cold water had been splashed in his
face. "What *I* did was wrong?"

And with sudden recklessness, wanting to do anything to
get away from the man he'd idolized, the boy threw open the car
door. Snow and chill air rushed in, and his father slammed on
the brakes, car skidding, but slowing enough for Michael to jump
into a snowbank, making a hole in its brittle icy surface, then
pick himself up and take off into the nearby woods.

The boy wasn't thinking—he was running, and he was feeling, but not thinking; the woods were brown and white and their
darkness promised shelter, not danger. The man running after
him—footsteps breaking the glassy surface of frozen water on
snow—was the danger...the man who had pretended to be his
father...

"Michael!" the man called.

And the boy ran harder, through the trees, feet crunching the sugary frozen sheet of ice and snow, cracking twigs and crackling leaves, a landscape as beautiful and forbidding as a fairytale forest, that childhood place where Little Red Riding Hood, Hansel and Gretel, and Snow White so often found themselves... but wolves and witches were in those woods, too, like the beast pursuing him, the creature that had been his father, a thousand years ago, tonight.

"Michael!"

The sound of his father's footsteps terrified the boy, but something in him longed to stop, to turn and run open-armed to the man and hug him, so Papa could explain away the blood and death...and then his feet made up his mind for him, tripping over a buried gnarl of root, sending him stumbling into the snow, breaking through its crisp crust of ice into something soft, soothing, but very cold.

Then his father was standing over him. The trees loomed, icicles hanging, melting, like long ghastly faces; the trees had faces, too, distorted ones...

But his father looked...like his father. His expression was sad—sadder than Michael had ever seen it, and his father hadn't ever been a particularly cheerful man.

"Michael...son..."

The boy couldn't help it—he began to cry...not in fear. Not anymore, not after seeing that look on Papa's face. Papa was sad. Michael, too.

He knelt beside his boy. "Son...are you all right?"

"Why...why did you kill those men?"

"Because they had guns, and they'd have killed me."

"But Uncle Connor...he shot first..."

"I know. Come with me. We can talk about it in the car."

"Have you killed other people?"

"Yes."

"In the war?"

"Yes."

"…But not *just* in the war."

Papa shook his head, then held out his hands. "Come on, back to the car…you'll freeze out here."

"How many did you kill?"

"Son…"

Michael felt more relaxed. Less afraid. And that enabled the physical pain to edge out the emotional upset, and assert itself; wincing, he said, "I think…I think maybe I hurt my leg."

"Here…I'll carry you."

The boy allowed his father to cradle him in his arms, to lift him from the snow, and carry him like the child he was, out of the woods. Michael even rested his head against his father's chest, wishing he could forget what he'd seen tonight, knowing he never would.

As they drove, they spoke—softly, in a grown-up way that was new between them.

"Why, Michael?" his father asked.

"I just…just wanted to see you in action. I wanted to be proud."

His father, eyes on the road, swallowed. Then he said, calmly, "It's natural for a boy to want to be proud of his father. But, son—what I do for a livin' is not to be admired."

The boy looked sharply at his father. "Then why do you do it, Papa?"

The night was dark, flecked by snow, the world vague on either side, the beams of the headlights dancing with white flakes; but the road ahead was visible enough.

"Do you know what a soldier is, Michael?"

"Sure. You were one in the war."

"Yes. But life is like a war, sometimes. You see that, don't you?"

The boy understood; on his paper route, he had seen the people out of work, hungry, huddling in the recessions of doorways, lining up for Mr. Looney's free soup.

Obviously choosing his words with care, Papa said, "I'm like a soldier, son. And a soldier does his duty."

"Even…killing?"

Papa's face was hard. "That's what soldiers do."

Michael thought about that for a while; then, shaking his head, he said, "Papa, it seems wrong…The Church teaches us thou shalt not kill…"

"The church is right…but I have a duty to my family. That means I have to work. And bein' a soldier, son…that's the only work I know."

Michael thought some more, then he blurted, "I don't want to be a soldier."

For the first time this evening, his father smiled—just a little. "Good," he said.

They fell into a silence—a slightly more comfortable one, though Michael remained torn within himself: this talk with his father, it was rare, it was special, a new bond had been formed between them. But that bond had been formed out of something bad. Sinful. Horrible…

When the car had rolled into the garage, Papa shut off the engine; through a window they could see their home. Michael sensed that his father felt what he felt: that they had changed, both of them. That going in that house would mean something different, now.

And Mama was in there—Mama who didn't know Michael had sneaked out, who—if she had discovered his absence—might well be distraught. These concerns seemed petty, somehow, after what Michael had seen and his father had done.

The boy asked, "Does Mama know?"

His father replied, "Mama knows that I love Mr. Looney like a father. She knows that when we had nothing, he gave us a home. A life. She knows we owe him everything… Understand, son?"

Michael nodded.

"Come on. Let's go inside."

"But Mama…"

"I don't think they're back from the concert, yet."

The concert—he'd forgotten. Real life, day-to-day activity, the little things that made up a normal life…the boy had forgotten all about the wonderful ordinary life he'd been living. Could he go back to that life? Could life ever be normal? Could he be an ordinary boy again?

Mother and Peter were not home yet. Papa put him down in the kitchen, and Michael could walk, with just a tiny limp. His father offered to carry him up the stairs, but the boy shook his head. The clock said it was surprisingly early, but all Michael O'Sullivan, Jr., wanted to do was crawl in his warm bed, between comforter and covers, where it would be toasty and safe.

His father looked in on him, but did not tuck him in.

"Goodnight, son," was all he said, from the doorway.

Michael said, "Night," and tried to go sleep, thinking he would, right away, as tired as he was.

But sleep did not come. Life wasn't that easy, anymore. And he lay awake, hands balled into fists outside the covers, as he stared up at the ceiling; the weather—snow, rain—reflecting weirdly, made shapes, strange drifting shapes he couldn't make out. He wasn't sure he wanted to, but he couldn't stop looking at them.

He was still awake when Mama—leading Peter in by the hand, his brother still dressed up for the concert (Mama, too)—whispered to her youngest boy, "Get dressed for bed, honey… quiet, now. You'll wake Michael."

And as the giggling Peter—Mama couldn't know the anticipation Michael's brother was experiencing, wanting to hear the scoop on the "mission"—got into his jammies, their mother crossed to her older boy's bed. She leaned in, to tuck him in, and he couldn't help himself.

Michael sat up and threw himself at his mother, hugging her tight, very tight, wanting to crawl inside her and hide.

Annie O'Sullivan, caught utterly off-guard, said, "Oh, dear," and held him, patting him, kissing his cheek, allowing the boy to disappear in her arms. She could sense his distress, could feel his fear, and said, "It's just a nightmare, dear."

"Oh yes, Mama," the boy said, "it's a nightmare...a nightmare."

When her younger son was in bed, she kissed Michael's forehead, tucked him in, and said, "You're safe, Mama's home, Mama's home." Then, after tucking in the younger boy, she slipped out.

Annie looked for her husband, but he was not around—the light in the garage was on. She did not make the leap from her son's distress to her husband's work-related absence, tonight. Vaguely troubled, but not overly concerned, she readied herself for bed.

In the garage Michael O'Sullivan, Sr., cleaned and oiled the disassembled parts of his Thompson submachine gun—a weapon designed for the Great War in which he'd fought, but developed too late for the trench action it was made for. He got grease on his hands and wiped them off with a cloth—seemed to take an inordinate amount of time, tonight, to get his hands clean.

Methodically, with ritualistic care, he packed away the parts of the machine gun into his plush-padded black carrying case. He stowed the case in the cupboard, with its ammunition drums, and locked away the tools of his trade.

But he did not go back into the house, not immediately. He stood there, staring at the closed cupboard, deep in thought, lost in the possible ramifications of what had transpired—worried for his son and the boy's emotional welfare, and most of all concerned about the safety of them all.

Connor Looney was an unstable, dangerous man.

And if Connor's father weren't John Looney, Michael O'Sullivan would have gone back out into the rainy, snowy night, and killed that homicidal lunatic, to protect his family and himself.

But in a strange way, Connor Looney was family, too—a brother of sorts. And John Looney—who, despite the wicked business they were in, was a kind, generous, benevolent soul—loved Michael O'Sullivan and Annie and especially their boys. O'Sullivan knew this with as much certainty as he knew there was a God, a Heaven and a Hell.

Yet even the most pious man, in silence, alone at night, can have doubts.

In their room, once their mother had gone, Peter sat up in bed, and demanded, "Well?"

"Well what?"

"What was it like? Did you see anything? Was it like the picture shows? Was Papa like Tom Mix?"

"It wasn't anything. Papa just had a business meeting."

The little boy sat forward even more, making the bedsprings squeak. "A *business* meeting? We went through all that for—"

"For nothing. And he caught me in the backseat, and I'm lucky he didn't get me in trouble with Mama…Now, goodnight."

Peter, bitterly disappointed, said, "Ah…good night."

Michael had promised his father he would never tell anyone what he'd seen tonight, and that included his brother. However mixed his feelings might be, Michael O'Sullivan, Jr., was no squealer.

At breakfast the next morning, Michael, Peter, and their mother were already at the table when their father entered, joining them. Annie smiled at her husband, but he seemed distracted, his attention—his rather somber gaze—directed at their oldest boy, who seemed to be avoiding that gaze.

Yet she sensed no anger in either of them.

Confused, she asked Michael, "Aren't you going to finish your breakfast?"

"Not hungry."

"All right. I'm not one to force food on anyone, even if there are t'ousands of starving people all around this great country."

O'Sullivan shook his head at her.

Still confused, Annie said to Michael, "Well, then at least clear off your plate."

"Can I do it later?"

"What, after school? Let that food just sit there and rot?"

The boy worked up a shrug—it seemed to take all his energy. "I don't have time now. You don't want me to be late, do you?"

Amazed, Annie looked at her husband for support; his eyes dropped to the table. What was going on? This wasn't like Michael—the words did not have a smart-aleck tone to them, nothing really overtly disrespectful; more like he was listless, that he somehow just didn't care...

But before this could turn into a confrontation—or not—the honk of a car horn outside the kitchen window drew everyone's attention away from the breakfast table.

"That's Mr. Looney's horn!" Peter said, and ran excitedly from the table, and out the front door.

Michael followed, with far less enthusiasm.

Annie, still seated at the table, watched with interest as her husband got up and went to the window. She rose and joined him—the sight a common one, the fancy Pierce Arrow pulling up before their house, the driver stopping, John Looney—in a rather shabby brown suit, unbefitting his wealth—stepping out of the back, just in time to catch Peter, who hurled himself into the old man's arms, for a hug Looney cheerfully delivered.

Annie stood close to her husband at the window, noting his oddly glazed expression as he took in what would normally be a cheery sight.

"What's wrong?" she asked. "Something's wrong."

O'Sullivan looked for the words.

"Has something happened?" She touched his shoulder.

"Michael was in the car last night when I went out."

"In the…oh no…"

"Tucked himself away inside the rear seat."

"Oh sweet Mary mother…what—"

"I've spoken to the boy," her husband said, cutting her off. "It won't happen again."

"But, Mike…"

He turned to her, his face a stony mask. "No questions, Annie. We won't speak of this."

And he left her side, heading to the front closet, for his top-coat and hat.

Outside, Mr. Looney had wandered over to where young Michael was climbing on his bike.

"Just the feller I wanted to see!" the old man said. Then he sidled up to the boy on the bike, and said surreptitiously, "This'll be our little secret, right?"

Michael pulled back, alarmed. "What do you mean?"

It was almost a shout.

Mr. Looney frowned. "Friendly game of dice, what else could I mean?" He held out a shiny silver dollar. "Here—take it…you won it fair and square. A man of honor always pays his debts."

Reluctantly, the boy took the dollar.

Mr. Looney stood so close, the grown-up smells smothered the crisp morning air—cigar smoke, liquor, coffee—and made the boy even more uncomfortable.

"And a man of honor always keeps his word," the old man told the boy, something hard in the ice-blue eyes, something Michael had never seen, or at least noticed, before.

So Mr. Looney knew about last night! Uncle Connor had told him.

"I'm...I'm gonna be late for school," Michael said, and pedaled off, the old man watching him go—the boy could feel the eyes on his back, burning holes.

When Looney turned, his man O'Sullivan was heading out of the house, shrugging into his topcoat. The wife, Annie, was in the window—she looked concerned. The old man threw her a friendly smile and a wave, as her husband got into the Pierce Arrow, in back. She waved back, but Looney could tell his gesture had done little to assuage her unease.

Within ten minutes, Looney and O'Sullivan were having coffee, seated across from each other in a wooden booth at one of the several restaurants the old man owned in downtown Rock Island. A glorified diner, the place did a brisk business, and was crowded with breakfast trade—of course, a number of the patrons were Looney bodyguards. Several more burly boyos were stationed out on the sidewalk.

Day after a dust-up like last night, the old man knew, extra precautions were called for.

"What an unholy mess," Looney said. "How's the boy? He seemed out of sorts to me. Is he okay?"

O'Sullivan seemed happy—or was it relieved?—to hear these words. He said, "I've spoken to him. He understands. He'll keep his pledge to me."

Nodding, Looney said, "Jesus jumping Christ, it's tough, seeing that kind of thing for the first time...such a tender age."

O'Sullivan paused—probably thinking about his first exposure to such like, Looney knew—and then said, "He's my son."

"Well," the old man said, and he bestowed a smile of warmth upon his loyal lieutenant, "you didn't turn out so bad, did you, lad?"

O'Sullivan didn't smile, however; his eyes had a haunted quality that disturbed Looney. "I shouldn't have let it happen."

"Boys will be boys—which of us didn't play stowaway as a whelp?...Anyway, you can't protect children forever. If it hadn't been one thing, it would have been the other."

O'Sullivan said nothing.

Looney waved at a waitress for the check, saying, "I fear it's natural law, my boy—sons are put on this earth to trouble their fathers."

O'Sullivan smiled, and Looney felt relief: the boy still loved him.

And now the waitress set the check in front of Looney, marked boldly NO CHARGE.

"Ha," Looney said, "I've been coming here forty years, and they never let me pay the check, yet."

O'Sullivan shrugged, sipped his coffee. "Well, you're the boss."

Looney laughed in agreement; but deep down the old man knew that even the boss, eventually, would have to pay.

SIX

As a younger man, John Looney's first ambition was to be an actor, and in Rock Island, in the late 1880's—when as a telegrapher he was working for Western Union—Looney organized a dramatics club that performed at the Harper Theater on 16th Street and Second Avenue.

When my father was working for Looney, I never knew the old man was an attorney. But in fact John Looney did study law, on his own and without formal schooling, and was admitted to the Illinois bar. Soon the amateur actor turned fledgling attorney began to make powerful associates in the world of business and politics. Nothing criminal, nothing shady, had yet emerged in the life of this ambitious young man, who ran as a Democrat for the state legislature.

But when he lost that election, an embittered Looney began to establish his own form of government. With his law partner, Frank Kelly, he defrauded the city over the construction of storm drains at the century's turn; and he began his scurrilous newspaper, the News, in 1905, proclaiming the publication would stand for "Truth, Good Government, and the Protection of the People."

And, over the next decades, he assembled a criminal organization that gathered (in the words of one scholar) "enormous tribute from any and all activities that were in conflict with the laws of the time."

With or without politics, sanctioned by society or not, John Looney would rule from his roost on the bluff.

Michael O'Sullivan, Sr., stood in the shadows. John Looney, seated at the head of a long table, had his back to O'Sullivan, who had a good view of most everyone else at this meeting of the Looney version of a board of directors. The confab was taking place in the Grand Parlor of the mansion, a room filled not long ago with partying mourners, only a few of whom were included in this esteemed company, the chief of police a prime example. Another was a snappily dressed Connor Looney, seated at his father's left hand.

The gathering included delegates of the various arms of the Looney empire—eight men representing distilleries, casinos, brothels, loan-sharking, extortion. This had been a working supper—coffee, drinks, the remainder of meals on plates, were in as much evidence as papers and file folders—and was now winding down, as night worked its way in the windows.

Jimmy and Sean, two of Looney's prime bruiser bodyguards, were on the door; but the great man's back could only be trusted to Mike O'Sullivan. The Looney family's chief enforcer did not like to think of himself as a glorified bodyguard, but in some respects, on some occasions, he was that very thing. Most of the men at this table had taken individual meetings, throughout the day, with John Looney; and, after last night's warehouse debacle, O'Sullivan had been primed and ready for retaliation.

Nothing, so far, from the McGovern forces; and many of the meetings, today, had been designed to unruffle feathers and smooth the way for a nonviolent transition. But the empty chair at the table—Fin McGovern's seat, which no one had dare take—provided an eloquent wordless reminder of the damage that had been done.

Speaking at the moment was Frank Kelly—in his fifties, the fleshily prosperous-looking partner in Looney's law firm. "I'd like to take this opportunity to thank our friend Alexander Rance for interrupting a busy travel schedule to make room for us on his dance card."

Kelly gestured across the table to Rance, a fussy little man in his forties, his clothes well tailored, his grooming immaculate; the man had already made a to-do about having to have a whole slice of lemon in his tea. Rance, in the company of Kelly, had met with Looney this afternoon, a meeting surprisingly short for such an important man to have rearranged his schedule to accommodate it.

Rance was, after all, the financial advisor to, and one of the top accountants of, the Capone organization, second only to Jake "Greasy Thumb" Guzik himself. And Guzik represented the old breed—Rance was the future.

Though he'd been sitting there throughout the meeting, Rance exchanged nods and polite introductions with everyone at the table, thanking Kelly for his "graciousness," but otherwise allowing the lawyer to carry the ball.

Adjusting his wirerims, his eyes on Looney, Kelly said to the assemblage, "Mr. Rance and I met with John earlier today, to make another bid for our involvement with this up-and-coming surge of unionism. Speaking on the authority of his position with our associates in Chicago, Mr. Rance's opinion is that Prohibition, unfortunately, won't last forever."

Nods and frowns and chuckles greeted this observation, which was hardly stop-the-presses news.

"Mr. Rance feels that we should be looking ahead," Kelly continued, "for new sources of income."

O'Sullivan wondered why Mr. Rance wasn't speaking for himself.

Perhaps the reason was John Looney, whose voice boomed from the head of the table: "And I gave our friend Mr. Rance the same answer I have given him before—no unions for us. Too much trouble, too much grief."

Connor, who'd been lying back but listening intently, sat forward now, leaning in toward his father. "Pa, much as I respect your view, I thought—since we have everyone here—it might be worth our time discussing the matter. After all—"

"What men do after work," Looney said, cutting off his son, "has made everyone at this table rich...including Mr. Rance and our friends in Chicago. Men like to drink, men like to place a bet, men like to wench...and they pay us dearly for the privilege. We don't need to screw them at work, as well...Next subject."

Connor almost spoke, thought better of it, and glanced down the table toward Rance, whose flicker of displeasure was not lost upon O'Sullivan, who wondered if Looney—the old man sat with arms folded, staring straight ahead—had noticed.

Kelly, who knew not to challenge his longtime law partner, had moved on to a new topic. "John also made it clear, in our meeting, that Fin McGovern's operation will be divided up locally among two territories."

A hand down the table from the manager of the Quinlan riverboat casino half-raised, but Kelly beat the man to his question.

"John will study the situation," Kelly said, "and will select personally how this division will be made, and to whom." With a less than subtle nod toward the empty chair of Fin McGovern, Kelly added, "Since everyone in Rock Island County and the surrounding area respects John, and his wishes, there will be plenty of help and protection, should there be anyone else with different ideas."

"And good luck to anyone," Looney said, "with different ideas."

Connor laughed at that, but no one else did.

O'Sullivan knew Connor had misread his father—laughter was not the appropriate response, here; no one in the room—except perhaps Connor himself, the man who'd pulled the trigger on Fin McGovern—took what had happened last night lightly.

Kelly was saying, "That wraps up what I have—any other business, anyone...John?"

Looney was staring at the empty chair. Then, without looking at his son, the old man said, "Connor—perhaps you'd like to say something regarding last night's unfortunate events."

And now John Looney turned his gaze upon his boy—O'Sullivan could not see the gaze, from where he stood, but in his mind's eye he saw it vividly: ice-blue eyes, a face as blank as a slate, but ready for rage to be written on it.

Yet the son—who clearly hadn't planned to speak on this subject, as unprepared as a kid in class with a surprise test sprung on him—said, awkwardly, with a touch of laughter in his tone, "Well, yeah—I guess I should apologize for what happened. Especially to you, Pa—two wakes in a week...what can I say? It's an embarrassment."

The two bodyguards at the door—who sometimes rode with Connor—found this funny. Their laughter elicited from the man at the head of the table a slap...against the wood, but it rang in the room as if against their collective cheeks, Connor's included.

The Grand Parlor went deathly still.

John Looney's face was long and pale, his eyes glittering with anger. "We lost a good man last night. A misunderstanding among associates led, tragically, to more death..." His head swiveled toward his son and his stare would have turned Lot's wife to salt as surely as Sodom and Gomorrah. "...And this you find funny? This you find an embarrassment?"

Connor, already shaken, did his best to maintain a shred of dignity. He said, without laughter, but so quiet it was difficult to hear, "I'd like to apologize for what I did—"

Looney cut his son off at the legs this time. "You'd *like* to apologize?" He slapped the table again, not as hard, but nonetheless a telling echo. "Try again."

Silence draped the room, a shroud of humiliation worn by Connor, but uneasily felt by all of them, except old man Looney himself. Much as he despised Connor for what he had done last night, O'Sullivan felt bad for the man, who now pushed his chair away from the table, got to his feet, head hanging, a disobedient child shamed before his peers.

"Gentlemen," Connor said. "My apologies."

Face flushed, Connor was looking nowhere; trembling under his father's censure. Anger would come later—right now it was all the man could do to hold back tears.

Kelly, who O'Sullivan had always found to be a decent man, for an abject crook anyway, said, "Oh, I do have another piece of business," and he launched into a short tirade about the affiliated businesses, roadhouses and brothels on the outskirts of Looney territory that had not been kicking in their share, of late…at least not on time.

Connor, let off the hook, was back in his chair, glazed, silent.

Looney said, "Our angel can wing his way to these misguided souls, and nudge them into righteousness…Right, Michael?"

"Just tell me who to call on," O'Sullivan said.

Kelly said, "That character Calvino, over in Bucktown, is way in arrears."

Looney said to O'Sullivan, "Come up to my study."

"Sure."

Then Looney placed both hands flat on the table and pushed himself to his feet, chair scraping back. "Thank you, gentlemen."

As the men stood, gathering their papers, Looney went to O'Sullivan, slipped an arm around his shoulder, saying, "I know you're wondering why I'd make an errand boy of you, Michael."

"No, sir. I wasn't thinking that."

Looney, his manner as warm as it was familiar, walked O'Sullivan out of the Grand Parlor, toward the stairs. His voice was affectionate, respectful. "…But when these recalcitrant lads see my angel of death on their doorstep, they'll know just how serious I am…that the next time they see you, the message you deliver might be from the barrel of a gun…"

Connor Looney, the only man still seated at the table, watched this bitterly—the men in this room, men who one day would be under his command, had seen his father disrespect him, and treat with favor that gunman, O'Sullivan.

When the room had emptied, Connor moved to the chair at the head of the table, where he could get at his father's bottle of whiskey. He sat and poured himself a healthy glass, and drank it, sitting alone, deep in thought, lost in the twisted passages of his mind.

Less than an hour later, after meeting with Looney in his study, O'Sullivan strolled to his Ford, parked in the driveway near the Pierce Arrow. He and the old man had gone over the list of bit-borrowers who needed nudging, starting with Tony Calvino.

"Word about McGovern will be out," Looney had said. "Can you drive over across the river, to Bucktown, and call on Calvino, tonight? We need to make a statement—to show our people it's business as usual."

So he called Annie from Looney's study—he'd been home already, for an early supper, a sandwich—and told her not to expect him for an hour or two, at least.

"Is Michael behaving?" he asked her.

"Yes—just a little quiet. He has a birthday party tonight, at St. Peter's. That should cheer him up."

"Should," he said, and they said good-bye to each other.

O'Sullivan had reached his car when he heard Connor's voice, surprisingly cheerful, calling out, "*Mike!* Wait up."

He turned and Connor trotted up to him. "Pa forgot to give you something—a message for Calvino."

Connor handed O'Sullivan the sealed envelope with Calvino's name scrawled on it.

O'Sullivan asked, "You going with me? Better grab your coat."

"No. You don't need my help, handlin' that fuckin' hophead Calvino...Anyway, I'm kinda sitting in the corner, right now. I'm a bad little boy, I guess."

"I guess."

"Hey, uh, Mike—about last night...sorry. I should've watched my mouth around McGovern. He always was a proud son of a bitch."

"Yes he was."

"I put you in a bad place...and I just want you to know that, uh...hell, you know."

"All right."

O'Sullivan got behind the wheel of the car, and Connor tossed him a wave and headed back into the mansion. The guy seemed in an awfully good mood for someone who'd been humiliated by his own father, not so long ago.

Of course, a lot of Connor's actions could be explained by one fact, O'Sullivan knew: the bastard was crazy as a bedbug.

On the Iowa side of the river, given over to sin of varying stripe, Bucktown nestled in the riverfront blocks of Davenport's west side. The wide-open area—where it was said you could buy anything for a buck—resided mostly in Tony Calvino's pocket. This seedy, trashy district was not O'Sullivan's favorite part of the world; he parked his Ford on the street, ignoring the devil-red glow of the CALVINO'S neon, walking around to the alley entrance.

Tony Calvino had once been a contender in local rackets, and Bucktown remained his stronghold. But Calvino had a reputation for indulging in his own merchandise—from booze to dames to drugs—and that had reduced him to just another acolyte of John Looney.

Breath smoking in the cold, O'Sullivan moved down a stairway to a basement door, a wooden sign next to which read SUBWAY POOL AND BILLIARDS. A size-48 bouncer in a size-44 suit stood guard at the door, arms folded, rocking on his heels;

a small kerosene heater kept the air warm. He had the bored, self-confident look of a guy who had beaten the crap out of countless others.

"Help you, sir?" the bouncer said, with a faint lilt of sarcasm. O'Sullivan, in his dark suit and topcoat, must have seemed like another slumming businessman. "Or just lookin'?"

"Tell Mr. Calvino I'm here," he said.

"Oh really? And who might you be? Mr. Calvino don't see just anybody."

"Mike O'Sullivan. I work for Mr. Looney."

The bouncer stopped rocking on his heels; his eyes widened, his complexion paled, as the blood in his face ran for cover. "Oh...Mr. O'Sullivan. Of course. I shoulda recognized you."

"Why? Have we met?"

"No, no...but everybody's heard of the Angel...if you don't mind my callin' you that."

"Just tell Mr. Calvino I'm here."

"Oh, well, sure—come on in, I'll show you the way..."

"Shouldn't you pat me down first?"

"Uh, should I?"

"Good idea to."

The bouncer gave O'Sullivan a quick frisk, found the .45 in the shoulder holster, and stuck the pistol in his own waistband, under his suitcoat, with an apologetic shrug.

"That's the only one," O'Sullivan assured him.

Then the bouncer—flustered and friendly—led the way through the pool hall beyond the door; in a room awash with green-felt tables under pools of light from conical hanging lamps, no one was playing right now. Tumbleweed might have blown through.

"I'll know you next time, Mr. O'Sullivan," the bouncer was saying, clearly nervous in his presence. "I'm kinda new, still putting names with faces—I'm from over Elgin way. I had no idea Mr. Looney's influence was so...influential."

O'Sullivan said nothing. The bouncer was showing him through another door, into a storeroom filled with barrels of liquor, which he led O'Sullivan across.

"They say Mr. Looney, he's as big as Westinghouse," the guy said, rapping his knuckles on another door, a coded knock.

The heavy door opened, revealing a bright bustling casino area, unleashing the near-hysterical sounds of laughter and dismay, roulette balls spinning, dealers calling out cards, dice clicking against wood. For the most part, however, the patrons here were not high-hat high rollers, just working men with their girlfriends or maybe even their wives, or anyway somebody's wife, risking money they were lucky to be making in these hard times.

A giddy group of little boys and girls—children!—were playing ring-a-round-the-rosy with some slot machines, getting in the way as the two men moved through the gambling hall. It sickened O'Sullivan, seeing children around this vice.

The bouncer seemed to agree. After shooing the kids out of the way, he glanced back at O'Sullivan, saying, "Not right, kiddies around a place like this; but some of the workin' girls got nowhere's else to put 'em. In my opinion, some things a kid just shouldn't see, know what I mean?"

They had moved into a barroom now, where couples were dancing and, on a stage at the far end, a colored jazz band was blaring away at "When the Saints Go Marching," making up for what they lacked in skill and musicianship with enthusiasm and volume.

The bouncer almost had to yell to be heard over the brass. "Hey, I'm a grown man, and this place gets to me, sometimes. Seems like every night there's trouble—I collected more knives from people than a busload of bus boys."

O'Sullivan said nothing.

"Answer me this, Mr. O'Sullivan—if nobody's got any dough in this Depression, what the hell are these chumps doin' in here throwin' it away? Seems like there's always money for frills and frails, never money for food and flop...If this is the human race, I say we're losin'."

Moving to the next circle of hell, a door opened onto the receiving area of Calvino's brothel, where low-key lighting didn't soften the reddish velvet drapes and black-and-red flocked wallpaper, the air ripe with the smell of cheap perfume and face powder. Ranging from their late teens to their early thirties, soiled flowers in overstuffed chemises on overstuffed settees perched and preened along the walls, like a buffet line of sex, working stiffs and men of means alike moving down each row, picking out their selections.

At the door, the madam, a hussy in her fifties with troweled on makeup, called out a number—as if this were an ice cream parlor—and the lucky girl who'd been chosen stood to receive the arm of the patron who'd picked her. With a smile worth every penny, the blonde floozy led her salesman-looking fellow down a dim corridor, and the bouncer and O'Sullivan followed after.

The hooker and her john ducked into a cubicle, shutting a velvet drape over the doorless doorway; the entire corridor was lined with such curtained doorways, and as the two men passed by, the muffled music of sexual intercourse—funny, O'Sullivan noted, how remarkably similar the sounds of pleasure and pain were—provided a backdrop for the bouncer's endless chitchat.

"You know, I'm a boxer by trade—nine consecutive wins, held the South Orange record. I got what it takes to make a hell of a bodyguard."

O'Sullivan remained mute as they moved down another corridor, at the dead end of which was a door labeled OFFICE—PRIVATE.

"What I'm gettin' at," the bouncer said, "and I mean Mr. Calvino no disrespect, but...you wouldn't happen to know if Mr. Looney needs another good man? I'm lookin' to move up in the world. Any chance you could ask him for me?"

"Sure."

A big grin broke out on the bouncer's mug. "Ah, thanks, Mr. O'Sullivan, I really appreciate that. It's been great talkin' to you—nice to chew the fat with somebody who really sees eye to eye with ya."

Aglow, the bouncer knocked on the door, and stepped inside without waiting to be summoned.

O'Sullivan, alone in the hallway, pressed his ear to the door and heard the following exchange:

"Mr. Calvino, sorry to in'erupt, sir...but Mike O'Sullivan's here."

Calvino's husky baritone, slightly slurred, responded: "O'Sullivan...Looney's enforcer?"

"Yeah, it's him, sir. Angel of..."

"I know who he is, I know who he is...aw, shit. What's he want?"

"To see you, sir."

"Fuck a duck. Is he packing?"

Pride colored the bodyguard's voice: "Not anymore."

O'Sullivan smiled as he listened.

Then Calvino's voice: "All right—show him in...but you stick around, see? Keep an eye on the mick son of a bitch."

"Sure, boss."

"Wait...wait a second..."

O'Sullivan's eyes narrowed—a drawer opened; he heard something being put away—dope paraphernalia, maybe? And a faint but unmistakable clunk on wood—a weapon?

Then the bodyguard emerged, smiling, friendly, as he said, "Come on in, Mr. O'Sullivan—Mr. Calvino's pleased to see you."

O'Sullivan went in, surprised by how slovenly the office was—buckets caught dripping water from overhead pipes, boxes were stacked precariously against wallpaper-peeling walls, newspapers and ledger books lay piled on top of file cabinets. Framed portraits of Louis Armstrong and other jazz greats who'd played Calvino's hung on one wall, at varying askew angles.

And behind the big desk was the man who at one time had been John Looney's only real competition in the Tri-Cities: Anthony Calvino, his dark suit and colorful tie a wrinkled mess, though not as much a mess as he was. Calvino was a big dark man, once a powerful person in every sense; now his rheumy eyes—and the sickeningly sweet smell of opium smoke—told another story.

On the big man's cluttered desk, in front of him, was a *RING* magazine, folded open, tented there, as if he'd been interrupted reading. Papers and paperweights alike were jiggling on the desk, and the framed photos on the wall were shimmying. The office shared a wall with the bar, it seemed—the loud jazz music was bleeding through, sending a slight reverberation through the room. Any boss other than the drug-addled Tony Calvino would have minded; Calvino probably hadn't noticed.

Without rising, the fleshy Calvino held open his hands, and beamed, as if he and O'Sullivan were dear old friends, not adversary acquaintances.

"Mike! Mike O'Sullivan—how the hell are you...and how is the old man? Things good?"

They did not shake hands.

O'Sullivan said, "Some things are good."

"How come ol' John never comes 'round to see me? We could talk old times."

"Mr. Looney doesn't like Bucktown."

"Ah, but he likes the money Bucktown puts in his pocket."

"That's why I'm here, Calvino. You been light of late."

"Yeah, yeah, I didn't figure you came for the quiff...but it's always there for you, Mike, on the house. Some very pretty ladies. There's one can pick up a dime off the floor with her—"

"No thanks. I'm not here to collect dimes."

Calvino raised his palms as if in surrender. "I know, I know...it's my goddamn overhead, expenses, grease for the cops and politicians...the Iowa side's no picnic, y'know. But I'm good for it. Don't I always render under Caesar?"

"Not lately...Mr. Looney sent this personal message for you...It's in my inside pocket."

Calvino made a magnanimous gesture with a plump jeweled hand, nodded toward the bouncer behind O'Sullivan. "My boy says you're clean. Go ahead."

But both Calvino and the bodyguard watched, tense and intent, as O'Sullivan reached under his topcoat into his suit-jacket pocket. And when he withdrew the sealed letter, the two men visibly sighed in relief...which amused O'Sullivan, some. Reputation did have its benefits.

Calvino took the envelope, saying, "So I'm behind again... the old man didn't need to..." As he reached for a letter opener—which jumped with the jazz beat, on his desk top—the king of Bucktown asked, "How much trouble am I in, son?"

"I don't know what's in the letter, Calvino. I'm just the messenger tonight."

O'Sullivan glanced at the tented magazine; was something under there?

Calvino unfolded the letter and read. His face gave away nothing—in fact, his reaction was so blank, it felt wrong to O'Sullivan.

As the walls reverberated with the frantic music next door—"Muskrat Ramble," at the moment—the objects, the papers on the desk, continued to do a little dance...and from beneath the tented magazine, something black and metallic peeked.

Calvino was holding the letter in his left hand, studying it, thinking, thinking...then he looked up at Looney's enforcer with a smile, but his eyes flicked toward the bodyguard behind O'Sullivan.

Perhaps if the fleshy Bucktown monarch hadn't been a hop-head, he'd have moved fast enough; probably not—the man merely shifted in his chair, his hand moving only a fraction when O'Sullivan reached under that magazine and grabbed the cold metal of the revolver there, hand finding the grip, finger finding the trigger, and as the open-mouthed Calvino stared at him, the whites of his eyes as big as his pupils were small, O'Sullivan squeezed off one round—on the downbeat of the music, right into the gangster's heart.

Calvino flopped onto the desk, his head hitting first, scattering everything, everywhere.

O'Sullivan had already turned to face the friendly bodyguard, who was fumbling for the gun in his waistband, O'Sullivan's own .45; but the man knew it was useless, and even as he went for the weapon, he was moaning, "Jesus, no...no..."

One bullet was all the job reference Mike O'Sullivan would ever give Calvino's ex-employee—the burly bouncer bounced against the wall, almost in time to the music, sliding down just as "Muskrat Ramble" came to a big finish.

O'Sullivan paused, waiting to see if anyone came charging into the room—but the raucous music had apparently covered the gunshots. He collected his .45 from the dead bouncer. The brothel was close by, and other than a few bouncers of their own—most likely unarmed—no threat should come from that direction.

Alive but confused, wondering what had prompted Calvino turning on him, O'Sullivan looked at the desk, where the letter lay discarded by its dead recipient.

O'Sullivan snatched up the missive he'd delivered, which consisted of one simple, boldly scrawled sentence...

KILL O'SULLIVAN AND ALL SINS ARE FORGIVEN.

A sudden realization gripped him—he knew he'd been sent on this mission for two reasons: to meet his death; and to draw him away from his family.

O'Sullivan had been one target.

But Connor Looney would have another target.

"Michael," he gasped, and he reached for the phone on the dead man's desk.

SEVEN

The great unanswered question, after all these years, remains: Was the betrayal of Mike O'Sullivan the work of Connor Looney alone? What role, if any, did John Looney himself play in the treachery?

Strangely, my father never spoke of this—to me, at least. The controversy rages, among true-crime authors, with depictions ranging from the old man masterminding the deception—sending my father to Calvino's with the orders for his own execution in hand—to Connor acting independently, out of jealousy and rage over his father's love for the O'Sullivans, as much as the need to remove an eye witness to the McGovern murder.

The latter view was seemingly confirmed around a decade ago by one writer, who located an elderly woman who claimed to have been a singer with a jazz band on the Quinlan riverboat, and one of Connor Looney's many girlfriends. The woman claimed she had been in Connor's apartment at the Florence Hotel, on the night of the tragedy. She had been in the bedroom, sleeping off a drunken two-person orgy that had apparently followed the McGovern slaying.

The sound of the old man hammering on Connor's apartment door had woken her, and she peeked out of the cracked bedroom door and witnessed a confrontation between the old man and his son, starting with Looney storming in, and hurling his son to the floor.

Oddly, Connor had not tried to defend himself, rather began to cry, as his father loomed over him, accusingly.

"I'm sorry, Pa," Connor had said. "I'm sorry."

"Why did you do this thing? Why?"

"That kid would've talked...he would've..."

The old man exploded with rage, excoriating his son for his stupidity, and his cowardice, and then—apparently unable to verbalize his rage, much less satisfy it—the old man began to slap his son, striking him, forcing him to his knees.

"Goddamn you!" the old man raged. "Since the day you were born you have brought nothing into my life but disappointment and shame...I curse that day, I curse the goddamn day you were born! I should have drowned you like a fucking cat...I should have...should have..."

And John Looney, exhausted, an emotional wreck himself, fell to his knees, beside his son, as if they were both praying. Connor was breathing hard, and blubbering like a baby.

And then the old man embraced his boy and soothed him, patting his back, there there, there there...

The alleged witness to this claims to have crept back to her bed and crawled beneath the covers. Within minutes, however, Connor burst in and threw her out of the apartment. He was leaving, he said, and didn't want any company.

Given two dollars for a taxi cab, the singer was soon in her own bed, where she lay for hours, wondering what terrible thing Connor Looney had done.

Troubled as she'd been the last few days—as disturbed as she was about whatever her son Michael might have seen the night before—Annie O'Sullivan could still laugh. Or at least Peter could make her laugh.

Mother and son were in the bathroom upstairs. This was one of those ordinary yet precious moments that she did not take for granted: a year from now, if not sooner, her youngest son would be uncomfortable having his mother help him bathe. He was really already too old for it, she knew; but to her, Peter was still her baby, even though he'd turned ten.

The child liked a hot bath, and the room was steamy, the mirrors fogged. She had told him to get out, now, "you're getting all pruney," and he'd splashed water at her, and she'd leaned over the edge, splashing him back—but the boy wasn't much dissuaded by that.

In fact, he seemed to find it very funny that his mother would be silly enough to splash somebody who was already dripping wet, and his childish laughter rang in the enclosed space. The little boy's infectious glee had caught her, and as she held out a towel for him, and he stepped out over the high edge of the tub into the towel, and her drying embrace, they were both still giggling.

Despite their laughter, Annie heard something in the hall. "That must be your brother, back from his party—or could that be your father, home so early...?"

"If it's Michael, I'll splash him," Peter said.

"You better not."

"If it's Papa, I'll splash *him*!"

"Don't you dare." She called out: "Which of my men is that?"

The door cracked open, giving them a glimpse of an adult male figure in a topcoat in the dark hall.

"Oh, it's you, dear," she said, toweling off her son.

But when the door opened wide, the figure there—in a dark topcoat and a knit stocking mask, balaclava-style—said, "No it's not."

Terrified, Annie drew Peter closer. The eyes in the knit mask were blinking—the intruder seemed almost as afraid as she felt. "What do you want?...Leave, please, leave now while you can. If you know who my husband is, you'll leave."

And the man in the knit mask raised his right arm, revealing the long-nosed revolver in his gloved hand. "I know who your husband is."

Annie put herself in front of her child, but the gun in the trembling grasp of the intruder barked once, a terrible explosion in the small room that had not finished echoing in her ears when the bullet in her heart ended her life.

She couldn't help falling away from her protective stance, exposing the towel-draped boy, who cried, "Mama!" staring down at his mother's open empty eyes and the spreading blossom of red on her blouse, and Peter wasn't looking when the intruder fired the second shot.

Naked as the day his mother had given birth to him, the late Peter O'Sullivan tumbled into his mother's lifeless arms, and their blood ran together on the white tile floor, making crimson pools, the towel a puddle of white flecked red.

"So much for my little squealer," Connor Looney said, with a bravado at odds with his trembling gun-in-hand, unaware that he had shot the wrong O'Sullivan boy.

After an evening of pin-the-tail-on-the-donkey, and several plates of birthday cake, Michael O'Sullivan, Jr., was pedaling home from St. Pete's. Tonight was clear and cold, and his breath was pluming as he tooled his bike down the street.

He'd had a long day, and kind of a lousy one—all the cake in the world couldn't make up for what he'd been through at the Villa today. At lunch, out on the courtyard, an older boy had made a crack about Papa working for "that gangster Looney," and Michael had lost control, punching, kicking, pummeling the kid. Neither boy had been the victor, and both stayed after school.

Michael's hand was still sore from writing I WILL NOT FIGHT WITH OTHER BOYS on the blackboard, a hundred times.

He was nearly home, just gliding into the driveway, when he heard the harsh crack. At first he didn't know what it was—a car backfiring maybe? But the noise had seemed to come from the house, and when he looked in that direction, a flash in the bathroom window, on the second floor, was accompanied by a second harsh crack...

...And he had heard similar sounds, last night, hadn't he? *Could those have been gunshots?*

He abandoned his bike in the drive, and ran toward the house, with no thought of the danger, or what this might mean; all the eleven-year-old knew was that his mother and his brother were in that house! Was Papa home, too? He hadn't noticed whether the car was in the garage...

These and a dozen other frantic thoughts tumbled through the boy's brain as he ran up on the front porch, and he was about to rush inside when the figure of a man appeared in the glass of the front door.

Michael froze: the man wore one of those stocking masks, a bala-what's-it, but the boy thought he recognized the figure—wasn't that...and the man pulled off the mask and confirmed Michael's suspicion: Connor Looney.

Who seemed to be staring right at Michael!

Michael wanted to run, but his feet wouldn't respond; and then, suddenly, he realized Uncle Connor couldn't see him—the man seemed to be trying to compose himself before going outside. Then the boy understood: with the lights on in the house, Connor couldn't see Michael standing out in the darkness—what Connor was doing was looking at his own reflection!

And now the man was reaching for the doorknob.

Michael plastered himself to the side of the house, so that when the door opened, he'd be tucked behind it.

Which was exactly what happened. Uncle Connor didn't notice him there, door open wide. The man stood on the porch, on unsteady feet, and fished a hip flask from inside his topcoat. He took a healthy swig.

Then, leaving the door wide open, Connor Looney—who the boy could tell was drunk, like those people at the McGovern wake—tottered off into the night, picking up speed, running, till the blackness swallowed him.

When Uncle Connor had gone, Michael came out from behind the door and just stood there, on the porch, staring at the open doorway for a long, long time.

He knew this had to be bad. The sick feeling in his stomach was only partly all that cake he'd eaten at St. Pete's. Maybe Uncle Connor had been here to do business with Papa; but Mama had said his father would be late, that he had to go do something for Mr. Looney.

And those noises had sounded like the gunshots at that warehouse, last night.

If something bad had happened in the house, he knew he should help—he should be running in there, at top speed; but he was a kid, and afraid, and perhaps he knew, instinctively, that if something bad had indeed happened, due to that crazy man he'd just seen leave, there would be no help he could give.

But Michael finally went in. The house was strangely still— the ticking of clocks, some dripping of faucets, nothing more. A droning sound turned out to be the phone—it was off the hook, in the hall. He thought about putting the receiver back in place, but didn't. Nearby the stairs yawned endlessly—and at the top, steam from the bathroom floated like fog, but other smoke was mingled there, too. He'd seen such smoke last night.

Guns had made it.

Trembling, he moved up the stairs. In his mind he was running; but the reality was, he'd never climbed them more slowly. At the top, he turned and headed down the corridor to the bathroom.

He went in.

His instincts had proven right: there was nothing he could have done. His mother and his brother lay sprawled lifelessly, eyes open, but with no more expression than marbles; they'd both been shot in the chest. Pools of blood glistened. The faucet dripped. The mirror was fogged up. They were dead.

He did not go to them. Somewhere inside, a voice was screaming, "*Mother! Mother!*"

But the boy only backed out of the bathroom, a sleepwalker caught in a bad dream, and moved down the hall, and down the stairs. Still in his trance, he found himself in the kitchen. His mother had left his plate on the table, the food spoiled, all nasty and crusty; he had told Mama he'd clean it off later, and she had left it for him, to show him. Teach him a lesson.

Michael cleared the plate off into the trash, then went to the sink to run water on it. Like his mother had requested. Lesson learned.

Then he went to the dining room table and sat there. He folded his hands, like when saying grace. The boy knew not to call the police; it was not what Papa would have wanted. And he was still sitting there when his father flew into the house, through the front door, his big pistol from the war in hand.

O'Sullivan—unable to raise the family on the phone, knowing he could call neither anyone associated with John Looney nor the police—had broken every speed law getting here, hurtling across city streets, passing traffic on the government bridge, earning outraged honks and curses from other drivers, and barely noticing.

He said nothing to his son, who was sitting at the table, dazed.

He took the stairs three at a time, and ran until the terrible sight stopped him at the bathroom doorway. The husband went to his wife, knelt beside her, touched her throat where a pulse should be; then the father did the same for his youngest boy. Finally, he stood, turned off the harsh overhead light, so they could sleep better, and he went out into the hall.

He leaned a hand against the wall, and then slid to the floor and sat there, gun beside him, his head in his hands. He had lost everything. Everything.

"Papa?"

Almost everything.

Michael was at the top of the stairs. "It was Uncle Connor. I think he thought Peter was me. It's my fault."

O'Sullivan just stared at the boy; then he got to his feet and joined him. They sat on the top step, their backs to the carnage. "Michael, it's not your fault."

"It is!"

"None of that...Were you were here when this happened?"

"I was coming home from the church—I saw him leaving."

"Did he see you?"

"No. He was drunk."

O'Sullivan thought about that for a moment, then said, "Son, go to your room and pack your things. We have to leave."

Michael swallowed. "Okay, Papa."

The boy went to the bedroom he'd shared with his brother, wondering why Papa didn't even seem surprised to have found Mama and Peter that way. He packed his clothes, and a few toys and the Big Little Books he hadn't read yet, thinking Papa didn't even seem all that sad.

But when he went to his parents' bedroom, to join his father, the boy changed his mind.

Papa had carried the bodies to the bed, and was tucking Peter in next to Mama right now. He'd put Peter's teddy bear next to him, and now was smoothing his youngest son's hair, then kissed his forehead, as he'd done a thousand times.

"Sleep well, son," Papa said.

Michael wondered if Papa really thought Peter was just "sleeping," and then his father turned to Michael and said, "Say goodnight to your brother, son."

The boy set his suitcase down, and went to his father, standing next to him alongside the bed.

"G'night," Michael said.

"You need to say good-bye to your mother, too, son—before we go."

Michael looked up at his father. "I don't want to say good-bye to her, Papa."

"You need to. Bid them both Godspeed, Michael—there'll be no wakes, no attending services for us. No graveside good-byes."

"Why, Papa?"

"Because the men who did this thing will come back for us."

The boy frowned. "Only one man did this, Papa."

"Son, if Connor Looney did this, all of them are our enemies."

"Even...Mr. Looney?"

"Especially him."

"Then give *me* a gun! We'll wait for them—this is *our* home!"

He put his arm around his son's shoulder. "We have no home, son. They took that from us...Say good-bye."

Michael kissed his mother's forehead, told her he loved her, said good-bye, and quickly his father packed a bag and the two of them were coming out of the front door, suitcases in hand. The boy had seen his father slip the .45 into his topcoat pocket, and his father's eyes seemed to be looking everywhere.

When Papa closed the front door, it was almost a slam—there was something final about it, the boy thought.

"Son, this terrible night isn't over," he said. "There are still things I must do. Can you be brave?"

"Yes...if I have to."

"Good."

The car was where his father had left it, when he'd pulled up to run into the house. Before they got in, Papa had Michael accompany him to the garage.

"Stay out here," he told the boy, "and yell if you see anyone... Anyone."

"Yes, Papa."

Papa went into the garage and came back a few minutes later, with the black hard-shell case in hand—the tommy gun would be making the trip with them, and somehow Michael was glad.

Before they got into the car, Michael paused, looking back at the house he'd been raised in—he'd never lived anywhere else. He'd even been born there, in his parent's bedroom, where Mama lay now.

His father touched his shoulder. "That's not our home anymore," he reminded the boy. "With Peter and your mother gone, it's just a house…an empty structure. Understand?"

"Yes, sir."

With their suitcases in the backseat, his father's big one and Michael's small one, and the black hard-shell carrying case as well, his father drove at a normal speed through the residential streets of Rock Island. Within ten minutes they were downtown, and Papa pulled the car into a parking space, where the shadows were dark.

Across the street a neon sign glowed: FLORENCE HOTEL.

The boy asked, "Are we staying here tonight?"

"No. I have something to do. I'll be back soon."

But when his father began to go, Michael grabbed onto his arm, holding him back.

The look in his father's eyes, Michael had never seen before—his expression was apologetic, and also sad. Papa's eyes were red, like he'd been crying.

"Son—tomorrow they'll realize we've gone, and they'll come after us—wherever we go. I have to protect you."

"Then stay!" Michael couldn't see how his father leaving him alone was any kind of protection at all!

His father sat there—thinking, almost like he was fighting with himself. Then he reached in his left-hand topcoat pocket and removed a small gun—a revolver with a very short barrel.

"You said you wanted a gun," Papa said, and handed it toward him.

But Michael couldn't make his fist unclench. "I…I changed my mind."

His father gently yet firmly opened the boy's fingers and placed the gun into his palm.

"Now, you may hear things—shouts, a gunshot or two. But sit tight, son—if I'm not back in half an hour, go to Reverend Landers at First Methodist, and tell him what happened."

"But that's a Protestant church, Papa! Why not go to St. Pete's, and Father Callaway—"

"Looney money built that church, son...and sent Father Callaway to Rome, last summer, to meet the Pope. You'll find no sanctuary, there."

Papa got out his pocket watch and handed it to the boy.

"Half an hour—and if you do have to go to that church, tell Reverend Landers not to go to the police. Tell him the Bureau of Investigation."

Michael swallowed. "The G-men?"

Almost smiling, Papa said. "Yes, son. The G-men. Remember...sit tight."

Michael said nothing, looking down at his hand, where the small gun seemed so big...

Papa, about to open the door, paused and his eyes held the boy—as if he were memorizing Michael's features—then he slipped out into the night, moving down the sidewalk.

In the shadows of a recessed doorway across from the Hotel Florence, O'Sullivan watched as men outside the building milled about, cars parked in front, more cars arriving, a small crowd of Looney thugs growing bigger as the group readied themselves to go after him. If any confirmation were needed, the brave talk among the strutting men occasionally contained the name "O'Sullivan" and the word "Angel."

Soon Looney's former chief enforcer—the sounds of cars starting up, heading off, the search party leaving—was in the alley behind the hotel. No one back here, somewhat surprisingly; he began to climb the fire escape cautiously, .45 in one hand.

At the second-floor landing, he looked in the window at an empty corridor; he forced the window open and stepped quietly in, all the while looking for an armed watchdog, but seeing no one. He walked down the hall to the doorway to Connor Looney's apartment; the lower edge of the door revealed the lights on in there. His first thought was to kick the door in, but that would be loud...

He tried the doorknob—and the door swung open!

Hurling himself in, gun raised, he found himself staring at a well-dressed, self-composed Frank Kelly, seated in the middle of the room, in comfortable chair, before a coffee table. Kelly's hands were on his thighs—to indicate that he was unarmed—and the portly, prosperous-looking lawyer seemed to have been waiting for O'Sullivan to appear.

O'Sullivan shut the door, and—looking all around the well-appointed apartment—kept the .45 poised to shoot, as he told John Looney's longtime law partner, "I have no business with Frank Kelly."

Genial, pleasant, the attorney held his hands open, palms up. "Ah, but Frank Kelly has business with you, Mike. You know as well as anyone that, as John Looney's partner...and his legal counsel...I've often represented him. That's what I'm doing now...Sit down."

"No."

Kelly shifted in his chair; he was walking a tightrope between keeping this friendly and yet serious. "I'm here, as I said, to represent Mr. Looney...to let you know that John Looney had nothing to do with the unfortunate...might I even say tragic... steps taken against your family."

"And I suppose he didn't send me to Bucktown with my own death warrant sealed in an envelope."

Kelly raised his hands in a calming manner. "All of this was Connor Looney's own doing, and may I say, a deplorable thing... and an unauthorized action, I assure you."

"Then Mr. Looney will understand why I have to kill his son."

Kelly sighed and his expression was suitably somber. "He understands the impulse—but as a grieving father yourself, surely you can comprehend why he has sent his boy into hiding…until it's safe for Connor to come out."

"In other words, when I'm dead."

Patting the air, shaking his head, the attorney said, "I didn't say that, I didn't say that—now, Mike, I know you're a reasonable man…"

"No I'm not."

Kelly tried a smile. "What is it about the Irish? Either full of blarney, like yours truly, or masters of understatement, like yourself." He shifted in the chair again. "Now I'm going to reach for something, Mike—it's not a weapon…"

O'Sullivan said nothing.

Kelly bent down and picked up a black satchel and set it on the table. "It's twenty-five thousand dollars, Mike. Mr. Looney wants you to know there'll be more. But at such short notice…"

"Money."

The lawyer shook his head again, his expression acknowledging the lamentable circumstances. "Insufficient to make up for your grievances, I know…but consider it a gesture from Mr. Looney, if you will. Mike, you have family in Ireland. Take Peter and leave."

"I can't take Peter. He's dead."

Confused, thrown, Kelly said, "My understanding…"

O'Sullivan shook his head. "Connor Looney didn't even know who he was killing. Tell John Looney his beloved younger godchild is in heaven. And tell John Looney, I'll see him and his son in hell."

The lawyer seemed, for the first time, afraid—almost as afraid as he should have been. "I…I understand your reaction…"

"Good. Now, where's Connor?"

Kelly shook his head. "He's in hiding. I told you that, Mike."
"Where?"

"Please! I wouldn't tell you even if I knew."

O'Sullivan raised the .45, leveling it directly at the lawyer's head.

Kelly was an old courtroom warrior and there was steel in his eyes as he replied, "You figure putting a gun to my head will make a difference? I can't tell you what I don't know, Mike. Now, go while you have the chance...and take the money. Make a new life with, uh...Michael's alive and well?"

"He's alive."

The lawyer sighed in relief, or pretended to. "Good. Thank God. Jesus, put that gun down! I'm not part of this. I'm just an emissary. A messenger!"

"Then you wouldn't mind giving John Looney a message for me?"

Kelly beamed benevolently. "Not at all. That's what I'm here for."

O'Sullivan thumbed back the hammer on the .45, a small click that seemed to echo in the room.

The lawyer's eyes widened in alarm. His mouth dropped like a trapdoor. "But...but you said you wanted me to deliver a message to Mr. Looney..."

"Oh, and you will," O'Sullivan said, and shot the man in the head.

Teeth chattering from the cold, Michael, in the car, thought he heard a gunshot, but he wasn't sure; it sounded far away. And then, before very long, his father was sliding in behind the wheel. He didn't look the same, somehow.

"Getting colder," Papa said. "I threw a blanket in back. Get it. Wrap it around yourself."

"Okay, Papa."

Michael got the blanket, bundled himself.

As he drove quietly away from the hotel, Papa asked, "No one bothered you, son?"

"No…but what happened in there, Papa?"

His father thought for moment; then he said, "I declared war."

Michael, not understanding, asked, "Where are we going?"

"To Chicago. There's a man there who runs things. I've done work for him, at Mr. Looney's behest. I have to find out where this big man stands."

"Oh." Michael leaned against the door, wrapped in the blanket. Despite everything that happened, he was so exhausted, the boy knew he would fall asleep at once. Before he did, he managed a final question. "What's the big man's name, Papa?"

His father let out a breath. "Capone," he said.

But Michael was already asleep.

EIGHT

I n the early months of 1931, Chicago suffering a typically chill winter, the city's most famous citizen—Alphonse Capone—was nearing the end of his criminal reign. Eliot Ness and his squad— who would enter American mythology as the Untouchables— had for several years been costing Capone dearly, seizing and/or destroying many of his assets.

Treasury agent Ness also collected tax ledgers that were turned over to Elmer Irey and Frank Wilson of the IRS, the second prong of the government's dual attack. With these and other confiscated records, Irey and Wilson would soon bring Capone down; but the criminal organization "Scarface" Al headed would go on without him, and even thrive.

Prohibition had been around for over ten years, and just about everybody considered it a colossal flop, unenforceable legislation that had paved the way for hoodlum Caesars like Big Al. For a time Capone had seemed a benign public figure, attending ball games, sending toys to orphanages, funding soup kitchens, an outrageous larger-than-life character.

But ordering the murder of a reporter in a busy train station was just one example of Capone's arrogance; and the bloody St. Valentine's Day Massacre was a notable other one. His shenanigans attracted the attention of President Hoover, which led to the efforts of Ness, Irey, and Wilson.

Many considered the real brains behind the Capone organization to be Capone's second in command, Frank Nitti. A former barber, and a cousin of the big man, Nitti had gone from the role *of Capone's chief enforcer—the job my father held in John Looney's organization—to his heir apparent.*

Nitti was at the fore of the new breed of gangster. He understood that the mob was like any American big business, and that the murderous ways so ingrained in thugs like Capone, who'd come up through the street, had to be kept in check. Under Nitti, the so-called Chicago Outfit would expand into legitimate businesses and, in particular, unions; the killing would continue, when necessary...but more discreetly.

When my father and John Looney fell violently out, the Chicago Outfit was already on the precipice of change. Capone was still in charge, but facing indictment on various charges. Almost certainly Frank Nitti knew he would soon sit in the chair, the throne, vacated by the most famous criminal America ever created.

O'Sullivan drove through the night, often taking back roads and circuitous routes on his journey to Chicago, though he did not expect Looney or his men to anticipate this move. His son slumbering beside him, O'Sullivan experienced a strange combination of clarity—he was not at all tired—and a dream-like state. His headlights cut through darkness like searchlights, and the winter-barren farmland—some of the richest land in the United States—seemed a surrealistic wasteland around them.

When night began its fade to morning, light easing over the endless fields, the rural landscape took on a stark reality, and beauty. Annie had an eye for such things. Like any woman, she would point out colorful flowers, in summer; but at this time of year, she might also draw his attention to a tree silhouetted against the sky like a ghostly skeleton.

The boy slept. O'Sullivan was thankful for that, and when Michael did finally wake, they were deep in Chicago's Loop, skyscrapers looming, safe and anonymous in the morning traffic.

"It's so big," the boy said, eyes wide, looking all around at the man-made canyon walls. "Is this Chicago?"

"Yes."

"Where are we going?"

"You're going to the library."

Michael looked at him curiously, but asked no questions. The boy was smart—maybe not as smart as Peter had been, but nobody's fool. O'Sullivan could tell that the boy understood a haven was needed for him, while his father did what he had to.

The Chicago Public Library faced Michigan Avenue between Randolph and Washington Streets. The turn-of-the-century classical-looking building was not a skyscraper, rather a massive elongated limestone structure, a fortress of knowledge. The boy would be safe, there.

Before long, they were on foot, just a man in a topcoat and fedora, and a boy in a jacket and cap, in a sea of early-morning workers—businessmen, secretaries, blue-collar types—and, again, O'Sullivan felt secure in their anonymity. He escorted his son—he'd instructed the boy to bring along his small suitcase—in on the building's Washington Street side, entering an immense world of glass mosaics and marble; Michael's reaction of wonder touched the father in O'Sullivan, despite all he had on his mind.

He walked the boy to a huge reading room, where students and other scholars mingled with the down-and-out, mothers with babies, and the elderly, all just escaping the cold.

Sitting Michael down at an individual table, O'Sullivan said, "I want you to wait for me."

The boy's anxiety leapt in to his eyes, but he merely said, "Okay, Papa."

"I won't be long, son. You'll be all right?"

Michael nodded.

"If you want to get up, and get something to read, you can. Otherwise—stay right here."

Michael shrugged. He lifted up his little suitcase. "I brought my own books," the boy said.

O'Sullivan almost smiled. "You still have that little gun I gave you?"

Michael patted his coat pocket.

"Good boy," O'Sullivan said. "Now if anyone comes at you with their own gun, do you know what to do?"

The boy thought about that. "Shoot?"

"Yes."

The boy thought about that, too. "Where do I aim? The Lone Ranger shoots the guns out of people's hands."

"The Lone Ranger isn't real. Shoot at their heads."

Michael swallowed. "Couldn't I just shoot at their legs?"

"No. Their heads, if they're close enough. Or their chests, if you need a bigger target."

"Oh, Papa…I'm afraid."

"That's not a bad thing, son. God put that feeling inside of us so we would protect ourselves. So we can survive."

Michael's head was swimming, O'Sullivan could tell; but his son needed to hear these things.

Then the boy asked, "But what about thou shalt not kill, Papa?"

The beleaguered father had known this would come up again, and he was ready: "God gives His permission for us to protect ourselves from evil men."

Michael thought about that. "What if a policeman comes?"

"Run."

"Papa…run from a policeman?"

"There are no police in Chicago, son. Just killers in blue uniforms…If I'm not back in an hour and a half, you find the nearest church."

"A Catholic church, Papa?"

"No…God, no. Protestant, Michael. Please."

"How will I find it?"

One of the librarians, a slender woman in her thirties, had been watching this whispered conversation—hearing none of it; her expression was warmly appreciative of the close bond between the boy and his father. She would have found the scene less heartwarming, had she overheard it.

O'Sullivan said, "Ask that nice librarian. Get directions."

Michael seemed close to tears, despite his efforts at stoicism.

Touching his son's shoulder, O'Sullivan said, "You've done well."

The boy liked hearing that.

His father continued: "I probably won't be gone that long. And I will be back…But you saw what Connor Looney did last night—you know what we're up against. We have to be strong—we have to consider the possibilities."

The boy was nodding. "Backup plans."

"That's a good way to put it." He patted the boy's shoulder. "You'll be fine."

On his way toward the exit, O'Sullivan noted his reflection in a mirrored wall—he looked pretty rough; unshaven. He ducked into a bathroom and threw water on his face, ran his hands through his hair, doing his best to spruce up.

With his father gone, Michael got into his little suitcase; there, among some clothes, were his pipe, his dice, and two Big Little Books, a Tom Mix and the Lone Ranger one that he was still reading. Selecting that one, the boy sat and thumbed it open. His eyes looked at the full-page picture at right, of the Lone Ranger holding a gun on a sheriff. The caption, redundantly, said: "The Lone Ranger had the Sheriff covered."

Five minutes later, in the vast room, surrounded by big-city strangers, the boy was still staring at the same page.

Then, his face blank, he shut the book, pushed it aside; he felt his lower lip begin to quiver and his eyes began to get wet, his whole face quivering, as if he had no control over it, which he didn't.

The boy put his head on the table, the way the nuns at the Villa had the students rest at their desks, and he wept, trying to stay quiet, and not attract attention, because his father wouldn't have liked that.

At 22nd Street and South Michigan Avenue, the Lexington had once been one of Chicago's most elite hotels, and the ten-floor structure still made an impressive appearance, with its turreted corners and bay windows. O'Sullivan had been here before—also at the former mob headquarters, the Metropole Hotel, just a block away. The Capone organization had the run of the place, controlling the third, fourth, and tenth floors and scattered rooms throughout, many of the latter taken up by the numerous hookers and showgirls Capone kept salted away for the convenience of himself and his boys.

Standing across the street, eyes on the marble pillars framing the entrance, O'Sullivan knew full well he was entering a mob stronghold. Capone had put in alarms, moving walls, hidden panels, and Christ knew how many other security measures. Though the hotel looked normal enough—doormen and bellboys thronged the glass doorways—the lobby would be crawling with Outfit gunmen. Nonetheless, as an expression of good faith, he was unarmed, the .45 and his other weapons left behind in the parked Ford. All O'Sullivan had on his side was the unexpected boldness of what he was about to do—that, and his reputation.

Moments later, O'Sullivan was walking across the magnificent lobby, across the black-and-white checkered tile floor, toward the iron-grille elevators. One of those elevators—which no one seemed to be using—stood vacant, while on either side of it, two watchdogs in Maxwell Street suits stood guard.

The brawnier of the two leaned against a wall, reading *The Racing News*. The other one—taller, skinnier—was smoking a cigarette, rocking on his feet, eyeing the floozies who were a part of the odd Lexington mix that included a surprising share of legitimate guests—salesmen and other professional types, in Chicago on business.

O'Sullivan approached, saying to the brawny watchdog, "How are you, Harry?"

Harry looked up from his racing paper, obviously startled to see this unshaven figure. "Mike!...Mike O'Sullivan. Yeah, uh...hello."

O'Sullivan looked at the taller watchdog. "Marco, isn't it?"

Marco nodded, warily.

Harry said, "Hey, uh, Mike—heard about what happened. Christ, it's awful. How you holdin' up, pal?"

O'Sullivan said, "I need to talk to Mr. Capone."

Marco, who didn't seem to know what Harry was talking about, said, "Mr. Capone is out of town."

"Mr. Nitti, then."

Marco shrugged. "You ain't on my list."

O'Sullivan smiled. "Like to be on mine?"

The watchdog paled. "I don't mean any offense, Mr. O'Sullivan. I just got a job to do."

Harry said, "Mike, Mr. Nitti's awful busy today."

"I'll wait."

The two watchdogs exchanged glances; both of them knew only too well who and what Mike O'Sullivan was.

Harry shrugged. "Okay—Marc, take the man to the top."

Marco stepped inside the elevator and so did O'Sullivan.

"Meaning no disrespect, Mr. O'Sullivan," Marco said, "you're gonna have to stand for a frisk."

"Fine. But I'm not packing."

Marco patted O'Sullivan down, found nothing, and said, "Friendly visit."

"Always."

Marco swung shut the grille-work doors. Ten floors took a while, and they rode in silence at first, then the watchdog asked, "How'd you remember my name? You only saw me, once. We never even spoke."

"I make it point to remember men's names."

"Yeah?"

"Men with guns."

Marco thought about that, then asked, "What was Harry talkin' about? What'd he mean, how are you holding up, you don't mind my asking?"

"I do mind," O'Sullivan said.

The elevator continued on its slightly jostling course, making no stops along the way.

"Quite a reputation you got," Marco said, perhaps starting to resent O'Sullivan's understated lack of respect.

"I don't know how that happened," O'Sullivan said.

"How do you mean?"

"I don't remember leaving anybody to spread the word."

And then they were there, at the top floor waiting room, where politicians and businessmen of varying degrees of respectability mingled with shadier-looking figures. Cigarette smoke floated like a blue haze as the men sat and chatted, talking business and sports and even family, drinking the coffee provided thoughtfully by the Capone organization.

Everyone was settled in for a wait, and O'Sullivan had left his son with that hour-and-a-half deadline. He gave the receptionist—a pleasant if officious thirtyish woman who sat near the focal-point door marked PRIVATE—his name, acknowledged he had no appointment, but suggested she tell Mr. Nitti that Mr. O'Sullivan was here. Then he took a seat.

After a while, when she had not yet done as he'd asked, he settled his gaze on her and, when her eyes met his, he checked his watch and raised an eyebrow.

The receptionist got the message—though she did not recognize O'Sullivan, she clearly could see that he was not a part of the political/business crowd taking up the other chairs. And, despite the pretense of normal business the Capone organization made, even a receptionist like this knew the score: the deadly-looking unshaven man should not be kept waiting.

She spoke to her boss on the intercom, then looked up at O'Sullivan and nodded.

He thanked her, as she held open the door for him.

The office was spacious, a lavishly appointed executive suite worthy of LaSalle Street, all dark woodwork, with a desk and a conference table, and of course a fireplace, over which hung an oil portrait of Al Capone.

Frank Nitti did not cut the imposing figure Capone did, either in the portrait or in life. A small mustached man in his midforties, Nitti was in his white shirtsleeves with dark suspenders, but his gray and black tie was not loosened, and there was nothing casual about the well-groomed former barber. As he approached his visitor—offering a hand, which O'Sullivan shook—Nitti seemed typically cordial yet distant.

"I didn't know you were waiting out there, Mike," Nitti said. He was smoking, a cigarette in his left, gesturing hand. "But I have to admit I'm not surprised to hear from you...Come, sit."

"No thank you. I can't stay long."

Nitti shook his head. "I'm pleased that you would think of us, in your time of grief...We all just heard. You want some coffee?"

O'Sullivan shook his head. "Thank you for seeing me, Mr. Nitti."

"Don't be silly. Al is in Florida, holed up with his lawyers. Some legal matters pending, and I haven't talked to him about your situation yet. But I know he'll be distressed by this loss. He's a family man, too..."

"I know. Thank you."

"And allow me to offer my personal condolences on your tragic loss." Nitti gestured. "Come! Please...sit..."

They sat facing each other across a small table, next to a window that offered a commanding view of the South Side of Chicago—the Capone/Nitti empire.

Sympathies expressed, Nitti's manner shifted to businesslike. "Now—what's on your mind, Mike?"

"You heard about my family. But what did you hear about Tony Calvino?"

Nitti lighted up a new cigarette. "That you killed him."

"Self-defense." O'Sullivan dug in his suitcoat pocket. "John Looney's son Connor sent me to Calvino's to deliver this sealed message…"

O'Sullivan handed Nitti the note; the bantam gangster read the words—KILL O'SULLIVAN AND ALL SINS ARE FORGIVEN—and said, "Jesus—the man sent you there to die. To be killed."

"And then Connor went to my house, my home, to kill my family. You seem to know that he murdered my wife and one of my sons."

"Yes. Yes…"

"Last night, before I shot him, Frank Kelly told me that Looney is protecting his son. He's hidden him away."

Seemingly unimpressed by the reference to the Kelly murder, Nitti shook his head, disgusted. "And you served Looney's interests well, and honorably, for years! There's no excuse for such vicious behavior. We're not animals—we're businessmen."

"Yes. And I have also served the *Capone* interests 'well and honorably,' over the years."

Nodding in a that's-old-news manner, Nitti said, "Through our alliance with the Looney family…Why did you come here, Mike?"

"I don't seem to be working for the Looneys anymore."

"That's a fair assessment."

O'Sullivan paused; rather formally, he said, "I would like to work for you, Mr. Nitti. For you and Mr. Capone."

That seemed to catch Nitti off guard; he exhaled smoke, then said, "Well now, that's a very interesting notion, Mike. You *are* the best at what you do."

"Thank you. But for me to join your ranks, and be your loyal soldier, I need you to turn a blind eye to what I have to do in the coming days."

"And what's that?"

"Kill the man who murdered my family."

Nitti blew out more smoke. "Connor Looney...And what about his father?"

"I have no desire to kill the old man. I would prefer he suffer the hell on earth of losing a son."

For endless seconds, Nitti said nothing, sitting still as stone. Then he said, "Mike, I'm afraid I can't accept your offer."

"Why?"

"Your wife and son are gone. So you kill Crazy Connor...Is one more body going to make any difference?"

"In my ledger book, yes. Mr. Nitti, you're a businessman. I've made a good sound business proposal—I'll work only for you."

Nitti stabbed out the cigarette in a tray on the table. "Mike, listen—I respect you. I'd like nothing better than to have you working for us. I know Al will feel the same way—he holds you, and your abilities, in high regard. But you put us in a difficult position."

"How?"

"You said it yourself, Mike. I'm a businessman. Much as I might personally loathe these despicable things that have been done to your family, the alliance between us and the Looneys is a long-standing one...and profitable."

"So if John Looney asks for your help—"

Nitti, impatient now, sat forward. "Let me tell you something you may not have realized. You've lived all these years under the protection of people who care about you. And those same people are trying to protect you now. Including me."

A chill passed through O'Sullivan's bones. "Looney's already come to you."

Nitti's mouth tightened, but his forehead was smooth. "If you go ahead with this thing—if you go through that door of vengeance, you'll be walking through it alone. And all that trust, all that loyalty we've talked about, will vanish...and, Mike, you can't make it, not on your own. Not with a little boy in tow."

This was over. O'Sullivan stood. "You're already protecting Connor Looney."

"We're not protecting Connor Looney, Mr. O'Sullivan," Nitti said, still seated, palms up. "We're protecting our interests."

Suddenly the weight of the worst hours of his life fell heavily on O'Sullivan's shoulders. He could not hide the disappointment in his voice. "I drove through the night to see you."

"I appreciate that. I appreciate the respect and trust you've shown—that you came unarmed...Now I suggest you drive yourself back to the Tri-Cities. I suggest you go home. Bury your wife and child. With our blessing."

O'Sullivan slowly shook his head. "It won't be that simple...I came asking only your neutrality. But the friend of my enemy *is* my enemy."

Nitti's eyes tightened. "Are you threatening me, Mr. O'Sullivan?"

"No. There'll be no bloodshed today. I don't think you want the newspapers to have a Lexington Hotel massacre to add to St. Valentine's day."

Nitti shrugged. "You're free to leave."

"Then I will."

O'Sullivan went out quickly, his eyes taking everything in as he moved through the reception area to where businessmen were stepping onto the elevator, Marco again playing operator. He stepped on, but then as the doors were about to be closed, thought better of it, and stepped off.

Down the corridor he found the service stairs and made his way to the lobby, where he blended into the throng of the thankfully busy hotel. Though he sensed no pursuit, he knew he could no longer trust Nitti—honor, loyalty, trust, all of those were old ideas, now.

But a new idea was forming. So this was all business, was it? Right now, the Capone crowd considered the Looney alliance a valuable asset. O'Sullivan aimed to change that view—he would hurt Frank Nitti, he would make the man bleed...not red, but green.

When O'Sullivan had left the room, Frank Nitti slipped through a doorway into a small side room, where two men had been tucked away, a mock grillwork vent enabling them to hear every word.

One of those men, a king in an easy chair, was John Looney, wearing a wrinkled, slightly shabby suit; more snappily dressed, in a chair at his left, sat his son Connor, anxious but sober.

Nitti approached Looney. "You heard?"

Looney nodded. To his son, he said, "Go upstairs. I can't stand the sight of you."

Connor sat forward, urgent but rational. "Pa, listen to me. O'Sullivan's in the hotel right now—you can end this. Mr. Nitti has more guns in this place than the Rock Island arsenal. We've got to take him now."

The old man shook his head. "In a busy hotel, with the resultant melee?...Connor—go upstairs."

Nitti almost smiled; how ridiculous it was, this grown man being sent to his room by his father! By all accounts, Connor was a fairly deadly character; he had been described to Nitti in varying ways, all unflattering: homicidal, unstable, volatile...

Yet the man wilted under his father's stare, and finally walked out.

And when his son was gone, Looney slumped in the chair, his head in his hands. "God help me. God help me...Christ, Frank, what do I do?"

Nitti took the chair Connor had vacated. "John...try to cast emotion aside. Think objectively. Suppose this O'Sullivan was just another soldier...Not someone you took a shine to, just some bird who got out of line."

But the old man only muttered, "God help me...God help me..."

"You know the answer, John."

Looney looked at Nitti with teary, rheumy eyes. "Make it quick, then. Has to be quick. Merciful."

Nitti nodded. "Done...and the kid?"

Dismay exaggerated the old man's features. "Oh, not the boy! Oh, Christ, no, no...I've already lost the wee one..."

Nitti had about had it up to here, from both O'Sullivan and Looney, with this operatic crap. "Right, fine, sure, and then one day, he's not a kid anymore, he's a man. You think Michael O'Sullivan, Jr., won't remember what your family did to his family?"

Looney considered that, then shook his head, violently. "Not the boy, Frank. Not the boy."

"I understand," Nitti said, already mulling over who to get for an assignment this important, this hazardous. Someone who had done jobs for the Outfit before, someone freelance but trustworthy, someone worthy of the Angel of Death, someone truly gifted...

Nitti smiled to himself; he knew just the man.

NINE

The true-crime writers call him "the Reporter." But that seems to be a latter-day appellation: no one has turned up any period reference, either in newspapers or the "true-detective" magazines of the day. This is probably because the public didn't become aware of Harlen Maguire until his death, after which the press—and later, researchers—put the facts together.

Maguire was a yellow journalist, and what was called a "picture chaser." He worked for Hearst papers in several big cities, Milwaukee and Chicago among them, and when a photo was too gruesome even for the tabloid press, he would peddle it to the even more exploitational newsstand crime magazines.

The gangland beat was his specialty—mob rubouts, in particular, though a good sex scandal or a celebrity autopsy also attracted his particular talent. His stature among the rags he worked for was based on his ability to show up at a grisly crime scene within moments of the carnage going down. He prowled the streets, with a mini-photo lab in his trunk. Some say he inspired the famed New York photographer WeeGee, who took Maguire's approach to truly artistic heights. Others say he was merely a ghoul with a camera.

Since no interviews with Maguire exist—and few who knew him, in his daily life, were aware of his dark, private existence—authors have been left to speculate, and dime-store psychology has it that Maguire became obsessed with his subject matter. Others wonder if some of the unsolved murders he "lucked" upon had been his own work—drumming up business, so to speak. An entire book has been devoted to Maguire photos and unsolved murders, *with analysis of a certain artistic, ironic staging that may indicate the shooter of the photo was also the shooter of the victim.*

How Maguire became aligned with the Capone crowd is unknown. One source claims that Capone hired Maguire to dig up the dirt on a ward heeler who was standing in the Outfit's way; another source says Maguire was tapped to find a racetrack manager who skipped town with a bundle of mob money.

At any rate, Harlen Maguire became one of Al Capone's most reliable and fearsome assassins, high on a short list that included "Machine Gun" Jack McGurn and Sam "Golf Bag" Hunt. A Chicago reporter who knew both Maguire and numerous Outfit mobsters claimed that Maguire worked directly under Frank Nitti, who reportedly relished the assassin's research skills and—under the cover of his profession—his access as a legitimate reporter. What else is a researcher but a hunter?

And Harlen "the Reporter" Maguire was the perfect hunter.

The portable camera, with extendible tripod, weighed around forty pounds, but the slender man carrying it—pale, boyishly handsome, but nonetheless thirty years of age—moved quickly along the sidewalk, as if the apparatus he was hauling were feather light.

Harlen Maguire might have been any reporter on the prowl for a good story, but the sharp cut of his suit, the rich fabric of his topcoat, and the snappy bowler said otherwise...though even a decent off-the-rack suit would have stood out in this neighborhood. This was Little Village, after all, a slum-ridden neighborhood on Chicago's West Side, where Italian blood often ran hot... and sometimes just ran.

Maguire figured the fire-escape entrance to the tenement block would be less crowded, but a small crowd—undissuaded by the bitter winter morning chill—had gathered here, as well. Most of them were out of work, and a juicy neighborhood murder was just the thing to warm the cockles.

Shouldering his way through, Maguire announced himself as press—"Out of the way! Excuse me, ma'am—thank you!"—and within a minute he was upstairs and inside the dingy one-room flat where, over by the kitchen area, police and a coroner's doc were dealing with a man of average build in work shirt and denims who was slashed here and there, some nasty cuts that the guy didn't even seem to notice, ranting, raving.

"I took the knife away from the son of a bitch! He was raping my wife...son of a goddamn bitch! Raping my wife..."

No woman was present, so the cops had already gotten her out of there. And while they were dealing with the killer, Maguire would take a gander at the killee...

His subject was in the bedroom corner of the flat, by a window looking out on the El tracks, a big oaf with his eyes and mouth open, sprawled on the floor with multiple stab wounds in his chest, like a bouquet of flowers: black entry gouges centered blossoms of red. His pants were embarrassingly down, his striped shorts discreetly up. The weapon was on the floor, a small hunting knife with blood smeared almost to the hilt.

Arms outstretched, there was a certain Pagliacci posture about the corpse that appealed to the photographer's sensibilities. This would be too much for the *Herald-American*, but the editor over at *Startling Detective* would pay through the nose—crimes of passion burned up the newsstands.

With swift precision he assembled his tools, camera out of its case, tripod legs extending, bellows growing, and soon the artist was ready to go to work. To create something permanent out of the temporary, to make a sort of life out of death.

But that bastard husband was still ranting, hands in the air, pacing around. "I tell you, it was self-defense! You saw her—her clothes ripped off. He was raping her, I tell you!"

A cop was trying to contain the guy, saying, "Come on, buddy! Hold still—you're tramplin' on the evidence."

"*Hey!*" Maguire said. "Could the deceased and I have a little peace and quiet? Trying to work in here. Let a guy make a living."

He'd already slipped the cop—O'Ryan, who Maguire had run into on several prior occasions—a sawbuck, coming in.

"Maguire," O'Ryan said, "we're all just trying to do our jobs."

The photographer went over and pressed another sawbuck into the cop's palm. "Why don't you do yours out in the hall?"

"No reason why not," the cop said, pleasantly, and hauled the killer's ass out of there, the medic tagging after.

Then it was only the photographer and his subject, who was not likely to give him any problems. Maguire stepped behind the tripod and began to focus, the image of the corpse upside-down in his viewfinder.

"Now smile," Maguire said softly.

But just as he was about to take his shot, Maguire heard a bubbling gasp...and he stepped from behind the camera and took a right-side up look at the stiff.

Only this wasn't a stiff: the oaf was gulping for air, blood bubbling, trickling.

Maguire shook his head—son of a bitch was ruining everything. What was a crime of passion without a murder? He glanced at the closed door, and the rumble of an approaching train out on the El already was blotting out the pitiful groans of the uncooperative would-be corpse.

The photographer took a handkerchief from his pocket, then knelt over the victim; the man's open eyes had lost their blankness, consciousness glimmering. So Maguire covered the man's bloody mouth with the hanky-in-hand, cupping it, and with his other hand squeezed the victim's nose closed.

As the El thundered past, the oaf struggled a little—not much, he'd have probably croaked on the way to the hospital, anyway—and Maguire looked into the man's eyes, watching the consciousness wink out, like the wind quenching a candle.

Then he wiped the fresh blood from the corpse's face, wadded up the handkerchief, slipped it in his pocket, and got back behind the tripod—with no more prima donna malarkey from his subject.

As his father drove the rural off-roads, Michael rode in the backseat, so he could stretch out and nap or just rest, if he felt like it. But right now he was wide awake, and he was glad when Papa—after a long interval of silence—struck up a conversation.

"Do you remember your Aunt Sarah? Your Uncle Bob?"

He sat forward, leaned on the seat. "I'm not sure..."

"Your mother's sister, in Perdition. Bob is her husband—your uncle...your *real* uncle."

"*Per* what?"

"Perdition. It's in Kansas. A little farm, next to a lake?"

"Was I little?"

Papa nodded. "We went there, all of us, when you were four, maybe five. Perdition's a bump in the road, near Fall River Lake. Peter was just a little tyke. It's beautiful...Do you remember?"

"Do they have a dog?"

Papa glanced back him, puzzled. "I'm not sure."

"Well, the place I remember, they had a dog and it jumped up at the table and took a bite out of Mama's sandwich."

His father glanced at him again, a tiny, tiny smile forming.

"And so Mama gave it to him," the boy continued. "I mean, once the dog took a bite, it was his, she said."

Michael could still remember their laughter, at the time; but he didn't feel like laughing, now. Neither did Papa, apparently. Because he was just staring at the road.

After a while, Michael asked, "What about it?"

"What about what?"

"Per...Perdition."

"Oh. Well...that's where we're going."

But that night they stayed in McGregor, Iowa, just another "bump in the road" with a town square and quiet streets. The Starr Motel was toward the edge of the little farming community, a typical roadside motor court. The room was clean but the furnishings were old and cheap, the lighting dim and yellowish, the covers and sheets worn, the kerosene space heater smelly, and, when the boy sat on the edge of the bed and its thin mattress, the springs squeaky. When they had traveled with Mama and Peter, the family stayed in nicer places than this. Not that he cared. The boy was preoccupied: he knew, he just knew, that his father was going to dump him at that place on some lake with this aunt and uncle who he barely remembered.

His father was sitting in a chair by the dresser next to the door, leaning forward, hands folded, thinking. The boy knew he probably shouldn't say anything. Then he did: "Papa—how long will we be staying at Aunt Sarah's?"

He looked up, paused, then finally said, "Michael, *you'll* be staying there…I won't. Not right away."

Michael didn't argue with his father—what good would it do? He just said, "How long are you going to leave me there?"

"I don't know. Until it's safe."

"How will you know it's safe?"

"I'll know," he said firmly, and stood. "Son, I have to use the phone, in the motel office…You know what to do, if anyone comes through that door."

Michael nodded and got up to get his jacket from the chair he'd draped it over. The boy took the revolver from the pocket and went back to the bed, setting the gun next to his Tom Mix Big Little Book on the nightstand.

His father was at the door when Michael asked, "Who are you calling, Papa?"

"Your Uncle Bob. To let him know we're coming for a visit."

And Papa went out, leaving the boy to think how normal that had sounded.

In the motel office, O'Sullivan gave the desk man a five-dollar bill to cover the long-distance call.

The farmer's husky voice, over the crackling wire, was strangely soothing to O'Sullivan's ear. "Sarah's in Rock Island, Mike...in your house. Seeing to the services for Annie and little Pete."

"That's damn decent of you, Bob."

"Wish we could do more. I wanted to go myself, the train fare for one purt' near broke us."

"I'll help you out, when I see you."

"I didn't mean...When will that be?"

And O'Sullivan explained how he hoped he could entrust his son to the couple, until he worked out his "problem" with the Looney family.

"You know we'll love to have the lad, Mike—we never had any of our own. It might be a balm for Sarah's busted heart."

"I know she loved Annie."

"Loved her like life itself. Guess I don't have to tell you what a saint Annie was—not a spoiled bone in her body, even if she was the younger girl, the baby..."

O'Sullivan couldn't hear any more of that. "Bob, before I turn Michael over to you, we have to make sure it's safe."

"Not sure I understand."

"Looney's men...maybe Capone's men...may be watching your house. They could be staying in town..."

"Understood. Give it a couple days and call me back—if the crows are sittin' on the fence, eyes on the corn, this old farmer'll spot 'em."

When O'Sullivan returned to the room, Michael was under the covers, shivering. It was cold in there, and the blankets were skimpy and threadbare, and the kerosene floor heater blew less hot hair than Uncle Bob.

"Didn't you pack a sweater?" he asked the boy.

"No. I forgot."

O'Sullivan almost reminded Michael that he certainly hadn't "forgotten" to pack those comic-strip books and toys; but instead the man went to his own suitcase, found a sweater, and started putting it on over the boy's head.

Michael pulled it out of his father's hands, putting it on himself, in a small show of defiance.

His son was obviously upset about his father leaving him at the uncle and aunt's. But O'Sullivan had said all he intended to on the subject, and went to the sink to wash up for bed.

From behind him, his son—his voice sounding very small—said, "I miss Mama and Peter."

"I know," O'Sullivan said, wishing he knew something about comforting a child. "I miss them, too."

That same evening, Maguire was in his studio in his Chicago apartment, in the red glow of the darkroom, surrounded by shelves of his beloved cameras, developing his photos. With tweezers, he fished a photo of the dead oaf out of the tray of fixing solution, then hung it up to dry. He was on photo number six, the last of the usable shots, when the phone rang.

With no sense of urgency, he wandered out into the living room of the small but nicely furnished flat, adorned with the artist's own work: framed photos of dead bodies, here a corpse in a pool hall, there a shot-up gangster in a corridor, here a bloody naked suicide in a bathtub. It was home to him—he just didn't bring his dates here.

Flopping on the sofa next to the phone on an end table, he answered with his usual, "Harlen Maguire."

"Frank Nitti," the assured voice said on the other end of the line.

Maguire scribbled on a pad as Nitti spoke, making notes, doodling, as the ganglord filled him in on the assignment, saying, "This may take some time—some real tracking, some real research. I can offer you sixteen hundred."

"Good...because that's my usual rate, Mr. Nitti. As you know...And anything I make on the photographs is mine."

"I'm not interested in photography, Mr. Maguire. But I do think creating evidence at the scene of your own crimes is reckless."

"I'm still around. You're still calling."

"I need you to drop everything. You need to go right away."

"That's no problem."

"The funeral's tomorrow afternoon—it's a three-, maybe four-hour drive to the Tri-Cities."

"I travel light."

Nitti paused. "You do know who Michael O'Sullivan is."

"Sure. Never met him. But I know his work...Angel of Death, pretty fancy moniker."

"Well deserved."

"You don't have to tell me. I'm a fan of his. So...he isn't traveling alone—there's a kid?"

"His son—Michael O'Sullivan, Jr. Eleven. Looks younger."

Maguire wrote the boy's name and age down and then turned the "11" into a square and made it into a face, drawing hair, ears, and two dots for eyes.

"So," Maguire said, "what do I do with junior?"

"What do you usually do with witnesses?"

"Okay." He drew a downturned mouth on the doodled face. "Will do."

And they said their good-byes, and he hung up, knowing he should have asked for more, for clipping the kid; but not wanting to cross Nitti. It wasn't a matter of being afraid of the gangster, though Nitti was not to be underestimated, former torpedo that he was. It wasn't that, at all...

Maguire got up to straighten one of the framed photos—he'd noticed it hanging crooked, as he spoke to Nitti. This shot was of a murder, or rather murders, he hadn't done; but one of his nicest compositions nonetheless: six corpses on the floor of S-M-C

Cartage, brains spilling out of their shattered skulls—the seventh corpse had crawled out of frame, toward the door, compromising but not really spoiling this record of the St. Valentine's Day massacre.

No, Maguire didn't want to risk losing the assignment.

He'd always wanted to meet the Angel of Death. And adding Michael O'Sullivan's portrait would be a crowning touch to his photo gallery.

The next day, when Michael awoke, the sun was filtering in brightly through the drawn curtains. An oily, metallic smell was in the air—like a machine shop. He looked over toward his father's bed and saw his father sitting there like an Indian, with newspapers spread out before him on top of the covers and the parts of the tommy gun arrayed like dishes of food on a picnic.

Papa had rags and various pipe-cleaner-like tools and little bottles of stuff. He was methodically cleaning the pieces of the weapon. The pistol lay to one side—either waiting its turn, or already finished with.

The boy rubbed his eyes. "What…what time is it?"

"After two."

The boy tried to make that work. He sat up. "In the afternoon?"

His father nodded. "You were tired. I slept a long time, too… We needed it. Wash up and get dressed."

"Are we going?"

"We'll eat. There's something we need to do…We're staying here tonight."

"Again? Why?"

"Resting up. Getting ready. Go—wash up."

They walked to the town square—it was only a few blocks— and ate at a little café. Michael asked if he could have breakfast instead of lunch, and they were nice and fixed him eggs and bacon and pancakes. Papa ordered the blue plate special, which was meat loaf and mashed potatoes, but he didn't eat much of it.

Afterward, Papa said, "Let's take a walk," and the day seemed cold and dreary for that, but Michael was in no position to argue. They crossed a little park and, a block off the business district, came to a small country church—a Catholic church. Michael quickly realized this was his father's destination—Papa must have spotted the church when they came into town.

In the gravel parking lot, Michael tugged his father's sleeve and the man stopped and looked down at his son.

"Why are we going here?"

"There's a funeral today."

"At this church?"

"Back home."

"For Mama? And Peter?"

"Yes. And we're not there. But we should go in, and light a candle for them. And pray for them."

This seemed reasonable to Michael, but something else didn't. Confused, he asked, "Are you sure we can go in there?"

"Of course we can."

"But, Papa...it's a *Catholic* church."

His father's smile was so faint, it could barely be made out. "The reach of our enemies doesn't extend here. We'll be fine."

Michael sat in a pew in the back of the church while his father knelt at the altar, praying before Christ on his cross. For a small church, they had a really big Christ—he looked real, and even from where Michael sat, the Lord's suffering was obvious. He watched as Papa lighted two candles—one for Mama, one for Peter. Then Papa lighted one more candle, which puzzled the boy.

After a while, the black-robed priest—white haired, well fed, with an expression that was both friendly and serious—stepped from the sacristy, and stopped to study the stranger, still kneeling, praying.

The priest introduced himself as Father O'Hara and then spoke with Papa—Michael couldn't hear the rest of it, they were almost whispering—and then the priest went back to the sacristy and soon returned, in his vestments. Then Papa stepped into the confessional.

Michael sat and prayed for his mother and his brother, and finally his father came out, having unburdened his soul. The priest came out, too—Michael knew that God had made Irishmen pale, but not as pale as that priest looked.

Of the ninety-five acres of Chippiannock Cemetery, five were reserved for Catholic families. The Indians had called the place Manitou Ridge, and Sauk wives had raised corn on the fertile, gently sloping summit, to feed the men, encamped for war. The white people who turned it into a cemetery called it Chippiannock—an Indian word for "village of the dead."

A statue of a dog lay faithfully at the grave of a boy, five, and girl, three, who back in pioneer days had died of typhoid fever. An elaborate monument with a soldier on either side and an eagle atop cannon balls saluted the local fallen of American wars. Colonel George Davenport, the man for whom the city across the river was named, lay here, not in Iowa. And stone cherubs and angels guarded the gray gravestones without complaint, underdressed though they were for the winter afternoon.

All of these made for good color, Maguire knew; he'd arrived an hour prior to the graveside services, and a sawbuck bought a nickel tour from a groundskeeper, with a few tidbits thrown in for free by a pair of gravediggers. The factual detective story magazines ate this stuff up almost as much as they did sex and slaughter.

As distant church bells tolled on cue, Maguire kept his distance, at the back of the gathering of mourners—perhaps two dozen—attending the burial of Anne Louise O'Sullivan and Peter David O'Sullivan. There had been no church service, no mass. The circumstances were too strained, and strange, for that.

He didn't expect O'Sullivan to show—but you never knew. Some of these tough men had sentimental streaks a yard wide.

So he kept watch, noting the armed bodyguards grouped around John Looney, who was weeping, the goddamn hypocrite. No sign of his loony son Connor.

After the two flower-draped caskets were lowered, various mourners came up to a pleasant-looking, white-haired woman in her late forties, dressed in dignified black; they would introduce themselves and then express their condolences. This would be the surviving relative, clearly from out of town, to whom these sad arrangements and duties had fallen.

He followed several cars—including the funeral-home limousine—to the house in Rock Island that matched the address Nitti had given him. The O'Sullivan family had lived in this fairly large two-story home—old Looney had treated his top gunman well, up to the point where the guy's wife and kid got bumped off, anyway.

Cars pulled into the driveway, and drew up along the street in front, as various mourners paid their respects, going up to the door in little informal groups. Maguire fell in with one of these mournful clusters.

With the bereaved relative occupied with her guests—food in the kitchen had been provided by neighbors—Maguire prowled the residence inconspicuously, taking in details like a hungry man took in a meal. He looked at old photos, family portraits of Annie and her kids together; O'Sullivan always seemed to stand to one side, vaguely detached.

Maguire understood that. Standing outside of yourself was necessary, when your profession was death. He had seen the same expression on the face of the mortician who'd been running the show at the graveyard that afternoon.

Some of the portraits had John Looney in them—arms around the boys, at age four and five he'd guess...so very grandfatherly. How goddamn touching, Maguire thought. A middle-aged woman—Looney's wife—was in some of the pictures, always standing next to the old man. She hadn't been at the services today. Dead, probably.

He asked where the bathroom was and someone pointed him upstairs. Glass of punch in hand, Maguire moved casually down the second-floor corridor; but once he was in the room that had been the boys' bedroom, he probed with surgical precision. In a drawer next to one of the boy's beds—the older boy?—he found a stash of Big Little Books, westerns mostly. Beneath the mattress he discovered a pouch of Bugler tobacco...definitely the older boy, he thought with a smile.

In the master bedroom he found little of note, except perhaps the Catholic trappings—a crucifix, devotional paintings, Christ revealing His sacred heart. Tasteful, traditional nonsense. Maguire wondered if these beliefs were the dead wife's alone—if O'Sullivan had a religious streak, that might prove an Achilles's heel.

Sentimental—these killers could be so goddamn sentimental. Was O'Sullivan one of those clowns who thought he could put the killing in one compartment, and his family in another? That was a weak mental outlook—the fabled Angel of Death was just a man after all, a flawed man...

Yet even as these thoughts flowed through his mind, Maguire knew he was trying to rationalize the intimidation he felt. He'd never had this big a challenge—and it was daunting.

And thrilling.

In the room at the Starr Motel, on his side of the nightstand, Michael placed a small plaster Madonna that he'd picked out from a basket of them back at that church; on his father's side of the nightstand, the .45 Colt rested.

The Madonna made Michael think of something he'd meant to ask his father earlier.

"Why did you light an extra candle, Papa?"

His father—washing one of the boy's shirts in the sink—didn't answer at first. Then he said, "That was for the man I killed, the night we left."

So that *had* been a shot, outside the hotel the other night...

"Papa?"

"What?"

"Do I have to go to Aunt Sarah's?"

"Yes. We had this conversation."

"I know, but...are you coming back for me?"

Hanging the damp shirt over a towel rack, Papa said, "Yes! Of course I am."

"When?"

Now his father was getting irritated. "Michael, I don't know. I'm doing this to protect you."

"If you want to protect me," the boy insisted, "you have to stay with me!"

Papa almost shouted: "Not until I deal with Connor Looney!"

The outburst surprised both of them.

Quietly, almost embarrassed, Papa said, "You won't be safe... not until I deal with him."

Michael knew what "deal with him" meant: one day, Papa would be lighting another candle.

Papa was drying off his hands. His voice gentle now, he said, "I have to make another call, son. You know what to do."

"You won't be gone long, will you?"

Papa was putting on his suit jacket; the .45 was under his shoulder. "No."

In the motel office, O'Sullivan handed the clerk another five-spot and made the trunk call. Telling the operator the telephone number—that familiar number—gave O'Sullivan a twinge. He half expected Annie to answer, and the voice that did answer—"Hello, O'Sullivan residence"—had some of Annie in it.

Her sister Sarah and Annie were much alike, after all.

"Sarah?"

"Mike. Thank God..."

"We're okay. Michael and I."

"Where are you?"

"On the road. We're heading to your place, if that's all right."

Relief colored the voice. "Of course. Have you spoken to Bob?"

"Yes. I thought perhaps you two had talked."

"No. I've been busy since I got here...with the arrangements. I kept it simple. I hope you don't mind...I know Annie would have preferred a full mass..."

"She would have preferred a long life. Merciful thing was to set her to rest."

"Oh, Mike...That man was there, the one you worked for."

"...Looney. Was his son with him?" He quickly described Connor.

"I don't think so. He did have two big men at his side, though."

Jimmy and Sean, probably, O'Sullivan thought. Bodyguards at a funeral—hell of a thing.

"How...how was it?"

"Dignified. Such lovely flowers. She had so many friends. Peter's class at the Villa sent a beautiful wreath. The cemetery, Chippiannock, is breathtaking...a bit austere, perhaps, but...oh, Mike...are you still there, Mike?"

"We'll see you soon," he said. He put the receiver in the hook.

And across the miles, in the house that had been O'Sullivan's, on the hallway phone that not long ago Connor Looney had taken off the hook, the mourner who was actually Harlen Maguire quietly hung up the phone, as well.

TEN

My memories of traveling with my father are something of a blur—when I think back, I see him behind the wheel, sometimes unshaven, sometimes not. When things between us were strained—as when I was pouting over him dragging me to Aunt Sarah and Uncle Bob's—I would ride in back, the whole seat to myself (me and the black tommy gun case, anyway), getting as far away from him as I could, in our little world that was the inside of the Ford.

My other memory is the heartland—middle America in all its vastness, sometimes rolling landscape, like a Grant Wood painting; other times flatness stretching to the horizon, winter barren, whites and browns and tans and grays. For every field there was a forest; for every ten barns, one church. The ribbons of concrete and gravel and dirt seemed to extend to eternity, endless sentences punctuated by the exclamation points of telephone poles—reminders that this pioneer country had been settled, that it was civilized now...even if I was sharing the backseat of a Ford with a Thompson submachine gun in a hard-shell case.

I can only speculate on what must have been going through Harlen Maguire's mind as he tracked us. Surely his photographer's eye had to have been struck by the abstract beauty of America's richest soil masquerading, in winter slumber, as wasteland. Or was he too consumed with the mission at hand—was he focused hard on the empty road, a pistol and camera on the seat beside him?

In later years, when Maguire's photographic gallery came to light, and researchers had access to the grisly photos he'd shot over his grim career, images of our room at the Starr Motel in McGregor, Iowa, were part of the inventory. They were published in a section of the book designed to show Maguire's interests extended to studies beyond the newly dead.

How odd it was, so many years later, to open up an oversized art book, with its slick pages, and find an introduction that noted, "Maguire's fascination with murder victims is perhaps as controversial as the Diane Arbus predilection for posing the retarded." How strange seeing Ansel Adams-ish midwestern landscapes in a section that included stark photographs of that empty motel room, with an emphasis on a plaster Madonna on the nightstand, "left behind by some nameless traveler" (the caption writer said).

Particularly odd, particularly strange, when that nameless traveler—me—knew full well that these were not abstract art studies at all, but evidence of the man who had tracked my father and myself, down lonely heartland highways.

Father and son were in Missouri now, traversing rolling prairie land, cutting down State Highway 13, where at a town called Collins they would take the road into Perdition, near Fall River Lake. O'Sullivan stopped at a roadside diner outside Bethany, a boxcar whose "We Never Close" neon made a ghostly glow at dusk.

They had driven all day, and said little to each other. O'Sullivan was lost in thought, working out a plan to force Nitti and Capone to abandon their support of the Looneys and turn Connor over to him. But he could not make it work, a man alone, and no matter how he mentally rearranged the cards, the hand he'd been dealt did not seem a winning one.

He knew his son was sulking, but that only made the boy less trouble, so he let it go. They'd eaten lunch at a small-town café, and the boy had again snookered the help into making him a breakfast. O'Sullivan's own appetite remained stunted, and he'd picked at his Salisbury steak.

Now, many hours of driving later, the man was ready to give eating a try again; and his son should have some food.

In the boxcar diner's parking lot, O'Sullivan pulled into a stall adjacent to the window on an empty booth. He turned to his boy, in the backseat. "Hungry?"

Michael was reading one of the little comic-strip books. He didn't look at his father when he grunted, "No."

"Might not be another diner for a while," O'Sullivan said.

The boy shrugged. "I'm still not hungry."

"You should eat something."

"I'm reading."

That was all the effort O'Sullivan was prepared to give it, and he got out of the car, leaving the boy to his book and his brooding. Inside the brightly lit green-and-brown diner, business was slow for this close to suppertime—a farm couple in a booth having a meal, a farmer drinking coffee at the counter.

Leaving his topcoat and fedora on, he took the booth next to his car, where he could see Michael's head in the backseat, looking down at his book; he could also see the diner's door, from here. A waitress came over, a blowsy brunette with plenty of lipstick and just as much personality. "Ruby" was stitched on her uniform blouse. She brought water and coffee.

"You look like a hundred miles of bad road, sweetie," she said.

"That's a low estimate," he said. Hunger was finally stirring, and he also thought he might be able to stir his son into eating by making a show of a meal. "I want a T-bone, rare."

"How rare, sugar?"

"When I stick in the knife, if it doesn't moo, it goes back."

"Okay, Dracula. Mashed or fries?"

"Mashed...Pay phone?"

"No public phone. I'd let you use ours, but the manager ain't here."

"I really need to use the phone." He held up a sawbuck. "I'll make it quick."

She snatched the ten-dollar bill out of his hands before he could change his mind. "It's by the register."

O'Sullivan was already heading toward the phone. "Okay—watch my booth for me?"

"Sure, honey." She eyeballed the nearly deserted diner. "I'll see if I can hold back the crowd."

He made the trunk call to Uncle Bob, who said, "No, Mike—not a crow on the fence. No strangers in Perdition, neither."

"Good. You should see us tomorrow, late."

"Fine. Sarah'll be home by midafternoon. We'll have ourselves a reunion."

"I won't be staying long."

"All things considered, that's probably wise. Meaning no offense."

"None taken."

He was saying his good-byes when the bell over the door dinged, and, just as the farm couple was leaving, a cop came in—a man in his forties who'd never missed a meal. The blue uniform indicated a town cop, not a sheriff's man or state policeman. The cop nodded and smiled to O'Sullivan, who nodded and smiled back, hanging up the phone.

The cop settled on a stool near, but not next to, the farmer, who was having a piece of apple pie.

O'Sullivan considered leaving, but Ruby was on her way with his T-bone, smelling very good indeed (the steak—Ruby's perfume was another matter), and his instincts said the cop's presence was innocent. So he sat in the booth and dug in, using a steak knife on the nicely rare piece of corn-fed Missouri beef. He glanced out the window, to see if this was tempting Michael, but the boy's head was no longer visible.

Knowing the boy was probably stretched out sleeping, O'Sullivan nonetheless wondered if he should go out there and check on him. Night had smothered dusk, and that was just enough to make O'Sullivan edgy. He was sipping his coffee, looking out the window at the Michael-less backseat window when the bright sweep of headlights, a vehicle coming into the diner parking lot, made him wince.

The driver parked, got out—O'Sullivan noted the uptown topcoat and bowler as atypical for this rural area—and glanced at O'Sullivan's car. Something about the glance was less casual than it tried to be. In his booth by the window, O'Sullivan craned his neck, trying to see the front license plate, couldn't, and as the bell over the door dinged, he returned to his meal.

O'Sullivan seemed to be looking at nothing in particular, but he noted the way the newcomer was registering the farmer at the counter…and especially the cop. Right now O'Sullivan was the only other patron. Dark-haired but pale, the guy had a narrow, angular face—youthful, though O'Sullivan made him as around thirty.

But the oddest thing about him was the camera: he had a camera in his hands, as if he'd come to photograph this mundane diner. That was no tourist camera, either—O'Sullivan recognized it as one of those reflex-and-view cameras the news photogs used. Those babies went for over a hundred bucks…

The man with the camera took the booth next to O'Sullivan's, but sat opposite him, the two men facing—and right now both were going out of their way not to look at each other.

Water and coffee in hand, Ruby approached the new customer, who said to her, "Pretty dead in here, huh?"

"You kiddin'? This is a stampede. Who has money for luxuries like eating, in these hard times."

"Well, I do."

"You look like it, handsome. What can I do you for?"

"What's tonight's special?"

"Honey, everything's special."

"Really?"

"Everything but the food."

The guy laughed at that—giving the remark a little more re-action than it deserved. "Ruby, you oughta be on the radio."

"Don't I know it. I wrote to Amos and Andy, but they didn't write back."

Still chuckling, glancing at the menu, the man said, "Didn't write back...Well, give me some of that honey-dipped fried chicken."

"Duck soup. Need any sugar or cream for that coffee?"

"No. Black is fine."

The cheerful waitress sauntered off, and the customer reached into his topcoat pocket and withdrew a roll of film. He began to load the camera, O'Sullivan noting all this, without seeming to.

Reaching in his own topcoat pocket, O'Sullivan withdrew his small silver flask. Putting a little weave into his actions, he poured whiskey into his coffee cup.

"Doesn't bother me," the man said.

O'Sullivan glanced up, seemingly unsteady, and—putting a tiny slur in his voice, not overdoing it—replied, "Bother what?"

The man leaned forward and whispered, as if keeping this conversation from the cop at the counter. "The hooch—used to be a free country. Man wants a little snort, no skin off my hindquarters."

Eyes half-hooded, O'Sullivan smiled, poured more whiskey into the cup, hoping he was playing his role more convincingly than the fellow in the next booth was. Too friendly, way too friendly...

O'Sullivan raised the flask, in offering.

The man raised a hand in surrender. "No thank you, sir." Then he returned to loading the camera, snapping it shut, fully loaded now.

"Profession?" O'Sullivan asked, voice wavering slightly, referring to the camera. "Or passion?"

"Little of both, I guess," the guy said with a shrug. He had cold eyes that didn't blink much; he'd probably worn that same smile, O'Sullivan thought, when he was a kid pulling the wings off flies.

"To be paid to do," the man was saying, "what you love to do...Isn't that the American dream?"

O'Sullivan lifted his shoulders, set them down, as if the action required both thought and effort. "Guess so."

"And yourself?"

"Huh?"

"What's your business?"

O'Sullivan blinked, thinking that over. "I'm *in* business."

"I knew it!" the guy said. "When I saw that fancy Ford, I thought, 'There goes a businessman.' And what is your business?"

"Salesman. Machine parts."

"Machine parts. The wheels that make the world go 'round—vital work. That's wonderful."

"Trus' me," O'Sullivan said, "it isn't...So who do you work for?"

"Can you keep a secret?" He sat forward again, whispering: "I'm afraid I'm a tool of the yellow press...for which I humbly apologize."

"No kidding? What paper?"

"Different ones. Also magazines. Ever read *Startling Detective*? *Real Fact Crime*?"

"No...I'm the squeamish type."

"Not me...I shoot the dead."

O'Sullivan tilted his head. "What say?"

"Dead bodies, at crime scenes. The grislier the better, my editors say. What, did you think *I* killed them?"

With a laugh, O'Sullivan said, "Should hope not."

Ruby came over to see if O'Sullivan needed more coffee. He said he didn't. She asked if he wanted a slice of pie. He said not. Then she refilled the photographer's cup and went back behind the counter.

The photographer picked up where he'd left off: "I know it probably sounds...sick. But death has always fascinated me. Dead bodies, particularly."

O'Sullivan shivered. "Hey, I'm trying to keep a meal down, over here."

"Now, friend, wait, think it over—the world needs people who aren't afraid to look at unpleasantness. Where would we be without doctors? Without morticians?"

"I suppose."

"The look of a person, right after life has left him—it's fascinating. Ever see a dead body? I don't mean in a coffin...I mean within minutes, seconds, of their last breath?"

O'Sullivan nodded.

"You have? Well, I'm sorry for you, friend, if it was a loved one or a friend...terrible thing, loss of life. But it sure does make you feel *alive*, doesn't it?"

O'Sullivan raised his coffee cup. "I'll drink to that."

The man was eyeing the cop at the counter, who was finishing up, paying Ruby.

Then those unblinking eyes narrowed. "Funny—you're sweating."

O'Sullivan sipped the spiked coffee. "Am I?"

"Beads all over your forehead. *Is* a little warm in here. Funny, though, seein' a guy sweating in the dead of winter. 'Course, the booze can make a man sweat."

"And piss, too," O'Sullivan said, scooching out of the booth.

"Hey, you need a hand, bud?"

"No—I'll be fine," O'Sullivan said, standing unsteadily. He began to make his way to the john, stumbling as he went.

"Take it easy, pal!" the man with the camera said.

"Thanks…watch my coffee for me."

And O'Sullivan staggered into the men's room.

Harlen Maguire sat, turned around in the booth, wondering if Mike O'Sullivan was as drunk as he seemed. Half a minute passed, and the bell over the door dinged—the cop going out.

Maguire reached in his jacket pocket, withdrew the .38 revolver, keeping it out of sight, beneath the counter. A car started up—pulled out. Good. With the cop gone, Maguire had no problem with what lay ahead of him—a farmer, a waitress, a cook. The gleaming tile of the diner, with its chrome fixtures, splashed with blood (red registering black on film), littered with corpses…what a picture. He wouldn't even need a flash…

The bell over the door dinged—okay, one more customer, just another element of his composition…*but it was the cop again!*

Ambling in, the officer said to Ruby, "I'm sorry, ain't got my head screwed on, tonight—I forgot your tip!"

And Maguire flew out of the booth, out of the diner, and the Ford was gone—he could hear it accelerating down the highway, roaring off.

Shit!

He ran to his own car—the Illinois plates screaming at him: *idiot!*—and found his tires slashed…four goddamn flats!

Cop inside or not, Maguire ran into the road, where O'Sullivan's taillights receded into the distance, and slowly, steadily, he aimed the long-barreled revolver…

In the Ford, O'Sullivan—not drunk at all, though rolling down the window one-handed, to combat the whiskey he'd chugged for the sake of show—was yelling at his boy: "*Down!* Get down—stay down!"

Michael, waking up in the backseat, popped his head up, saying, "What? Why? What's goin'—"

And his father reached back and physically shoved him down as the rear window exploded.

Behind them, pleased at the sound of the shattered glass, Maguire fired again, this time with no success.

"Damnit," he said, standing in the road.

The cop, having heard the shot, came running out, one hand unbuttoning a holstered sidearm. "*Hey!* What the hell you think you're—"

Maguire turned and shot him in the head.

Blood mist blossomed in the night, as the dead cop tumbled onto his back. With a sigh, disappointed but willing to salvage the evening, Maguire and his gun and his camera headed back into the diner, to finish up.

O'Sullivan drove the speed limit, relieved that no headlights were coming up behind him, grateful for the dark night and the empty highway. He was heading up Highway 13, back toward where they'd come, the turn-off to the Perdition road no longer an option.

In his cap and heavy winter coat, pushed down by his papa, Michael hadn't been hurt by the flying glass—neither had O'Sullivan—and shards lay in the backseat like scattered ice.

Questions were tumbling out of a frightened Michael. "What happened back there? Who shot at us?"

O'Sullivan answered, watching the boy in the rearview mirror. "A man in the diner was sent to kill us."

"How did you know he was? Did he point a gun...?"

"No. I saw him and knew, that's all."

"But, Papa—how could you know?"

Now he turned and looked back at his son and told him— flat-out told him: "Because, Michael—I used to have his job!"

O'Sullivan took a side road. A few miles later, he drove up into the entry of an open field and after perhaps half a mile stopped the car, cutting the lights. The man with the camera would not find them here.

Out of breath, he turned to his son, who was wide-eyed and also breathing hard. Fury rose in O'Sullivan like lava, erupting: "When I tell you to do something, goddamn *do* it!"

"Papa..."

"When I say get down, you get down. You don't ask questions. There's no time for questions. You can die in the time it takes to ask a goddamn question!"

"I didn't—"

"You didn't *listen*. From now on, if I say we're stopping to eat, you stay with me! At my side. You will listen to what I say and do as I say, or you can get the hell out of this car and take care of yourself."

The boy's eyes were huge. "What?"

"Make up your mind, Michael. I can't fight them and you. Not at the same time."

And now the boy got mad, shouting defensively, "I can take care of myself just fine! You never wanted me along, anyway! You blame *me* for this—you think it's all *my* fault!"

"Stop it, Michael...stop that talk."

"He meant to kill me and Peter died instead and—"

"It was not your fault! The fault lies with the betrayers—Looney and his son. Listen to me—listen! You are not responsible for the deaths of your brother and your mother...and neither am I. But I am responsible for their retribution."

The boy seemed to understand; but he still sounded angry when he said, "Just take me to Aunt Sarah's."

"I can't."

"...What?"

"Not now."

"But...why?"

He answered the boy's question with one of his own: "How did that man find us tonight?"

"I don't know—how did he? How *could* he?"

O'Sullivan shook his head. "There's only one way, son—he knew where we were heading."

"So I can't go stay with Aunt Sarah and Uncle Bob."

"Someday, maybe we both can."

He could tell this terrible turn was, to his son, good news.

Trying not to smile, the boy said, "So…what are we going to do, now?"

O'Sullivan sighed. "Get in front."

"Okay," Michael said, and scrambled up next to his father.

O'Sullivan touched his son's arm. "I've been thinking about doing something…but I couldn't figure out a way to do it alone. With you helping, I can make it work. But it's dangerous."

Michael shrugged. "I don't care. I just want to be with you. I just want to help."

He held his son's eyes with his. "Then you need to listen to me…all right? You can't be a little boy—you have to be the man helping me. Or we'll both be dead."

Michael nodded.

"This is what we have to do," O'Sullivan said. "We have to convince the Chicago gangsters to give us Connor Looney."

"How can you make them do that?"

"'We,' son…'we.' Now, these men in Chicago, they talk about loyalty and honor and family, but what they really care about is money."

"Root of all evil, Bible says."

"The Bible's right. These big men, Capone and Nitti, they keep their money in little banks all over the Midwest. It's sort of…spread around, for safety sake."

"What banks, Papa?"

"They're the same ones your godfather John Looney uses, for the same purpose…hiding money from the government, for tax reasons. I know where these banks are, son."

The boy was shaking his head—grasping some of it, but not all of it. "But Papa, they won't just give you the money."

"That's right, son—we have to take it."

Michael's eyes got big again. "Like robbers? Like Pretty Boy Floyd and Baby Face Nelson?"

O'Sullivan frowned. "How do you know those names?"

"From the newsreels at the moving pictures."

"...Think of it more like Robin Hood. Are you going to help me, son? Can you do this?"

This time the boy answered with a question: "Do *you* think I can?"

"Yes."

Michael smiled—eager. "When do we start?"

"Not until I teach you something."

"What?"

"How to be a wheelman."

"What's a wheelman?"

"First thing tomorrow, after breakfast...you'll see."

ELEVEN

For my father and me, the road to Perdition, Kansas, was ever-winding, and (or so it seemed to me then) never-ending. We could have been to the farm by the lake a thousand times in those long months. We traversed the same midwestern states often enough—dirt roads, gravel roads, occasionally concrete, ever traveling, ever nearing, never arriving.

When my father would call my uncle in Perdition, the answer would always be the same: crows on the fence. Looney (or were they Capone?) men were posted on the road outside the farm, "sittin' out in front of the place in broad daylight," Uncle Bob would say. And another group of Capone (or were they Looney?) men had a room over the hardware store, in the little downtown of Perdition itself. Two sets of four, at the house, downtown, watching in shifts...

And of course my father wouldn't allow my uncle and aunt to bring in the sheriff, and Papa's "no" was emphatic when Uncle Bob suggested, "Should I take my own shotgun, and pay 'em a visit?"

So, in a way, the real start of our journey began the morning after that man with the camera tried to kill us at the diner.

And on that morning—when I had my first lesson as my father's underage wheelman—I accomplished something that all of Capone's thugs (and Looney's too) never could: I frightened my father. Not that my father was immune to fear, and I don't mean to suggest that the various scrapes and shoot-outs with gangsters and assassins didn't affect him.

But no gangster, however hardboiled, however ruthless, managed to do what I did—turn my father's face as white as a *sheet, as white as a ghost, as white as that priest stepping out of his confessional.*

The next morning—while a service station repaired the Ford's rear window—Michael's father gathered some items at the motel, and they had a nice breakfast at another diner, where, between bites of toast and nibbles of crisp bacon, Papa gave Michael the first part of the driving lesson. He told the boy about the gears and the clutch and brake, and the boy—so excited he could barely eat—grinned and nodded and took it all in...or anyway thought he had.

Before long they were on the road again, Papa behind the wheel in his dark topcoat and fedora, looking serene, even comfortable as he turned off the main highway onto a farm road, where right now they seemed to be the only traffic. Soon he pulled over, and got out, telling the boy to do the same.

From the compartment under the backseat Papa collected the items he'd rounded up at the motel—a stack of newspapers he piled on the seat behind the wheel, and pieces of block-like wood that he tied with twine to the various pedals. His father didn't explain, but Michael realized this was to enable him to sit higher, and reach those pedals easier.

This took quite a while, and by the time Papa had finished, Michael's heart was a triphammer—he wasn't scared, not really...more exhilarated, and even astonished. How many fathers would entrust their car to a boy his age? Who needed a bicycle, anyway? Kid's stuff.

"Get in," his father said, gesturing to the driver's door.

Delighted, the boy climbed behind the wheel, and his father came around and got in on the passenger side. Doors closed, they were ready. And Papa still seemed calm, relaxed—apparently confident in Michael's abilities.

"Do you remember everything I told you?" his father asked.

"Sure."

"Would you like me to go over it again? I'll point things out to you."

"…Sure."

And his father gave him a refresher, the abstract instructions from breakfast becoming real, gaining context…

Then Papa asked, "Ready?"

"Sure."

"Okay, then…ignition."

"…Now?"

"Yes, now."

Michael turned the key in the ignition and it seemed wondrous, the way the engine burst to thrumming life. How many times had he sat in this car with his father (and his mother) and taken that magic for granted.

Michael turned to his father, who remained casual, composed, the car throbbing. "Now what?"

"You remember what the clutch is?"

"Of course I remember what the clutch is!"

"What's the clutch?"

"It's the clutch. It's the thing that…clutches. You know—grabs."

"Right. And which pedal does the clutching?"

Michael put his foot on one of the blocks-tied-to-pedals and pressed. The engine roared, and he reared back from the wheel.

"That's the gas," his father said. "The accelerator."

The boy blinked. "Sure. Yeah—it…accelerates."

"Right. That's right. Let me show you which one is the clutch…"

Then the car was moving forward, a few feet, and Michael tried to put it in gear; but the car shuddered to a stop.

"Don't worry," Papa said. "It just stalled. The engine died."

Alarmed, Michael asked, "Died?"

Papa smiled just a little. "It's not hard to bring it back to life, son…Let's try again."

His father reached over, started the car again, and Michael looked at him, asking, "Release gas, clutch, shift gear, hit gas?"

"That's right. That's right."

Michael tried that sequence—and the car lurched forward!

"And shift!" Papa said.

And the car stopped—died again.

They sat in silence for a moment, then his father asked, gently, "Might I make a suggestion?"

"No! Pop, I have to do this myself."

His father's eyebrows were raised, and the boy didn't sense the man's amusement.

Before long, however, Michael was driving, the car crawling along the country road...but moving.

"Is this better, Papa?"

"Very good, son. Very good...but I'm going to need you to go a little faster."

"When?"

"I would say...any time now."

"Right now?"

"Son, when I come out of a bank with the bank's money, I don't want the police to be able to catch us by running alongside the car."

"Police?"

"It's a good idea to practice. Faster."

And before long Michael wasn't just driving, he was really driving—zooming! But the boy was steering the wheel like in the moving pictures, like a cartoon bug driving a cartoon car, and his father settled him down, and then the car moved straight and steady...and fast.

Farmland seemed to whiz by on either side of them.

"Okay, son, easy now."

But the boy was having a great time, unaware how barely in control of the vehicle he was.

"Easy, Michael! Forty-five miles an hour is too fast."

Suddenly, as if it materialized, a tractor was up ahead of them, moving very slow; had this been a field, the tractor would have been doing fine, clipping right along—but on a road, the machine beast was crawling, and the boy was stunned by how fast they had come up on it...

"Watch out for the tractor, son...the tractor...*watch out for the—son of a bitch!*"

Instinctively, the boy whipped around the tractor, shrieking past, and when he glanced over, his father was white, his eyes wide...afraid, really really afraid...

"We made it!" Michael said, excited, relieved, elated.

"Yes we did," his father said dryly, settling into his seat, color climbing back into his face.

They had a few more close calls, and when a haywagon crossed the road ahead of them, the boy hit what he hoped was the right pedal and the Ford squealed to a stop, thrusting son and father forward.

"Papa, these brakes are swell!...Are you all right? Are you sick?"

"No...no, son. I'm fine. You're doing fine...Looks hilly a few miles up ahead. Let's practice taking curves."

Other than the scrape with the tractor, Papa never raised his voice, once. He stayed at it, working with his son, guiding him, giving him confidence; and by midafternoon, they were in St. Louis, Missouri, where the boy—sitting high enough in his seat to pass for a teenaged driver—got his first taste of sharing the road with other drivers, not all of them considerate. This came easier than his father had expected—but ex-paperboy Michael had, after all, maneuvered his bike through all kinds of traffic back home.

And by the end of the day, Michael O'Sullivan, Jr., was ready for his new job.

The next morning, O'Sullivan—his fedora and topcoat brushed, his dark suit, too—approached the entrance of the St. Louis Bank and Trust Company. With his no-nonsense manner, a black leather bag in his right hand, he looked better than just presentable—he might have been a doctor, or perhaps a businessman, lugging a valise filled with important papers.

The boy waited down the street, in a legal parking place, motor running. O'Sullivan nodded at his son who, behind the wheel, swallowed, and nodded back.

The high-ceilinged marble lobby was less than crowded, but a share of farmers, housewives, and businessmen stood at the teller windows in lines that weren't moving fast. He paused inside the door, nodding to a bank guard, who nodded back—an older man, retired cop probably, but armed.

Heading across the lobby at a leisurely pace, O'Sullivan gave the place a slow scan, mentally recording the layout, the positions of people and things. He approached the teller windows, heading toward one that was closed, where a small brow-beaten man in glasses and bow tie and shirtsleeves was getting chewed out by an older, heavier man, also in glasses, but wearing a crisply knotted striped tie and a tailored suit amidst these off-the-racks.

"…You ask for proper identification or you'll find yourself in the bread line. Do I make myself clear?"

"Yes, sir."

O'Sullivan waited until the officious man seemed finished, then said through the window grating, "Excuse me, gentlemen— I understand Mr. McDougal is your bank president."

The bow-tied teller pointed. "This is Mr. McDougal."

After frowning at the stool pigeon, McDougal said, "You'll have to make an appointment with my secretary, sir."

"I'm sorry I didn't have a chance to call ahead, Mr. McDougal. But this concerns a major depositor…from out of town."

McDougal began to speak, but the words caught as he took a closer look at O'Sullivan. Then he said, "Yes...of course...step this way, please."

McDougal led the way, even opened the door for O'Sullivan with an after-you half-bow, closing the door behind him, making a fuss over showing his visitor to the chair across from the big desk in the medium-sized office dominated by a huge safe. Officiousness had been replaced with obsequiousness, as the bank president took the chair behind the desk, eyeing the black bag O'Sullivan had placed on its glass-covered top, to one side, by framed photos of wife, grown children, and grandchildren.

"I've come in regard to the Chicago money you're holding," O'Sullivan said.

"Well, this is a pleasant surprise," the bank president said, hands folded like a man sitting down to a big fine meal. "I wasn't expecting a deposit until the end of the month—business Chicago-way must be good."

"Actually," O'Sullivan said, reaching over for the bag and undoing its clasp, "I'm making a withdrawal."

And O'Sullivan reached down into the bag and came back with the Colt .45.

McDougal's ass-kissing smile disappeared—fear painted the man's face a pale shade.

"Hands on the desk, sir...Listen carefully—I want dirty money only, the off-the-books money you're holding for Capone."

The banker didn't miss a beat. "It's...it's all right here," McDougal said, smiling sickly, gesturing to the big safe filling a corner of the office, behind his desk.

"Good. Open it."

The terrified banker got up and went to the looming iron box and dialed the combination—it took several tries, nervous as he was; but soon McDougal was hauling out a safety deposit box, which he rested on the desk, opening it to reveal stacks and stacks of cash.

"Fill the bag," O'Sullivan instructed.

The banker did as he was told.

During which, O'Sullivan said, "I read anything in the papers about this...if I read that the savings of innocent farmers were wiped out by a cruel and heartless bank robber...I'll be unhappy."

As he piled the bricks of cash into the bag, the banker—still nervous but past the shock, somewhat—asked, "Are you insane, man? You obviously know whose money you're taking. You must know what kind of animals you're stealing from. They'll find out who you are, they'll track you down and—"

"The name is O'Sullivan. Michael O'Sullivan. Would you like me to write it down for you?"

O'Sullivan took the bag of money from the banker—who was more astounded now than afraid.

"They'll kill you," the banker said, trying to fathom this event.

He pointed the gun at the banker's chest. "Tell Frank Nitti, tell Al Capone, that Michael O'Sullivan will stop bothering them if they give up Connor Looney. Until then, I'll feed at their trough. Tell them!"

"I will! I will..."

O'Sullivan removed two fat wads of cash from the satchel. "This is for you. Call it a handling charge. The boys in Chicago will never know—I sure as hell won't tell them."

The banker, blinking, shaking his head, asked, "Why cut me in? The upper hand is yours..."

"It's tidier this way. Less risky for both of us. This way you won't be apt to press a button and cause something unfortunate on my way out. You see, Mr. McDougal, if I start shooting, people are going to die...and you'll be one of them."

McDougal nodded. "I understand." And he opened a desk drawer slowly—knowing the standing O'Sullivan could see his every move—and placed the two bricks of cash inside, covering them with some papers.

"Good decision," O'Sullivan said. "How would you like to do a little advertising for me?"

"Advertising?"

"If you have any trusted colleagues looking for an opportunity...you might want to spread the word. Let them know that when I come around, they shouldn't hit any hidden alarms. It'll be safer...and more profitable...if they cooperate."

"And...if I do this?"

"You'll receive a bundle in the mail, now and then. A surprise from Santa. You just *think* Christmas is over."

The banker was shaking his head again. "You really trust me not to say anything?"

"If you can't trust your banker, Mr. McDougal," O'Sullivan said, hoisting the satchel of money, touching the tip of his fedora, "who can you trust?"

Within a minute O'Sullivan—black bag in one hand, other hand with the gun in it shoved into his topcoat pocket—was standing outside the bank, stepping out to the curb, waiting in the chill St. Louis air. Then the Ford drew up ever so slowly.

O'Sullivan looked through the window at the anxious boy behind the wheel.

"No rush, son," he said with a faint smile.

He got in, and they drove off.

The boy was amazed by how smoothly it had gone. And as he tooled confidently through downtown St. Louis traffic, he realized he was indeed his father's wheelman, his accomplice...if not his confidant.

Papa had told Michael he hoped there'd be no bloodshed, no fuss, but did not reveal to the boy how he hoped to achieve that.

"You didn't say it would be this easy," Michael said.

"You have to be prepared for anything," his father said. "I need you alert...pull over. I'll take the wheel, now."

"Do I have to?"

His father just looked at him, and Michael pulled into a restaurant parking lot.

Still in the passenger seat, Papa repeated, "You have to be prepared for anything."

"I know." Michael shrugged. "I'm a Boy Scout, aren't I?"

And his father leaned back in the seat, covered his face and, at first, Michael thought Papa was crying.

But he was laughing—softly...The only time he would do that, in the time they'd spend on the road together.

TWELVE

O ver the next two weeks, my father and I knocked over four banks, and that was just the beginning. At the time I wondered why we put so many days between robberies; looking back, I realize my father was craftily creating a nonpattern, a patchwork of plunder that defied analysis. It made for a lot of driving, but a bank in Illinois would be followed by one in Nebraska; Iowa might be followed by Oklahoma, with him filling his satchel in Wisconsin next.

We could certainly afford the gas.

The compartment in the backseat, where I had hidden myself away on that rainy night, was stacked with bricks of money, decorated with various bank wrappers. And we were probably on the fourth robbery before my father finally explained the absence of gunfire and police.

His pattern was always the same—politely announcing himself as a representative of Chicago, revealing his gun in the bank president's office, the gathering of Capone money, a sharing of the proceeds with the banker, and a threatening but almost courteous exit. After the first several robberies, the word had spread and most of the bankers seemed to be waiting for my father—in a good way...eager for their bonus.

It was a good thing, too, that these hold-ups were so nonviolent, because I didn't get the hang of my wheelman role all at once. The lack of a parking place, on our second job, sent me around the block, and I got turned around somehow, and left my father cooling his heels at the curb with a bag of money in one hand and gun in the other (in *his topcoat pocket). He probably stood there less than a minute, but it must have seemed a lifetime before I showed up—coming in the wrong direction, hitting the curb, making Papa jump back.*

But every time I got better, and I was probably as smooth and professional a getaway driver as anybody in the outlaw game— Bonnie and Clyde, and Ma Barker and her boys, had nothing on the O'Sullivans.

It didn't take long for the Capone forces to get wise to our tactics—not the aiding and abetting of the bankers, but that Michael O'Sullivan was plundering their hidden coffers. After all, Papa advertised it—encouraged the bankers who were in collusion with him to tell Chicago the looting would stop, when Connor was turned over to him.

So after the fourth robbery, we found a farmhouse where the people were away, and borrowed their barn to turn our green Ford into a maroon one. Good thing, too, because on the fifth robbery, we rolled up to find a contingent of Capone thugs milling around outside the bank Papa had chosen.

My father nodded at me, and I drove away. No problem. And the Capone money was spread around in too many banks all over the Midwest for goon squads to be sent to all of them.

My father didn't smile much—not ever, but especially not after my mother and brother were murdered. Sometimes at night, though, in our shabby little motel rooms, he would sit and grin. I would ask him what was so funny, and he would tell me.

"I'm just thinking about Frank Nitti," Papa would say, "and how he must be taking all this."

In the executive suite on the top floor of the Hotel Lexington in Chicago, Frank Nitti—impeccable in a gray pinstriped suit, immaculately groomed right to every hair on his mustache, exbarber that he was—listened on the phone as the president of the Loose Creek, Missouri, Farmers' Savings and Loan explained what had happened.

Nitti listened quietly. His secretary, a handsome, professionally attired woman of about thirty who'd been taking shorthand when the call came in, sat with her legs crossed, waiting to get back to it. Her boss seemed placid.

Then he exploded into the phone: "*How* much did he take?"

The voice on the end of the wire said, "As I said, seventy-five thousand, Mr. Nitti—all of it, everything you had with us. He said he'd kill me, otherwise!"

Relaxed again, seemingly, Nitti replied: "I'm sure he would have."

"I'm glad you understand, sir. He said to say his name was O'Sullivan and that he was prepared to give up his 'fun,' as he called it, if you'd turn over a Conrad Looney to him."

"That's Connor Looney," Nitti said patiently.

"It may well have been. I do apologize. I wish there were some way—"

"May I just ask, Mr. Ingstad, one small question."

"Certainly, sir."

"Do you have security guards on staff?"

"Oh, yes. Two at all times. Former police officers. Very efficient."

"Are they armed?"

"Certainly. We take all reasonable precautions."

"Well, perhaps not all. One last question?"

"Yes?"

"*What the fuck are we paying you for?*"

And Nitti slammed the receiver in the hook, glancing at his secretary, shaking his head in disgust. "Where were we...?"

The door burst open and Connor Looney stalked in, the bodyguard Nitti had assigned to him, Little Louis Campagna, on the man's heels. Looney was not drunk at least, but he looked terrible, his suit rumpled, his complexion gray and waxy—like he hadn't slept in days. Weeks.

"I'm working," Nitti said tightly from behind his desk, not rising. "What the hell's the idea, barging in on me? You make an appointment like anybody else."

"The hell with that," Connor said, standing right across from Nitti. "Where is my father?"

Nitti flinched a nonsmile. "What do you mean, where is he?"

"I've been calling the house—his office—trying everywhere. He's either not there, they say, or there's no answer."

"How should I know?"

The slender gangster began to pace. Campagna took a step back, but kept an eye on his charge. Connor was saying, "Has my own father turned his back on me? Now, you want me to make a fucking appointment? Why the hell is no one talking to me? I don't know whether I'm a leper or a goddamn prisoner!"

Nitti, arms folded, composed in the detached way he preferred, said, "You're not a prisoner, Connor. You're my guest—under my protection. That's what your father wants."

Connor came back over to the desk, leaned on it, his expression indignant, eyes flaring. "I can protect myself. I'm not afraid of Mike O'Sullivan."

"You should be."

"What, you believe these stories about him? Angel of Death? He's just a man."

"The night of the Market Square Riot, how many men did he kill? Protecting your father? And where were you?"

Connor ducked the question. "Listen, I can handle myself. Let me out of here—I'll find the son of a bitch and—"

"Just what O'Sullivan would love." Nitti stood behind the desk. "And you *can't* handle yourself. That's the point, here. You're a big baby, all confused, sucking his dick like it's his thumb."

Connor's eyes flared again, nostrils too, like a rearing horse. "Go fuck yourself, Nitti!"

Nitti was cool, calm, as he replied: "Sonny…listen carefully. The only thing keeping you alive is you're John Looney's kid. Your father covered Al's back a thousand times, and Mr. Capone does not forget such favors."

"My old man covered Capone's back, and *your* back, with Mike O'Sullivan! Explain that, Nitti!"

The diminutive ganglord held up his hands, in "stop" fashion; Campagna continued to monitor the conversation closely.

Nitti said, "I don't have to explain anything to you, you worthless little prick."

Connor paced again, in front of the desk, now. "Worthless, huh? Aren't you being a little shortsighted, Frank? Aren't you forgetting who your real friend is? The Tri-Cities area, it's a goldmine—a goldmine my old man owns. And he *is* an old man—and what you're really protecting is your future…'cause I *am* your goddamn future, you dago bastard. And talk to me like that again and I'll be *your* angel of fucking death. *Capeesh?*"

Connor stormed out, followed by Campagna, who threw Nitti a shrug on the way out.

Nitti sighed and looked at his secretary in a what-are-you-gonna-do manner. "Sorry for the unpleasantness. The language."

"That's all right, Mr. Nitti."

He sat back down. "But if that clown's the fucking future, we should all go straight."

And before Nitti got back to his dictation, he rang up Harlen Maguire, and told him to find O'Sullivan and the kid.

"I'm taking steps," Maguire said.

"Steps don't make it," Nitti said. "Try leaps."

"He's hopping around a seven-state area."

"Look, I didn't call to shoot the breeze," Nitti said. "Just do what you have to do," and doubled the photographer's retainer.

"That's generous of you, Mr. Nitti."

"Wait till you see how generous I am," Nitti said, "the day you find them."

Maguire, back in his Chicago flat, hung up the phone, after telling Nitti "this might take some time."

He returned to what he'd been doing—not work in his darkroom, for a change, rather a wall map he'd tacked up in his living room, removing a few of his framed death photos to make space. He had already indicated which midwestern banks held Capone money with a bold red dollar sign.

Now he used red thumbtacks to show which banks had already been robbed. Once that was done, he traced between the red dots with a spread forefinger and thumb; try as he might, the photographer could find no pattern. Which of course was a pattern in itself, just not a very useful one.

He spent the rest of the evening deep in thought, even as he cleaned the lenses of his cameras with methodical precision, and then identified—and studied—the photos he'd taken inside the O'Sullivan house, when he and other mourners had dropped by to give their condolences.

Then Maguire went back to his wall map, looking at each bank that had not yet been robbed, as he rolled a cigarette, licking the paper, finally firing up with a golden lighter. Still seeing nothing, he walked away, doing make-work, like replacing the bulbs in his carrying case...and adding bullets to a secret compartment in the camera he'd carried into the diner a few weeks ago.

He poured himself a glass of whiskey, smiling bitterly at the thought of O'Sullivan playing drunk, fooling him, making a patsy of him. Sipping the liquid, he idly, almost unconsciously, shot off flashbulbs with his other hand, as he sat on his couch and looked at the map on the wall...studying the nonpattern of O'Sullivan's trail amid the lightning-like bulb bursts.

They had robbed their fifth bank—in Loose Creek, Missouri—this morning; it was evening and the father and son were in a small family restaurant in Farmington, Iowa. The place had a homey feel—a few booths, more tables, picnic-style tablecloths, curtains on the windows, the light soft and warm and yellow.

O'Sullivan and his son sat at a small table near an improvised dance floor, where a couple of couples danced to the radio—right now that new jazz singer, Bing Crosby, was singing "Where the Blue of the Night Meets the Gold of the Day." The singer's warm voice, his casual style, pleased O'Sullivan. Both he and his boy were having the meat loaf with mashed potatoes and creamed corn; both ate heartily.

Their waitress—whose name BETTY was stitched on her neck-high apron—freshened O'Sullivan's coffee. She was probably forty, a slender brunette with dark red lipstick, though not heavily made up. A nice girl. Nice woman.

She noticed him looking her over, and their eyes met, and hers told his she didn't mind the friendly onceover.

"What brings you boys to the middle of nowhere?" she asked.

Michael, turning a piece of white bread brown by mopping up gravy, said brightly, "We're bank robbers!"

His father gave him a look, but Betty just laughed. "If so, there are nicer places for men with money to eat!"

"In Farmington?" O'Sullivan asked.

She laughed again. "Well, you got me there."

"We're just traveling through."

"On your way somewhere?"

"That's right."

She accepted this nonanswer with another smile, and he watched as she headed behind the counter, taking off her apron. The restaurant was about to close.

His plate clean, Michael pushed it forward and, as if inquiring about dessert, asked, "So—when do I get my share of the money?"

O'Sullivan thought about that. "How much do you want?"

The boy clearly hadn't expected such an open-ended response, and O'Sullivan watched with amusement as his son's face registered the effort to come up with a suitably high, but not outrageous, figure.

"Two hundred dollars," the boy said, firmly.

"That's a lot of moolah."

"I coulda asked for half. But I figure you got the hardest job. You're the brains of the outfit."

O'Sullivan shrugged. "Doesn't say much for the outfit. Okay—two hundred it is."

Michael frowned. "I coulda had more, couldn't I?"

O'Sullivan sipped his coffee. "I guess you'll never know."

One of the dancers went over to the console radio and turned it up, not long before Crosby came to his big finish, the music swelling.

Working his voice up over this pleasant racket, Michael said, "I gotta go to the bathroom."

"What?" his father asked, innocently.

"I gotta go to the..." And the music stopped, but Michael blurted on: "...*bathroom!*"

His voice seemed to echo through the room, and the boy covered his mouth, embarrassed but grinning, as the patrons and dancers laughed and smiled.

"You're only human," O'Sullivan said. "Go on. Go."

Michael left the table, and Betty walked over—not a waitress now, just an attractive woman, who'd been watching O'Sullivan from across the room (he'd noticed).

"Hi again," she said.

"Hello. Closing up?"

"'Bout that time. You fellas ate kinda late."

"You know how it is when you're on the road. Trying to make time."

She smiled, and he realized what he'd said; he hadn't intended the double entendre, and felt almost as embarrassed as his son had.

"I can get you another cup," she said, nodding to his coffee.

"Thanks. But aren't you off work now?"

"Yeah, but…I don't like going straight home. House is empty since…Maybe I oughta get a cat."

O'Sullivan smiled, wondering if it was a divorce or if death had taken someone from her, too.

She brought over the coffee pitcher, topped off his cup, then took the chair next to O'Sullivan, leaned an elbow on the table, her chin on her hand. Her eyes were hazel—as lovely as they were sad. "You men traveling alone?"

O'Sullivan nodded, sipped his coffee. "His mother passed away, not long ago. My wife, I should say."

Her eyes tightened. "Oh…gee, I'm so sorry."

"We're just driving through, you know?"

A new song started up on the radio—Kate Smith, singing "Dream a Little Dream of Me."

"Oh, I just love this song," Betty said.

"Nice song. Nice voice."

"Oh yeah…Funny, doesn't matter how long I been on my feet, I can always make these dogs get up and dance. I just love to dance…Would you like to? Dance?"

She looked just enough like Annie to tempt him; but too much like Annie for him to say yes.

Gently, he turned her down: "I don't think so."

"Okay. Too soon?"

He swallowed. Nodded. "Too soon."

"I understand. Really I do."

"But, Betty…"

"Yes?"

"Thank you."

Michael was walking back toward the table. The boy watched his father and the waitress sitting, listening to the music, smiling at each other. It made him think of his mother, and that made him sad...but it was nice to see his father smiling just the same.

They drove a few hours, and took a motel in another Iowa town, Muscatine, on the Mississippi River, at a motor court that was awfully shabby for a couple of bank robbers in the money.

In the room, before bed, Papa counted the "take" (as he called it), removing the packets of cash one at a time from the black satchel. Michael took his two hundred dollars and sat like an Indian on the bed and counted it over and over.

"Are we rich, Papa?"

As he counted the bundles of cash, Papa said, "No, son. We're very poor."

"But, Papa—so much money!"

"Without your mother and brother, there can never be true prosperity."

The boy thought about that, but it still looked like a lot of loot to him.

Papa was saying, "All this money is much more than we need right now. Most of it will be yours one day."

"Not just the two hundred dollars?"

"Not just the two hundred dollars." He came over and sat next to Michael on the boy's bed. "As we travel, I'll deposit what we don't need for expenses at more honest banks than the one we stopped at today."

"That's a good idea. We don't have enough room in the compartment anymore."

Papa touched Michael's shoulder. "This money, when it's yours, son...you must promise me you'll put it to a good use."

"What sort of use, Papa?"

"That'll be your decision. You could go to school...college. You could buy a business. Perhaps a farm."

"I wouldn't want to be a farmer, Papa."

"Be whatever you want, son...as long as it's not like me."

But as the boy lay in the darkness, waiting for sleep to come, he knew he did want to be like his father. Papa was a courageous soldier, and a resourceful one, too—hadn't he found a way to take money from his enemies without firing a shot?

Maybe it was a sin to steal this money; the boy wasn't sure— Papa had said it was like Robin Hood. And, anyway, he could go into a confessional, like Papa had, and be forgiven for his sins. After all, everybody was a sinner—the sisters at the Villa said so. But everybody could be forgiven, too—like soldiers who God forgave for the sins that war made them commit.

Seeing Papa talking to that pretty waitress had reminded the boy of his mother, but Michael would have thought about her, anyway, in his bed. He missed her so much, and every night he would think about her and the pain would be real, the emptiness awful; and he missed Peter, too—he'd give anything to be hit by just one more snowball by that little assassin...

Nonetheless—and despite what his father had said—Michael O'Sullivan, Jr., trying to sleep in the Muscatine motel, did not feel poor. Prosperity may not have been around the corner, but it sure was in the satchel between their beds, and in the backseat compartment of their Ford.

And never in his life had he felt closer to his father.

They were still a family, Papa and Michael.

Still a family.

THIRTEEN

As the weeks rolled by, my father filled his black satchel at banks in Iowa and Illinois, Nebraska and Oklahoma, Missouri and Kansas, even Indiana and Wisconsin. Never was a shot fired, and our hold-ups became as close to routine as bank robbery could get.

Still, my father warned me: "Keep alert, son. Never forget what we're doing and why we're doing it...or who it is that's pursuing us. Complacency kills as surely as a bullet."

We did stop at other banks, as my father had indicated we would—not to rob them, but to place our excess cash into safety deposit boxes. As we traveled, Papa would read the papers religiously, looking for mention of our robberies, never finding anything, which pleased him.

He was less happy about the lack of other news. He never said, but upon reflection, I understand he was thumbing through the pages of papers looking for a mention of Connor Looney's body turning up in a ditch somewhere, signaling Chicago's surrender, and an end for our journey.

Sometimes at night, when my father grew sleepy behind the wheel, we would sleep in the car. I disliked this, and most of the time, he tried to find motels, or at least campsites where, when we parked, a few of the amenities of civilization were on hand.

And when we stopped to eat at a diner or cafe, he would call the farm at Perdition, at least once a day, talking to my aunt or uncle, who continued to report that crows were indeed on the fence. I was not aware of it at the time, but historians of the mob, including two Capone biographers, claim that among the phone *calls my father made along the road were several that went directly to Frank Nitti.*

At his desk, in a crisply knotted four-in-hand tie and his long-sleeved white shirt and dark suspenders, Nitti leaned over the phone, saying, "Mr. O'Sullivan—what can we do to put an end to this little misunderstanding?"

"Mr. Nitti, I have no misunderstanding with you," O'Sullivan's voice said, calm, reasonable over the crackling lone-distance wire. "I've no grievance against the Capone organization—I think I've made that clear from the start."

"And I hope I've made it clear," Nitti replied smoothly, "that the Looneys are business associates of ours, of long standing, and such alliances must be respected."

"I still have friends back home, Mr. Nitti—and they tell me John Looney is a shambles. Not tending to business, his mind strictly on this present matter...and the welfare of his son."

"You have a son, too, Mr. O'Sullivan. You can understand that view, certainly."

"I hope that's not a veiled threat, Mr. Nitti."

Nitti, having just lighted up a cigarette, waved out the match. "Of course it isn't. I merely—"

"I have a son, and if any harm comes to him, all of you best pray the breath has left me—because as long as I have one breath, all of you will pay."

"Now who's making threats, Mr. O'Sullivan?"

"I don't threaten, I take action. Do you have a wife, Mr. Nitti?"

"I do."

"A son?"

"Yes. And if that is—"

"No. I would never touch them. I would feed you your eyes, if necessary—but your family...no."

Nitti blew out smoke. "Well, I do appreciate that. There are lines even men like us mustn't cross."

"Then you would you agree that some things in life are more important that money?"

"...I would."

"Well, then I remind you: the murderer of my wife and son is in hiding, with your help."

Nitti sighed, shifted in his swivel chair. "Mr. O'Sullivan, despite what you say, the Looney interests in the Tri-Cities continue to flourish. It would not be good business to—"

"Then I'm going to continue disrupting *your* business. Just keep a running tally and when it's costing you more to be friends with the Looneys than not, make a business decision."

"Back to threats, Mr. O'Sullivan?"

"Either turn Connor Looney over to me, or kill him yourselves in a way conspicuous enough to make the papers."

And the line clicked dead.

Nitti looked across his desk at the well-dressed, moon-faced figure with the high forehead and parallel scars—a long and a short—on his plump left cheek, his forehead beaded with sweat; the man had been fighting a fever for several days.

"Find the prick," Al Capone said, clenching a fist, "and kill him."

"It's not that easy, Al," Nitti said, leaning back. "He stays on the move. And he knows just enough about our inside operations to really do us financial damage.

"Isn't Ness and his goddamn metal-prow truck costin' us enough these days! Legal fees up the ass...we're drowning in negative fuckin' cash flow."

Nitti shrugged. "And when O'Sullivan finishes with banks, he can start knocking off casinos—or a brothel on a Saturday night. Where does it end?"

"Where the fuck *does* it end?" Capone lighted up one of his pool-cue Havanas, while Nitti fired up a fresh cigarette. "You suggestin' we should do what he says? Give up Crazy Connor?"

Nitti was thinking.

Capone said, "The Looney interests in the Tri-Cities are still a goldmine, Frank—and the feds ain't touching us there."

"Fine, but if we gave Connor Looney to O'Sullivan, without making it look like we betrayed him, or his father, we could step in and take over those interests ourselves...with no cut going to the Looneys."

Capone got up. He seemed unsteady. "Fuckin' flu..."

But Nitti knew it wasn't the flu: Big Al's syphilis was kicking in again. The Big Fellow had started really having problems with the old Cupid's itch lately, a doctor on staff fulltime at the Lexington these days.

"Al, the Looneys killed his wife and son. O'Sullivan was a loyal soldier, and they sold him out."

"The old man didn't do it," Capone said. "That old mick and me go way back...Life ain't all ledger books and balance sheets, Frank. Life—and business—has to do with respect. We cave in to O'Sullivan, we look soft."

Nitti could see that. "Well, I have my best man on it. A real pro..."

"What, Maguire? That screwball photographer? He makes my skin crawl."

"You're not takin' him home to mother, Al—he's a cold-blooded killer, and a kind of bloodhound...and that's what it'll take to find O'Sullivan, and stop him. Already caught up with him once."

"Yeah, and he slipped through this so-called pro's fingers." Capone, cigar in his mouth, flopped onto a couch and mopped his brow. "Call the old man, in Rock Island. Call Looney, tell him to get his ass up here. I want to talk to him."

"All right."

"And this photographer—this 'pro' of yours, Maguire, him, too. Tell 'em both to come with answers."

"Answers to what, Al?"

"Questions."

"What questions, Al?"

"The answers are their problem, Frank—I'll handle the fuckin' questions."

And the next afternoon, in the executive suite at the Lexington, John Looney and Frank Nitti were seated on a small sofa adjacent a larger couch where Al Capone—suitcoat off, in the vest of his sharp green suit, his green-and-black floral tie loosened, his shirt soaked with sweat, forehead beaded—lay propped up behind a pillow, a thermometer in his mouth.

The most famous criminal in America, on his back, removed the shaft of glass from his full, sensual lips and studied the line of mercury, muttering, "Fuck Mike O'Sullivan...and fuck this flu."

Nitti exchanged glances with Looney, in a dark vested suit and tie. Both men knew what the "flu" really was. To Nitti's left, arms folded, his expression as cool as it was unreadable, stood Harlen Maguire, bowler hat in hand.

"Well, this goddamn thing says I died Tuesday," Capone said. "Close my eyes, strip me down, and fry fuckin' eggs on me, already!"

The gangster hurled the stick of glass across the room, into the fireplace, where it made a small breaking sound. With surprising grace for a big man—and speed for a man as sick as he seemed to be—Capone climbed off the couch and began to pace. In his left palm he was tossing a baseball—a signed gift from Babe Ruth—up and down.

"How can this be, gentlemen? How can one man...one man and a goddamn kid...cause me so much pestilence?"

Nitti asked, "Pestilence, Al?"

"Pestilence, Frank—biblical shit, curses and plagues. Raining down frogs on our ass—and me, I'm hemorrhaging from his shit...He's got me bleeding C-notes all over six states!"

Maguire, quietly, said, "Eight."

Capone stopped and looked at Maguire, hard—it was a gaze that would send Medusa running, but the photographer just received it placidly. "Don't you ever fuckin' *blink*?"

Maguire just shrugged.

Scowling, Capone paced like a caged cat now, in front of a wall that already bore a series of mysterious dents, as if a hailstorm of mythic proportions had had at it. The gangster stopped and threw the ball into the wall, catching it on the rebound.

Capone did this again and again, and every time he did, both Frank Nitti and John Looney flinched—they were hard men, fairly fearless men, Nitti and Looney; but they were not crazy, and one thing that separated Nitti and Capone...and Nitti knew this well...was Big Al having a screw loose. This advancing VD wasn't helping, either.

Perhaps the baseball reminded Nitti of the time Capone threw a banquet for John Scalise and Albert Anselmi; in the midst of his guests-of-honor speech, Snorky (as his pals called him) had declared them disloyal soldiers and caved in their heads with a baseball bat. Few murders have ever been committed before more witnesses; and yet no one had ever dared whisper a word to the authorities...though the act had served to seal Capone's legend, locally.

Maguire, on the other hand, neither flinched nor (as Capone had pointed out) blinked, when Al Capone played catch with himself, rattling every object in the room.

"People are laughin' at me, Frank," Capone said, punctuating his speech with more hurls of the ball against the wall. "I don't like bein' a laughingstock. I got a phone call from Luciano, last night, expressin' his concern, laughin' up his fuckin' sleeve... This morning Dragna out in LA calls, to see how he can help... Probably bust a gut when he hung up."

"Al," Nitti said, pacifyingly, "nobody's laughing at you. Your friends in the business know they could be hit the same way. Remember what your doctor said, Al...sit down."

"Fuckin' useless quack," Capone said, smacking the ball in the wall, catching it in a fist.

Nitti was saying, "You need to relax, doc said, drink lots of water..."

Capone, calmed down a little, turned to Looney. "John, I ask you—what is this shit? Drink a lot of water!"

Looney, who'd been trying to disappear into the woodwork, said, "They say water's good for a fever."

"And this you'd know how? You who never had a drink of water in your life...'cept maybe bourbon and branchwater!" But Capone wasn't as worked up now, and he walked over to his old friend, stood before him, and said, "John, explain this to me...I extend a helping hand to an old friend, take in his one and only son, protect him like he's my own."

Looney nodded, his expression conveying his deep appreciation.

Capone continued: "And in return, what do I get? Robbed. I get robbed...Does this make sense to anybody? I got a biblical goddamn plague rainin' down on me, and I'm supposed to write it off to, what? The Lord moves in mysterious fuckin' ways?... Why doesn't the Angel steal *your* money, John? It's your beef."

Looney, quietly, stated what they all knew: "Mike O'Sullivan thinks you'll give up Connor to stop him. He doesn't understand our friendship...or that you're a man of honor."

Capone smiled, paced a little, playing gentle one-handed catch with himself, obviously not taken in by this shameless blarney. "So, then, maybe you can tell me, John—how much of *my* money is *your* son worth?"

Looney's eyes flared. "Is that what this performance is about, Al? *Money*? Well, then, I'll write you a goddamn check! I'll fill it out and leave it fucking blank...Is that what you want to hear?"

Capone stood there quietly. Nitti tried to read him—and couldn't. After all these years, a quiet Al Capone remained an unreadable thing to Frank Nitti.

Looney, the eruption over, his voice weary, melancholy, said, "If it had just been about the money, all these years, Al...none of us would be alive today."

Capone was a statue in a sweat-stained shirt and vest with a sweat-beaded forehead and a blank expression. His thick lips puckered, as if he were about to blow a kiss.

Then he exploded in laughter: "I love the fuckin' Irish!...So full of shit, but full of heart, too. Thank you, John, I appreciate your remarks. We need, now and again, to be reminded not just of who we are, but who we were."

Looney nodded sagely.

"And I mean no disrespect," Capone said, his tone reasonable now, "but the fact remains, I am bleeding money at a time when this Ness character is killing me and these revenue clowns are throwing indictments around like fuckin' confetti."

"It is a problem," Looney admitted, gesturing with open palms. "I am sincere that I will help, financially."

Capone waved that off. "And as if all this isn't enough, I'm spending a small fortune...the figure grows daily...bankrolling the efforts of somebody supposedly workin' at stopping the O'Sullivan problem...a man I am assured, by those closest to me, is a 'pro.'"

And Capone again cast his gaze on Maguire, who stood quiet, unflappable, as unreadable as Capone in his silences, but without the explosions of clarification.

"And what's that mean?" Capone demanded of Maguire.

Maguire shrugged a little. "What does what mean, Mr. Capone?"

"That look."

Not in the least afraid, Maguire replied, "I'm just giving you my undivided attention, Mr. Capone."

"Every face has a look, kid. Except maybe the Invisible Man's mug...is that who you are? The Invisible Man? Who's got no 'look'?"

"Al, come on," Nitti said, the tension building, "he ain't looking at nothing."

"He's looking at me, Frank. And I'm something. But the point is, he's not *doing* anything. He's takin' pictures, he's takin' rides in the country, he's standin' there in my suite with a fuckin' look...and I'm bleedin' money all over the Bible Belt."

Capone made a face, tasted his own mouth thickly, and went to his massive mahogany desk, where a pitcher of iced water and several glasses waited on a silver tray. He poured a glass and gulped it down.

"Satisfied, Frank?" he asked. "I'm drinking the water. I'm drinkin' the fuckin' water, like the doc wants. That should solve everything!"

Nobody said a word while Capone had another glass of cold water. Nitti exchanged a glance with Looney, then both men looked toward Maguire.

"Al," Nitti said, "Mr. Maguire has a proposal for how we might resolve this difficulty. A way to stop your 'bleeding,' and at the same time bait a trap for O'Sullivan."

Capone, affable all of a sudden, turned to Maguire. "Hey, I'm all ears. I'm a fuckin' elephant, I got such big ears for ways for me to stop bleedin'. Propose to me, Mr. Maguire—show me why Frank Nitti says you're the best...but do me a favor?"

"Anything, Mr. Capone," Maguire said, with a tiny smile.

"Fucking blink once in a while."

And Capone wiped off his brow and poured another glass of ice water, then headed over to the couch to flop there, and listen.

A week later, at the Grand Prairie State Bank in Grand Prairie, Oklahoma, Mike O'Sullivan was sitting across the desk from a bank manager, a younger man than most in his position. Very professional in dress and manner, the young bank manager was nervous, and clearly frightened.

"No need for fear," O'Sullivan assured him. The black bag was open on the desk, the .45 in O'Sullivan's hand. "This is strictly business. You won't get hurt—no one will."

"Mr. O'Sullivan, I'm sorry...I really am..."

"Sorry?"

The bank manager, his eyes wide, shrugged helplessly. "There's no money here for you."

The gun snapped into position, leveled directly at the bank manager's head.

"You don't understand! Please...give me a chance to explain."

"Do it, then."

"I can get you money, of course we have money. But I know who you are, I've heard about you, I...it's just, I don't have *Chicago* money for you. They came around two days ago, and took it all out."

O'Sullivan had been studying the man; the truth was written on his smooth, young face.

"Who took it out?"

"He was going around, with armed men, to all the banks. He's been doing it for days."

"Who?"

"The accountant. From Chicago."

Alexander Rance, O'Sullivan thought; the mob accountant Frank Kelly had brought to the Looney board meeting, to try to make the case for getting involved with the unions.

"What was his name?" O'Sullivan asked, knowing.

"Rance," the bank manager said. "Alexander Rance."

O'Sullivan thought about that; then he asked, "You wouldn't happen to know what Mr. Rance's next stop is, would you?"

"Actually, I do. He left word where he could be reached until day after tomorrow, I believe."

"Write it down for me."

The banker did.

O'Sullivan dropped the slip of paper into the otherwise emp-ty satchel, fastened it, put his gun-in-hand in his topcoat pocket, rose, and was almost out the door, when the banker asked a question.

"Is that…all?"

"I don't want your money," O'Sullivan said. "Just don't men-tion the information I asked for—or that you gave me."

"All right."

O'Sullivan looked at the man, hard. "It's important."

"All right!"

"You don't want to see me again, do you?"

"No."

"Then keep your word."

And he went outside, where his son—like clockwork—picked him up, eager to hear about the latest haul.

FOURTEEN

N ot much is known of Alexander Adams Rance. He represented Frank Nitti's shift toward a big business stance, including moving into legitimate enterprises, a radical approach for the
criminal empire Johnny Torrio had founded and Al Capone made
flourish. Rance was a Chicago boy—he grew up on the mid-South
Side not far from State Street, ironically not far from where Capone
maintained his Chicago residence. A graduate of the University of
Chicago who worked on LaSalle Street before the crash, Rance was
recruited by Nitti shortly thereafter.

That Rance exemplified a new generation, a new approach,
can be demonstrated with a quick comparison to the one Capone
man above him in the area of financial wizardry and creative ac-
counting. Jake "Greasy Thumb" Guzik came up from the streets,
a portly teenage pimp who had overheard a murder plot against
Capone, reported this to Big Al, and earned a friend for life. Years
later, when the porcine mob treasurer appeared before the Kefauver
committee, he took the Fifth Amendment, saying he wouldn't answer questions that would "discriminate against me."

The smooth Rance, on the other hand, was like so many accountants and lawyers in that small white-collar army who did
the bidding of thugs-made-good like Frank Nitti and, later, Paul
Ricca, Tony Accardo, and Sam Giancana. By all accounts, a fussy
man, particular about his food, dress, and lodging, Rance operated
on Outfit finances in a fashion that isolated him from the violence
inherent in such criminal activities as gambling, loansharking,
prostitution, and bootlegging.

The accountant probably had no idea how much danger he was in when Nitti directed him to personally supervise the removal of mob money from midwestern banks. Rance was to select a hotel from which he could operate, in a given area, withdraw the money, and send it home to Chicago under armed guard, where the funds would go into safety deposit boxes in the kind of large, reputable Chicago banks that would be unlikely targets for my father.

Researchers—seeking information on the Chicago mob's financial guru, whose reign was cut so prematurely short—discovered that Rance would seek a luxury hotel in a smaller town. He would then check into the bridal suite, apparently because that would represent the nicest accommodations available, and take all of his meals via room service, asking to speak to the chef, to whom he gave copious instructions on the preparation of his meals.

Breakfast in particular was a ritual to Rance—boiled eggs, runny, with crisp bacon...but not so crisp that the strips would break off when he inserted them into the yolk. This detail made it into the newspapers, when a reporter interviewed both the chef and the startled room service clerk, who'd been delivering the kitchen's second attempt at Rance's breakfast, shortly before the trouble began.

When father and son pulled into Stillwater, Oklahoma, the wear and grime of the road showed on them. They were a grubby, hardened-looking pair, the boy behind the wheel of the maroon Ford well aware that his father was possessed by a quiet apprehension that seemed a notch up from recent days.

On a gentle slope of Stillwater Creek, the idyllic small town spread northwest; large, comfortable-looking residences sat in big yards half-hidden by trees, and the business district consisted of low, trim buildings, though the relative grandeur of the aptly named Grand Hotel belied the town's modest appearance, and gave away its secret: this was a center of business and agriculture, within easy driving distance of most Oklahomans.

Fedora low on his brow, O'Sullivan directed Michael to a parking place on the main street, across from the Grand Hotel.

Pulling into the spot like the seasoned driver he now was, the boy asked, "Should I shut off the engine?"

"Yes." O'Sullivan was checking the clip in the automatic. He had an extra clip in his topcoat pocket. Going into unknown territory like this, such preparations were key.

"Papa?"

"Yes?"

"Can we stay at a motel tonight? I hate sleeping in the car."

"All right." He slapped the clip into the .45. "Now if you see anything, what do you do?"

"Honk twice."

"And then what do you do?"

"Nothing. I stay in the car. Wait for you."

"Good—stay sharp, now." O'Sullivan leaned close to the boy, locked eyes with him. "You could hear shots, screams...you could hear nothing. Don't leave this car. No matter what."

"Yes, sir."

"You ready for this?"

The boy took a deep breath. "I'm ready."

"I know you are," O'Sullivan said, and got out of the car.

From where they had parked, the boy watched in the driver's side door mirror as his father strode confidently, yet casually, into the fancy hotel.

In a dreary, functionally furnished apartment above a storefront across from the Grand Hotel, Betty Lou Petersen was sitting on the edge of the bed, pulling on her silk stockings.

Otherwise, the curly-haired blonde teenager was fully dressed, the first time in the two days since she had hooked up at the Stillwater Tap with the man who stood opposite her, his back to her, in his T-shirt and shorts, at a window looking down into the main street.

A year ago Betty Lou had been a cheerleader at Stillwater High School; now she was an unwed mother and one of the town's youngest, most attractive prostitutes, although she had not admitted that to herself, yet. She knew she was attractive, but at this point considered herself just to be a party girl who took favors from men. Betty Lou lived at home with her widowed mama, who looked after little Violet when Betty Lou was out "having a good time."

The man at the window, in his underwear, was a handsome date, but an odd one. His clothes (when he was wearing them) were uptown, and he had good manners; he smelled like pomade and talcum and was very, very clean. Also, he was fairly young and nicely slender, not like some of the traveling salesmen and businessmen she entertained, who had flabby bellies and body odor.

Still, she wasn't sorry this party was over. Moments ago, when she'd asked him how many more days he wanted her to hang around with him, he'd just ignored her, given her the cold shoulder while he stared out that window, which was all he did, except for when he was on top of her, making her lie still while he did it to her. He was weird. A real Count Screwloose, even if he was good-looking in a Robert Taylor kind of way.

On the bed next to her were the two crumpled twenty dollar bills the creep had just tossed there, irritated when she'd asked him to close the curtains; didn't he know it was hard to sleep with all that sun!

On the other hand, he *was* cute, and when she paused at the door, before going out, she said, "I'll be at the Tap tonight."

He turned his head toward her, his blue eyes cold and unblinking; he said nothing—didn't even shrug. Creepy...

"See you," she said, and went out, his gaze still on her.

And that was why Harlen Maguire, standing watch, did not see Michael O'Sullivan, Sr., cross the street and go into the hotel.

For a town this size, the lobby was spacious and opulent, in a vaguely decadent, late-nineteenth-century way, potted ferns and plush furnishings and an elaborate mahogany check-in desk, behind which a harried fellow in pince-nez eyeglasses was talking on the phone. In a dark suit and tie, with a gold breast badge giving his name in small letters and MANAGER in bigger ones, the poor guy was dealing with a difficult guest.

"The chef isn't available, sir...can I help you?"

O'Sullivan paused just long enough to eye the key rack, where most of the keys were back on their hooks, their businessmen guests up and out of there. One hook, however—labeled 311 BRIDAL SUITE—was empty.

"Mr. Rance, I'm writing it down," the manager said.

O'Sullivan paused.

The manager was continuing: "Runny eggs, yes sir...You do not want your bacon to break off, I understand...Right away, sir."

The hotel was old enough not to have elevators, and O'Sullivan trotted up the central stairway to the mezzanine, where he found more stairs, which he climbed to the top floor, the third.

At room 311, the bridal suite, O'Sullivan glanced around at the otherwise empty corridor, withdrew his .45 from his right-hand coat pocket, and knocked with his left.

"It's open!" an irritated voice called from within.

Gun poised, O'Sullivan went in. The living room of the suite was expansive and expensive—chintz and crystal, overstuffed sofas and chairs, woodwork washed ivory. At a room-service table—its silver tray arrayed with a plate of a largely uneaten breakfast of boiled eggs in twin silver cups and crisscrossing crisp bacon—a man in a green silk dressing robe stood pouring himself a cup of coffee, his back to O'Sullivan.

"Well, at least you're prompt," the man said, his manner fussy and patronizing. "Top marks for speed, anyway…if not for preparation of cuisine."

Dripping with indignation, Alexander Rance turned and held up an egg in its silver cup. "Perhaps *you* would like to attempt to consume this hardboiled monstrosity?"

Rance's eyes were on the egg in the silver cup, as he spoke, but his peripheral vision caught something that drew his attention to the man standing before him…

…Pointing a .45 automatic at his head.

O'Sullivan said, "Put that down."

Rance's eyes showed white all around. "It's…it's just an egg."

"This isn't. Put it down."

Rance did as he was told, muttering apologetically, "I'm sorry…I thought you…I was expecting…Mr., uh, O'Sullivan, isn't it?"

"You know it is, Mr. Rance."

A plush pinkish-red brocade sofa was between them. The accountant held his hands high; his eyebrows were almost as high, as he asked, "How did you find me?"

O'Sullivan, not about to betray the manager of the Grand Prairie State Bank, said, "This is the best hotel in the area, and you're so very particular."

Rance, working hard to regain his dignity, lowered his hands to waist level, saying, "What may seem 'very particular' to you, Mr. O'Sullivan, may simply be another man's rather more discriminating tastes. But I will be 'particular' enough to ask you to do me the courtesy of lowering your weapon."

"Keep those hands up," O'Sullivan said.

Not taking his eyes off the accountant for longer than a second, he went to the door, which had the key in it; he then locked the room and went to the bedroom door, opening it, leaning in, gun ready. He quickly scanned the room—large double bed and floral brocade wallpaper; though no maid had been here yet,

Rance had made his bed, at the foot of which was a large metal steamer-type trunk that was clearly not part of the bridal suite's florid furnishings.

O'Sullivan returned to the accountant, said, "You can put your hands down—we're just going to talk," and lowered the .45.

"Thank you," Rance said with exaggerated distress. "Now—what can I do for you, Mr. O'Sullivan?"

"I'd like your files."

"My files?"

Nodding, O'Sullivan said, "The ledgers, the record books—you had to bring them along, if you were going to close out all those accounts."

Rance seemed almost amused. "Suppose I did—what good would they do you?"

"They wouldn't do me much good. But those feds who're readying indictments against Al Capone could really use them."

This notion seemed to alarm the accountant. "You wouldn't even think of doing—"

"Mr. Rance, I've obviously already thought of it. But I won't give them to the G-men if Capone and Nitti give me Connor Looney. Like the wanted posters say—dead or alive. Either one is fine with me."

Rance was shaking his head. "You're completely out of my arena, Mr. O'Sullivan—I'm strictly a man of books and numbers."

"Good. Because that's what I want: the books with the numbers."

But Rance was still shaking his head. "I can't give you those files. My life would be—"

O'Sullivan raised the .45 and cocked it—the click made its small, deadly point.

"All right! All right…They're in the trunk in my bedroom."

"Get it. Bring it in."

Rance gestured, exasperated. "Well, I could use some help."

"I'll hold the gun. You get the trunk. I'm particular about that."

Rance, understandably nervous with the gun pointed his way again, glanced toward a window onto the street. O'Sullivan noted this, and as Rance went into the adjacent room, leaving the door open, O'Sullivan went to that window, and closed the curtains.

In the boarding house across the way, Maguire had already perked up, several minutes before, realizing Rance was talking to someone. Half the time the accountant would deal with room service and other hotel staff, making their lives miserable; so Maguire spying Rance through the window, speaking to someone in his suite, did less than set off an alarm bell.

And then Mike O'Sullivan was in the window, closing the curtains—perfectly framed there, if only for a moment.

That Ford he'd spied earlier...maroon, but the same make as the green one. Had they painted it? Had he been asleep at the wheel?

These and other thoughts rocketed through Maguire's mind, as he dressed quickly but with his typical methodical precision, omitting his tie. Under the bed he had stowed a canvas bag, and from this he withdrew a long-barreled pump-action rifle. Bowler atop his head, the rifle concealed under his topcoat, he flew down the stairs and strode across the street, paying little heed to the downtown traffic, which was light anyway in this hick burg.

As he headed toward the entrance of the hotel, he didn't even look up when a car screeched its brakes, swerving to avoid him.

Someone else looked up, though: Michael—who had gotten bored on his watch and started reading his Tom Mix Big Little Book, missing the sight of Maguire passing right by on the driver's side of the Ford—was startled back into vigilance now, by the squealing brakes. In the driver's side door mirror, he could see the man in the bowler hat, jogging across the street.

The boy hadn't seen the gunman very well at that diner; but his father had described the man in detail and, besides, the snout of a rifle was sticking down like a skinny third leg that didn't quite reach the ground.

The man in the bowler was approaching the hotel now, and Michael slammed his hand into the horn—twice.

The sounds made the man glance back, but he didn't make eye contact with Michael; and then the man was inside the hotel.

Heart racing, Michael hit the horn again, and again. He paused and repeated the action, and kept it up, getting scared, holding the horn down for a long time, so long that people on the street were stopping and staring.

But where was his father? Why hadn't the sounds sent him running out of the hotel?

About the time Maguire was reaching under the bed for the bag with his pump-action rifle in it, O'Sullivan was in the bridal suite, keeping his .45 trained on Alexander Rance, who was huffing and puffing as he pushed the large metal trunk out of the bedroom.

Rance glanced at the window, where O'Sullivan had shut the curtains, and complained, "I can't see well enough—open those back up."

There was no overhead light, but several of the crystal lamps were on. Sunlight filtering in through the closed curtains cast an eerie glow.

"You can see fine," O'Sullivan said. "Push."

Rance continued to push the apparently heavy trunk into the room. "What do you think you're accomplishing by interfering with our business, Mr. O'Sullivan?"

"This doesn't have anything to do with business. It's personal."

Breathing hard, still pushing the trunk, nearer the light of the lamps by the couch, Rance said, "It's nothing *but* business—all of life is business, that's what you fail to grasp. And in business, to get what you want, you must have something valuable to trade."

"Those files are a start."

"Not…" The accountant grunted as he pushed the trunk. "…Not for someone as valuable as Connor Looney."

O'Sullivan frowned. "What makes Connor Looney valuable?"

Rance's expression clouded, as if he'd said too much, bantering with this intruder.

A mechanical chatter—loud as hell!—drew O'Sullivan's attention away from Rance, who was rising from his crouch, the trunk pushed to the center of the room, now.

"Opening bell on Wall Street," Rance explained, nodding across the room.

In the shadow of an alcove, a ticker-tape machine stood, spewing tape, making a racket like a miniature machine gun. Under the glass jar covering the machine, a pile of yesterday's tape was strewn.

The machine's chatter was loud enough to blot away the outside world—including the sound of O'Sullivan's son, desperately honking the horn.

Rance withdrew a big ring of keys from his dressing-gown pocket, sorting through them, muttering, "Now which one is it?"

"Find it—now."

"I'm trying!…I believe this is the one…"

The accountant knelt at the trunk, tried the key. "No…not that one…"

"If you're stalling, I'll shoot the lock off. Then you."

"Please…I'm doing my best!…Here it is…no, I tried that one already…"

"Mr. Rance…I may look like a patient man, but I assure you I'm not. Move it!"

Rance threw a glare at O'Sullivan. "That tone isn't helping! You're making me nervous!"

O'Sullivan went over and jammed the gun into the accountant's left temple and asked, "Does this help?"

"Uh...uh..."

"One more try, and we do it my way."

Rance selected another key, and said, "This is it—it has to be," inserted it into the keyhole and, with a click, unlocked the trunk. O'Sullivan took a step around, to get a look inside, as Rance opened the lid...

...on emptiness.

At that moment the ticker tape ran out, its chattering ceased, and the blurt of the car horn...the signal repeated over and over...finally made itself known to O'Sullivan.

Rance took that opportunity to scramble into the bedroom, slamming the door, locking it behind him.

And Mike O'Sullivan—with a second futile glance at the bare inside of the "heavy" trunk the accountant had struggled with so—knew he'd been set up. Rance had been the bait, and he knew he was the mouse...*so where was the fucking cat?*

A gunshot trumped the car horn, punching a hole through the bridal suite door—a rifle blast at close range!—splintering the wood, the honeymoon over.

O'Sullivan took cover behind the trunk, its metal lid up, as somebody kicked the door in with a forceful boot heel, wood crunching, metal snapping, and the man in the bowler filled the doorway and—not seeing O'Sullivan—fired off five loud sharp shots in quick succession, all around the room, including the bedroom door and wall.

Two shots slammed into the open metal lid, which was providing a shield of sorts for O'Sullivan, who stayed down as low as possible, the body of the trunk serving better cover.

As the man with the rifle paused to reload, stepping inside what appeared to be an empty room, O'Sullivan popped up from behind the trunk and blasted away with the .45. But he'd been shooting somewhat blindly, and the slugs thudded into the sofa near the door, as the guy with the rifle, losing his bowler, scrambled behind an end table that supported a crystal-shaded lamp, crouching there to finish reloading.

O'Sullivan, huddled low behind the trunk, could see where the two slugs had dimpled the lid; breathing hard, he mentally counted how many rounds he had left, as time itself seemed to pause, and the room took on a ghostly silence broken only by the sound of his opponent reloading the rifle. In the wall and the door to the bedroom adjacent, where Rance had fled, daylight was slanting through bullet holes like swords in a magician's box. Dust motes floated. Crystal lamps stood mute and the elegant surroundings seemed at odds with the conflict at hand.

O'Sullivan didn't see his adversary pop up from behind the end table, but the punch of the bullets from the rifle—two more rounds—pounded into the trunk, which slammed into O'Sullivan, knocking him backward and to one side, robbing him of cover. The second he realized he was exposed, O'Sullivan squeezed off three fast rounds, and one of them shattered the crystal lamp on the end table, showering his opponent with flying shards of glass, hitting him right in the face, like a dozen terrible bee stings.

The gunmen screamed in pain and surprise, and dropped to his knees. O'Sullivan, still on his side on the floor, out in the open, kept firing with the .45, though his bullets only served to send his bleeding moaning adversary seeking refuge behind the overstuffed sofa.

And then O'Sullivan was clicking on empty chambers, and he got a glimpse of the man with the rifle cowering behind the sofa, his bloody face in one hand, the rifle impotent—at least for the moment—in the other.

O'Sullivan took the opportunity to get to his feet and run over to that bedroom door, and—in a panel that had bullet holes punched in it already—kicked, then kicked again, letting daylight flood in, and he reached in and around and turned the key in the lock.

Pushing into the room, O'Sullivan quickly turned, staying in a crouch, in case the man with the rifle advanced on him; he slammed a fresh clip in his .45 and, as he backed in, he finally saw Rance—flung on the bed, on his back, his eyes and mouth open, and a blossom of red on the green silk robe, a spray of scarlet on the headboard and wall. One of the rifle slugs had caught the accountant, and taught Rance a final lesson about the business of crime.

O'Sullivan almost stumbled over something, and he looked down and saw a small black strongbox, amid a scattering of file folders and accordion envelopes next to the bed; too much stuff to grab up and carry...but the strongbox had a tiny label that said something big: CHIEF ACCOUNTS.

With his left hand, O'Sullivan grabbed the strongbox by its little handle, his right hand still ready to send death flying at that bleeding bastard in the next room.

The bedroom had a separate exit, and O'Sullivan took it, running down the corridor. On the second floor he found a window out onto a fire escape that brought him to the alley; and within seconds he was sprinting across the main street, toward where Michael was parked.

He didn't realize that Harlen Maguire had managed to stagger to the window and draw back the curtains and, pulling a revolver from his topcoat pocket, blinking away blood—no shards in his eyes, one small miracle—took aim.

Michael had spotted Papa, exiting that alley, and threw the Ford into reverse, backing the car toward his advancing father, neither of them wasting any time. But two gunshots discouraged them—holes punched in the roof of the car, sunlight streaming in!—and the boy heard his father yell, "*Go!* Get out of reverse, damnit—go!"

And Michael knew not to disobey his father. He changed gears, as professional as any outlaw wheelman, and began to pull away, his father running alongside the car. The boy's reach wasn't long enough to open the door for his father, but Papa managed to get the door open himself and was almost inside when another gunshot rang out, and Papa's shoulder flinched, even as he winced from the impact and pain.

Still, Papa somehow flung himself in the car, and shut the door, saying, "*Go! Go!*"

Frightened as he was, knowing his father had been shot, Michael did his job, hitting the accelerator, speeding and winding and weaving in and around and through the morning traffic, as sirens wailed behind him.

On the outskirts of town, he allowed himself to look at his father, who was holding onto his left shoulder with fingers that had blood seeping through them, making red trails down his hand.

O'Sullivan could see the panic on his boy's face, and he snapped, "I'm okay! Eyes on the road! I'm okay..."

The boy drove.

And in the bridal suite, Harlen Maguire dropped to his knees, as if about to pray, only he didn't clasp his hands: he held them before him, palms up. In the other room, through the open door, the corpse of Alexander Rance beckoned.

But Maguire didn't have his camera. And he was busy looking at his hands, anyway, the hands that had been holding his poor glass-ravaged face...

...hands covered in blood, dripping with red, and he was startled. It was as if all the blood he had on his hands was finally showing.

FIFTEEN

A s the great film director John Ford put it, "When the legend
becomes fact, print the legend." Depictions of my father and
myself paint us as well-known figures in the outlaw Midwest of the
1930s, placing us side by side with the likes of the Dillinger gang,
the Barker boys, and Bonnie and Clyde. In truth, latter-day stories
of my renown as the Angel of Death's "boy getaway man" are gross
exaggerations.

The only time we made the papers was the shooting at the
Grand Hotel in Stillwater, when witnesses indeed saw me fleeing
the scene at the wheel of the Ford, my father slumped on the rider's
side. Those contemporary newspaper accounts, however, were
even more inaccurate than subsequent speculation about us at
the hands of Hollywood and the more sensationalistic true-crime
writers.

In recent years, the truth has been sorted out, somewhat, as
Alexander Rance's role as a Capone organization financial wizard
has come to light; and research into photographer/reporter/assas-
sin Harlen Maguire's bizarre life has helped clear our record.

At the time, "the Bridal Suite Bandit" was painted as a
homicidal thief who murdered a respectable accountant—one
Alexander Rance—robbing him of hundreds of thousands of dollars from his rooms at Stillwater's Grand Hotel. Of course, my father took no money at all, merely records—ledger books and files.

And, at the same time, Harlen Maguire was portrayed in the
press as Rance's bodyguard, who bravely did his best to ward off a

murderous brigand, suffering injuries in the process. Which was how Maguire managed to walk away from the carnage, or rather was gurneyed away, spirited like a hero to the Stillwater hospital for emergency care of his glass-ravaged face.

Rather crude suspect sketches of my father and me hit the papers, though until subsequent events put Michael O'Sullivan, John Looney, Connor Looney, and Harlen Maguire back in the papers (and on the radio and in the newsreels), neither Papa's name nor mine was associated with the story headlined "ARMED ROBBERS SOUGHT—Getaway Driver a Young Boy."

At the time, of course, my father and I had other, more pressing concerns—chiefly, survival. Fortunately for us, other families—perhaps most families—in those hard times were scratching out a modest living and knew what it was to struggle just to exist. None of what has been written about my father and me has covered—no amount of diligent research has uncovered—the identity of the people who helped us, in the aftermath of the Grand Hotel shoot-out.

They are gone now, and their deeds—whether interpreted negatively or positively—cannot harm these good Samaritans. I would ask that you think of them as representative of a breed of American who lives no longer—hearty pioneers who managed to wrest a livelihood of sorts out of hardscrabble land.

Farming in the Great Plains never really made a recovery after the collapse of farm prices in 1920 and '21. Though even worse adversity lay ahead—droughts and dust storms would soon place Kansas, Nebraska, and Oklahoma in the middle of the so-called Dust Bowl—farmer families were already barely scratching out a living, after the Depression drove prices into the cellar.

Thus the landscape into which I drove my wounded father was topsoil rich and money poor, a desolate paradise that promised us, if not salvation, respite from the road.

Frightened though he was, Michael could handle the situation as long as his father was conscious, giving him directions—*turn here, stay at the speed limit, take a left.* Papa had managed to get the bleeding stopped with a piece of cloth torn from his own shirt, wouldn't even let the boy stop to help wrap the makeshift bandage around himself.

That may have been what finally taxed his father's considerable stamina and willpower, sending this strong weakened man into unconsciousness.

And then panic rose in the boy like water overtaking a sinking ship. Instinctively, he pulled off the main road, knowing he had to find a residence, a farm maybe, to seek help for his father. The Ford did well on the rutted dirt road, but Michael had to slow, not wanting the jolts to cause his father pain, even in his unconscious state.

Up ahead were some rickety buildings—a farmhouse, a barn, shack-like structures constructed of paint-peeling planks—that might normally have put the boy off. Right now, he was happy to see any sign of civilization, even if this spread was more like the hillbilly houses he'd seen in moving pictures and funny papers than the nice farms around Rock Island.

A pair of old people—in their fifties, maybe—were working in a field that looked pretty rough; warmer here, spring easing out winter, already. The couple was moving along slowly, kneeling at tilled soil, the man digging, the woman planting; their clothes were old and worn-out looking, the man in overalls and a ragged shirt and raggedy hat, the woman in a calico dress—both she and the dress had probably been pretty once, before the boy was born.

Michael pulled up at the edge of the field, where the couple worked, the boy thrilled to see any human being, particularly any that weren't shooting at him and his father. He ran between tilled rows, desperately waving his arms, and the couple glanced at each other, knowing help was needed, ready to give it.

What followed was a frenzied blur to the boy—a heated knife digging at his delirious father's shoulder, a bloody bullet dropping into a tin cup like a coin in the offering plate at church, his father shivering with fever on a makeshift cot in the front room of the shack-like house.

"Night sweats," the farmer said. His name was Bill; he had kind blue eyes, a grooved face, and mostly white hair. "It's good he sweats out the poison in him...but tend him, son. Stay with your father."

Michael didn't have to be told that. His father had tended to him, over these long weeks, and now he removed his father's shirt, buttoning cuffs that were frayed and stained from their travels. He folded his father's tie, placing it over the end of the cot, ritualistically, in the way he'd seen his father do, so many times.

The farmer and his wife—her name was Virginia, and she had blue eyes, too, in a face as pleasant as it was weathered, and dark-blonde graying hair—stayed in the room, but out of the way, mostly over by the kitchen part. They wore concern in their features that seemed unusual to Michael, considering he and his father were strangers. They didn't have Catholic icons in their house, so they weren't of the faith of his family; but Michael knew these were Christians, because they did Christian things... unlike some people who said they believed in Jesus.

Their name was Baum, but he thought at first they said "Bomb," which struck him as a funny kind of name. Later his father corrected him, saying their name was like Balm in the Bible—"The Balm of Gilead," Papa said.

By the next night, his father was awake, but groggy, still not really communicating very well. Michael sat beside him and fed him soup with a spoon that was a little too small for the job; he would have to wipe Papa's mouth with a frayed napkin Mrs. Bomb had provided. It was as if Papa were the child, and Michael the father, and the change felt good, made the boy feel older, that he was somehow paying his Papa back for all the wonderful things his father had done for him.

When the Bombs had gone off to their own bedroom, Michael settled on the threadbare sofa opposite his father's cot—Papa was still feverish, but not as bad, not near as bad—and the boy was settling his head on a pillow Mrs. Bomb had given him, when he noticed the gun in the holster under his father's jacket, on a chair where Mr. Bomb had draped it.

Papa was asleep, and so was the farm couple. The boy crept off the sofa, carefully removed the gun from the holster, and he stood and looked down at the weapon, huge in his small hand—rough and cold, not smooth and warm, like you'd imagine, from Tom Mix and the Lone Ranger.

But the longer he held it, the more natural it felt—he stood at the cracked mirror of a dresser off to one side of the room and pretended to be Tom Mix, drawing his gun at himself—looking fierce, a bad, bad man...

Then he pretended he was the Lone Ranger, and at some point, in his imaginings, he was his father...

O'Sullivan was not exactly sure how many days had passed. Three at least; probably no more than five. Unshaven, topcoat over his tieless white shirt, he sat in an old wicker chair on the porch of the timeworn farmhouse, feeling not bad, a tin cup of coffee steaming, cradled nicely in his hands. In the world around him, green was overtaking brown, and snow was nowhere. When had spring crept up on them? It had been winter, an eye blink ago.

Yet somehow it was not a surprise. They had been on the road together, he and Michael, forever—and yet there was no way to put enough time and space between them and the taking of Annie and Peter to give any solace, to make it seem anything but terrible and fresh in his memory. Out in the field—what a hard life these people had, but it was a life, wasn't it, better than their own—Bill was allowing Michael to help in the planting, the boy doing the digging with energy and enthusiasm, while the warmly amused farmer followed along, dropping seeds.

Mrs. Baum, a grizzled goddess in a frayed checkered dress, peeling potatoes, was watching the boy, too. Then she glanced toward the ramshackle barn, where the maroon Ford could be glimpsed, since the door was half off its hinges.

"'spect you'll be leavin', soon," she said.

O'Sullivan knew what she meant.

"We've enjoyed our visit," he said. "I should be strong enough, by tomorrow…Don't want to cause you any trouble."

"No trouble a'tall."

"Thank you for not asking questions."

"Our own business is enough to keep us occupied."

"But you took us in—strangers. Bullet holes in our car…bullet in me."

A smile grooved her face, a thousand smile lines joining it. "This is Oklahoma, mister. We don't like the banks much."

O'Sullivan didn't correct her false assumption.

"You know," she said, "that boy Choctaw's from around these parts."

"Pardon?"

"That Floyd fella."

Now O'Sullivan knew: Charles "Pretty Boy" Floyd.

"He's a wild one," she continued, "but he helps folks out. Law says we oughta give him up—so far nobody has. Sayin' is around these parts, sometimes a person's got to sift the law."

O'Sullivan said nothing.

Then Mrs. Baum, her smile almost glowing, said, "Boy of yours—he's a good worker."

Nodding, O'Sullivan felt a smile of his own blossom—he was enjoying his son's antics out in the field. He asked the woman, "Any children of your own?"

"No...Bill and me hooked up a little late in life, for that. This *is* a family farm, though, Bill's people—once was right somethin' to see. No, no children...Can't have everything."

These people had next to nothing, O'Sullivan thought; and yet they were grateful for their lot in life...

Almost too casually, the woman said, "Dotes on you, you know."

"Pardon?"

She turned her smile on the confused O'Sullivan. "Boy of yours! Worships the ground you walk on...Don't you see it?"

Frankly, he didn't, and just shrugged by way of response; but the next moment, his eyes caught Michael's, the boy looking up from his work, joy in his face, and he threw a casual wave at his father, before returning to his digging.

O'Sullivan did not understand the rush of emotion. It came up somewhere deep inside of him, rolling with an awful warmth up his chest into his face and moisture welled behind his eyes, overtaking him. He excused himself and went back into the house.

He did not want these kind people to see him weep, nor did he want his son to witness that shameful action.

Michael awoke on the sofa, startled out of sleep by a dreadful dream.

In the dream—the nightmare—he'd been in the Looney mansion, and he and his father were kneeling at the coffin again, like at the wake. But when Michael peeked inside the box, his father was inside—with pennies on his eyes! And when Michael looked to his side, where a moment before Papa had been kneeling, too—it was Mr. Looney now, smiling in that grandfatherly way, his arm around him. Then the boy ran away and Mr. Looney started to chase him; at some point Mr. Looney turned into Connor Looney and then Michael ran into a room and it was the bathroom of their own house, white tile and red blood and dead Peter and dead Mama and he made himself wake up.

He stumbled over in his pajamas to where his father sat at a table, going over books and records in the light of a kerosene lamp. Papa was in his T-shirt and suspenders and trousers, his bandaged arm showing, blood dried there, a reddish brown.

Papa looked like he was having trouble—it reminded the boy of himself, trying to do his schoolwork, really struggling.

When Michael approached, Papa looked up—the boy had been expecting reproval, for not being asleep, but instead his father's expression was warm, the man obviously pleased to see him.

That really helped, after the bad dream.

"Hello," Papa said. "What are you doing up? It's the middle of the night."

"Nightmare."

"Want to tell me about it?"

The boy shook his head.

His father pulled out the chair next to him at the table. "Come. Sit with me...if you want."

Michael sat. The papers his father was going over were figures, numbers in columns and rows.

"Math, huh?" the boy said, making a face.

Papa smiled at him. "Yeah—I always hated that subject, in school."

Michael had never thought about his father ever having been a kid at all—let alone in school. This was a minor revelation... and sudden common ground.

"Me, too," Michael said, and grinned.

Then his father stopped and he had a funny look—almost like he felt guilty about something. "I...I guess I never took time to find that out, son. What, uh, subjects did you like?"

That came out of left field! The boy thought for a few moments, then said, "Bible history, I guess."

This seemed to really surprise Papa. "Why?"

"I don't know. Maybe it's the stories. I always liked stories."

Papa smiled again, then asked, "You like stories with happy endings?"

"Sure...but not all good stories have happy endings. The ones in the Bible have really bad endings, sometimes, sad endings."

O'Sullivan thought about that, then he nodded. "But maybe they teach us something...the sad-ending ones."

That seemed reasonable to Michael. "Yeah...Pop?"

"Yes?"

"Don't get mad."

"I won't."

"...Did you like Peter better than me?"

His father's expression was blank; but something in the man's eyes made Michael wish he hadn't asked the question.

"Oh Michael, no," he said, and he touched the boy's arm. "I loved you both the same."

"But you couldn't have."

"...Why?"

"Because if you loved us the same, you wouldn't treat us different."

His father blinked. "Did I do that, son?"

"...Well. Yes. Sure."

Papa sighed, then he said, quietly, "I didn't love you the same...I loved you equally. Understand?"

"I think so."

"I may have seemed to love Peter more, because..."

"Because he was the baby?"

Papa swallowed. "Yes. Because he was the baby, and...he was just a sweet boy. You know? Sweet."

"He never hit you with a snowball."

Though his eyes remained sad, Papa laughed, once. "No, he didn't. But he did have a sweetness about him that...you and I don't have, son."

"We don't?"

"You were more like me. Peter was more like Mom."

The boy thought about that.

Then his father said, "I didn't mean to treat you different."

This was getting hard on both of them, so Michael just shrugged and said, "Okay. It's okay...'Night, Papa."

And, on impulse, he hugged his father around the neck, being careful not to hurt the man's sore arm. Papa hugged back, not being so careful.

After his son began softly snoring on the couch, O'Sullivan was able to get his mind back on the task before him. Something Rance had said—or maybe it was something about the accountant's attitude—made O'Sullivan think an answer of sorts might be waiting to be found in these figures.

So he sorted through the documents, setting some aside, looking at others, overwhelmed, out of his element. Finally a buff-colored file almost seemed to appear in his hands...

...CONNOR LOONEY, it was boldly marked.

Surprised, interested, he began to look carefully through it— at letters, accounts, bills of lading, receipts, dockets, and more. He pushed the other books and ledgers and files aside and concentrated on this one.

And when the sun came up, O'Sullivan—fully dressed, ready to ride, .45 under his arm, new information in his brain—gently shook Michael awake, saying, "Up up up."

The bleary-eyed boy leaned on an elbow and asked, "Where's the fire?"

"Time to go. We don't want to wear out our welcome."

Michael gave him no argument, though the boy was clearly conflicted about leaving behind his new "family," and yet obviously anxious to get back out on the road with his father.

As they rolled out of the barn in the Ford, O'Sullivan waved at the farm couple, who waved back. He leaned out the window, and said, "We left a little thank you," and pointed to the barn. Then the car rolled out onto, and down, the dirt road.

The Baums were already heading into the barn, and O'Sullivan smiled at his son, who smiled back. The couple would soon find out it sometimes paid to be hospitable: the O'Sullivan "gang" had left them stacks and stacks of money packets on a bale of hay…hundreds of thousands of dollars in Capone money. Let Choctaw top that.

They were on a paved highway when he told the boy they were heading back to the Tri-Cities.

"Why are we going back?" Michael asked.

"Something doesn't add up, son," he said, nodding toward the back, where the ledger books and files were now stowed in the compartment under the seat. "Men lie, but numbers don't. Facts and figures…It's always about money."

"You mean, math?" the boy asked.

"Math," his father said.

SIXTEEN

*J*ohn Looney had a ranch in Chama, New Mexico, an adobe *fortress where he had gone from time to time, to rest or to hide out from his enemies. After the Market Square riot, when Looney was fined by the court for incitement and his newspaper (temporarily) shut down, the patriarch went to the ranch to recover from injuries delivered by local cops who were in the pocket of a Looney rival. Another time Looney holed up at the ranch recovering from wounds received in a duel. Many true-crime historians have wondered why Looney stayed around the Tri-Cities when the trouble with Mike O'Sullivan started. Some contend that he did flee, briefly at least, to his New Mexico "home away from home," and one account has federal agents arresting him there.*

Though I have no direct proof other than my recollection, I believe my father had heard from a friend on Looney's payroll that the old man was packing up for another of these New Mexico "vacations." This was in part why we rushed from Oklahoma back to Illinois, while Papa was still weak from his injury.

That, and the discovery he had made in that strongbox he'd taken from the suite of Alexander Rance.

A sunny Sunday morning, crisp but not quite cold, found the bells ringing and the Irish Catholics of the Illinois side of the Tri-Cities converging on St. Peter's. The parking lot was full outside, the pews full within. God was doing a hell of a business today, John Looney thought, eyeing the throng—better business than he had, of late, his mind on this goddamned O'Sullivan matter.

Looney—along with his trusted bodyguards Jimmy and Sean (on his right and left hand, respectively), as well as other more respectable members of the parish—knelt at the altar rail to receive communion. Among the morning's last group to receive the Eucharist, Looney rose and returned down the aisle, the congregation all around kneeling in their pews in meditation. The choir sang in the Latin gibberish that the old man found so soothing—all this ritual was reassuring, the pomp and circumstance of it such wonderful theater, the trappings a delightful blend of fear and forgiveness, mass itself a droning reiteration of tradition and order in a cruel, chaotic world.

John Looney had no use for the empty cross of the Protestants, who insisted their Christ had risen, and that the cross should be a symbol of redemption. He embraced instead the cross of the Catholics, with Jesus in plain view, suffering, bleeding, living the life of hell-on-earth His father had willed to man.

The old man in his well-pressed, somber dark suit and tie looked like a Methodist preacher himself; but the irony was lost on him. Looney sidled into his pew, and with Jimmy and Sean's help lowered himself at the padded kneeling bench; moments later—in the row behind him—a man spoke, not in a whisper, but softly enough that only Looney (and perhaps his boys) would hear.

"Hello, John."

Looney did not need to turn to know Mike O'Sullivan knelt at the bench in the pew directly in back of him. "I'll be damned," the old man breathed.

O'Sullivan said, "Not a good churchgoer like you...Sean, Jimmy. Morning."

Looney, almost smiling, said, "You're a clever boy, Mike. Neutral ground—sanctuary. What do you want?"

"I want to talk...in private. Downstairs."

Looney sensed the man behind him standing, and he got to his feet—batting off the help of his chowderheaded bodyguards—and, with a nod to Sean to let him pass, moved out of the pew. In a brown suit that looked somewhat the worse for wear, O'Sullivan stood waiting for Looney to fall in alongside him, and the two bodyguards followed as the two men moved together up the aisle toward the church entrance. Around them heads were bowed, as Latin call and response echoed throughout the cavernous church and sunlight filtered in colorfully through stained glass.

Near the front doors, to the left, were stairs that went down into the basement. Then the little group, footsteps ringing off cement, was in a corridor, off of which a large room could be used for various meetings and even banquets; Michael O'Sullivan, Jr., had attended a birthday party in that very room, the night the boy's brother was killed in his stead.

Looney nodded to Sean and Jimmy to wait outside, and he and his former chief enforcer went through a small door into another room. O'Sullivan snapped on the lights, a few bare hanging bulbs exposing in their yellowish glow an unfinished windowless concrete area that had a crypt-like atmosphere, littered with religious artifacts, some of them stored, others just abandoned.

The old man and his younger ex-associate stood facing each other—no chairs were available, though they might have used one of the pews stacked around, amid kneeling benches, various plaster saints, and a bloody Jesus on the cross leaning against the wall, a bystander with more on His mind than the two of them.

Looney had a flash of the basement of his home, and the last good time he'd had with his two godsons, playing dice, rolling the "bones" against the concrete wall, losing to Peter. He was still losing to Peter, after all these weeks.

Above them the muffled sound of mass made the Latin even more indecipherable, providing a strange, otherworldly accompaniment to their conversation.

Emotion swelled through Looney's chest; seeing Mike O'Sullivan—his other son, the better son—filled him with emotion, much of it contradictory: love, hate, pride, shame.

"And here I thought," Looney said, letting the brogue roll, "I would never see you again."

"Not alive," O'Sullivan said flatly.

That hurt the old man, and he flinched as O'Sullivan thrust something toward him: a file, a manila folder, stuffed with papers and such.

"Read that," O'Sullivan said. "Take out your glasses, if you like."

Looney did not reach for the file his former soldier offered him.

O'Sullivan made his sales pitch: "It's interesting reading, John. The kind of story the *News* specializes in...crime, sin, betrayal...It's all there."

Looney waved a hand: no. Shook his head the same way.

"Read all about it, John," O'Sullivan said, as if hawking an extra edition of Looney's paper. "Your son has been working for Chicago. When you turn down something as beneath your dignity...narcotics, forcible white slaving, union racketeering... Connor goes right ahead with it, with Capone's blessing."

Looney held up a palm. "Mike, please stop. Don't waste your breath."

Above them, Latin droned.

"Of course," O'Sullivan was saying, "your boy's been stealing from you for years...in league with your good friends, your business partners Nitti and Capone. He's been keeping accounts open under the names of dead men—men like the McGovern brothers. I stood and watched him kill Danny, and I helped him kill Fin, and I did these distasteful things under the mistaken impression I was working for you. Doing your bidding—but I wasn't."

O'Sullivan dropped the file to his side; it was clear Looney would not accept it.

Finally the old man said, "Do you think I'd give up my son?"

"He's been stealing from you, John."

"You're a father, Mike. My own son?"

"He betrayed you. Sold you down the river."

"And you think I don't *know* that?"

The simple question almost knocked O'Sullivan back.

The old man was smiling bitterly, shaking his head again, as if disagreeing with himself. "I *know*, Mike...I know what Connor's done, and what Connor is. Hell, those things in that folder, I'm proud of him for 'em...it's the only time he ever showed any goddamned initiative!"

Michael O'Sullivan had not expected this response from the old man. Right now, he felt as if he'd been struck a blow to the belly. This had been his last effort, one final chance to get through to the one man who could end the nightmare.

The old man's face was a wrinkled mask of intensity, his blue eyes cold as ice, and yet blazing. "Listen to me, boy! I tried to avoid more bloodshed—I sent you an emissary with an offer of amnesty and money and freedom, and you butchered him to send me a message. Well, you wouldn't accept my offer, so I did what was necessary."

Above them, the congregation said, "*Ah-men!*"

O'Sullivan said, "I loved you like a father."

"And I love you like a son...I always have. And I am begging you, boy, to leave...before there's no leaving."

"That sounds like a threat."

Looney sighed. "I am too old and tired for threats. When did either of us make such idle comments? You can leave this town, this country, with your remaining son, and live long happy lives. Open a shop, buy a farm, or sit back and spend Capone's money till Gabriel calls."

"And if I don't?"

The old man looked at him gravely. "Then you know how it will end."

O'Sullivan felt he was talking to a brick wall, whose response to whatever he said was to fall on him; but he had to try again—he and this man had been close, so very close, and their heart-to-heart talks had gone long into many nights.

"Think it through, John. Capone and Nitti are protecting Connor, now—but when you're gone, they won't need him. They've been using him, manipulating him, positioning themselves to take over the Tri-Cities action."

Looney's smile was like a skeleton's. "But I'm still alive, Mike—and as long as I'm alive, they won't give you Connor. Now, Capone might steal from me—and if I were to look at that file, I believe it would be Frank Nitti's fine Sicilian hand I would see at work, not the pudgy fingers of Capone—but in any case, the Big Fella would never have me killed."

"I have a strongbox of Alexander Rance's ledgers and files—this..." O'Sullivan hefted the manila folder, "...is just the small part of it that applies to you."

Looney grunted a humorless laugh. "And what would you do with this strongbox of information? Trade it back to Capone and Nitti for them giving you my son?"

"That's right."

"If you believe that, Mike, why are you here? Why take this risk? Or have you already figured out that those records wouldn't have been in that hotel suite if someone didn't *want* you to have them."

O'Sullivan had considered this, but had not been able to sort it out; so he had to ask, "What do you mean, old man?"

"I mean Frank Nitti wants Capone's chair, but he wants it to come to him by rights of succession, not violent overthrow. Voices within the Capone organization whisper to me that

Nitti has paved the way for these federal indictments dogging Capone's heels."

O'Sullivan tried to absorb this twisted news. "Nitti is helping the feds?"

Looney nodded. "Oh, they don't know he is...but he is. So you do not hold the cards you think you hold, Mike."

O'Sullivan pointed at Looney. "When you're gone, Nitti will kill Connor and take over here in the Cities. You *know* that, John—either way, this ends with your boy dead."

"That may be. But I won't be alive to see it. Anyway, do you expect me to give you the keys to his room and point the way for you to walk in, put a gun to his head, and pull the trigger? No. He's my son. I'm his father. I will not do that."

Quietly, as if praying, O'Sullivan said, "For your godson— Peter. For my wife—Annie."

"*No!* No...Mike, how many men have you killed? Do you imagine they didn't each have a wife? Children? A mother, a father? Didn't Danny McGovern have a brother? Who were these men we killed, you and I—clay figures? Phantoms? Or men who lived and breathed, until we took that away from them, forever?"

"Soldiers kill soldiers. Your boy murdered a woman and a child."

Looney's eyes and nostrils flared; his false teeth flashed. "Open your eyes! Look around you—who do you see in this room? Only murderers, nothing but murderers, here. This is the life we chose, Mike...and the only certainty in this life is that we'll be damned in the next one."

Muffled Latin filled the silence.

Then O'Sullivan said, "My boy Peter is in heaven, with his mother. Michael will join them one day—many years from now."

Looney winked at him. "If that's what you want, boyo, do everything you can to make sure that happens. But never mind the next life—there's still a life here on earth for you and your son. Reach out for that life, Mike...and take it! Leave us; go! It's the only way out."

"Not the only way."

Looney nodded. "You could kill me," he granted. "And then Nitti might give up Connor. But can you do that, son? Can you look me in the eyes and see me off to hell?"

"Suppose..." For the first time O'Sullivan considered the possibility of taking Looney at his word. "...Suppose I do go."

Looney nodded, pleased. "Go with my blessing, and take the money you've stolen with you."

"Capone's money."

"I'll replace it."

"I took a lot."

"I have a lot."

O'Sullivan stared at the old man; the old man stared back.

"And what will you do, John, if I go?"

"Why, I'll mourn you, Mike...mourn the son *I* lost."

O'Sullivan wondered if this was more self-serving blarney, or came from Looney's heart; then he had a sudden revelation: the answer to that question didn't matter! When the time had come to choose between loyalty and blood, between sentiment and blood, even money and blood, Looney had chosen blood.

As he stepped from the room, leaving Looney to the plaster Christ, backing out into the corridor with his .45 drawn, keeping a close eye on Sean and Jimmy, O'Sullivan could not shake that thought: *Looney had chosen blood.*

And by the time he slipped away from the sanctuary of the church—the mass loud now, muffled no more, though still its arcane Latin self—O'Sullivan knew what had to be done.

SEVENTEEN

My father took me to Chippiannock Cemetery, or rather I took him—drove him there, from St. Peter's. When he was sure we weren't being followed, he gave me directions, and my next memory is Papa and me all alone in the vast sloping graveyard, surrounded by stone cherubs and crosses, the snow gone, patches of green trying to overtake the brown.

So we had our graveside good-byes, after all.

I remember kneeling at Mama's simple gravestone, next to Peter's, and saying, "We should have brought flowers."

And Papa said, "That's all right, Michael. It's still too cold for flowers."

That had troubled me, and I asked, "Is Mama cold?"

"She's free of earthly concerns, son."

My father is buried next to them, now; and one day—one day soon—I will join them in the Village of the Dead. Connor Looney is buried in Chippiannock, too. When I first heard, I thought that was a terrible thing—even the ground should be more discriminating.

But with the passage of years, I've come to see the rightness of it. We were bound together in life and death, all of us, and my father, mother, and brother will be forever linked to the Looneys, as will I, at least as long as people are interested in the history of that lefthanded form of human endeavor called crime.

John Looney, unfortunately, is not buried at Chippiannock. His grave is at his ranch in New Mexico, next to his wife's, one last getaway from Tri-Cities trouble.

They say he was packed and ready to go to Chama, that rainy Sunday night; he could have caught an afternoon train, but instead he lingered, for reasons of his own. Perhaps he had pressing business that needed tending before he could leave.

Or maybe the old man had a sense of his destiny. Maybe he believed in fate—though I'm not convinced he believed in anything at all.

The Paradise Hotel was in downtown Prophetstown, near the Tri-Cities, on the way to Chicago. Nondescript, almost rundown, the three-story frame building was anything but paradise, the kind of lodgings the less successful traveling salesmen resorted to in these hard times.

The boy was asleep in his clothes on top of one of the twin beds in a room whose yellowish wainscoted walls had grime and stains from the decades that had passed since the hotel's heyday. A naked bulb screwed in the wall provided the only illumination; O'Sullivan switched it off, and sat on the bed next to the boy. Rain streaked the windows, and its reflected shimmer made patterns on the slumbering child. Thunder rumbled, sounding distant, but a threat nonetheless.

O'Sullivan was in the same suit he'd worn to the church today. He wore no tie. This was the end of the road and he knew it—and he knew what had to be done, knew now the only way that Capone and Nitti would give up Connor to him.

Because he had phone calls to make, and other preparations, O'Sullivan had taken the adjoining room, as well; and he'd made his arrangement with the desk clerk for the long-distance calls.

From that adjoining room, he sat at a table, a work area where salesman and businessmen could go over their receipts and records, and used the phone. Shabby, sparsely furnished, these two rooms did not constitute a suite worthy of, say, Alexander Rance. But it suited Mike O'Sullivan's purposes just fine.

He did not reach Nitti at first. Someone at the Lexington asked for a number where Mr. Nitti could return the call, and O'Sullivan refused to play along.

"Tell Nitti," he said into the receiver, "that Mike O'Sullivan will call again—in one hour."

Then O'Sullivan hung up. Still seated at the table, he made out a list of banks and safe deposit box numbers on a sheet of Hotel Paradise letterhead; he wrote "Michael" on an envelope and inserted the sheet into that, with eight little keys folded up inside—also included were Uncle Bob's phone number and directions to the farm on the lake. Then he slipped in a fat wad of cash, enough to carry the boy for weeks, perhaps months, and licked the flap and sealed it shut.

O'Sullivan went back in where his son slept, and placed the envelope on the scarred nightstand, where a fat little Lone Ranger book lay folded open next to the boy's small revolver. Again he sat beside Michael and looked at him for a long time—studying him, committing to memory every detail of the child, as if he hoped to recognize the boy in some other lifetime.

Then he stroked his son's hair, thinking how much he loved the child, hoping Michael knew, and got up and returned to the next room, not realizing the boy had only been pretending to be asleep.

Alone in the room now, Michael eyed the letter on the nightstand suspiciously. The word "good-bye" seemed to rise off the envelope like steam. Glancing toward where his father had gone, the boy saw a strip of light along the doorway's edge. He rose and went to the door, nudging it open another crack, and peeked in.

His father sat at a table, the hard-shell black case before him, closed; like a master musician, he unsnapped the clasps, lifted the lid, and revealed the protectively nestled parts of his instrument—the tommy gun, which had been with them on their journey, but had gone as yet unused.

Michael was amazed by the speed, the precision of it: piece by piece, checking each one, his father assembled the gun quickly, efficiently, snapping the parts together, tiny loud mechanical clicks and clacks, each one making the boy flinch. Michael had seen his father like this many times on the road—intense, methodical, precise; but something seemed different tonight. Papa was preparing not just the gun, but himself—snapping his own parts together, somehow.

Steeling himself.

Finally, the drum of ammunition was clicked in place onto the assembled machine gun, and the boy went in.

O'Sullivan turned to him, with an expression almost like a kid getting caught doing something he shouldn't—the gun before him like the contents of a forbidden cookie jar.

"What are you doing?" the boy asked sternly.

"Preparing myself."

"For what?"

"For the one last thing that has to be done."

"And then?"

"Then we're free of it, son."

Michael just stood there in his rumpled clothes, and stared at his father with blank accusation.

Papa, not irritated, even gentle, said, "Go back to bed, Michael."

"Who are you going to kill?"

"Michael..."

"I know I should want you to kill Mama's and Peter's killer. But right now I just want us to go off somewhere. Even if it is Perdition."

"This is perdition, son."

"What?"

"Son—go to bed."

"Shall I say my prayers, Papa?"

"If you like."

"Because I'm a sinner, too, Papa? Helping you like I have?"

He shook his head. "We're all sinners, son. That's the way we enter this world. But we can leave it forgiven."

The boy knew what that meant—more candles. But he had been skeptical when the nuns at the Villa taught him theology, and he was skeptical now, when a man holding a machine gun was giving the lesson.

"You're leaving me here," Michael said—the accusation boldly out in front of them both.

"…I'll be gone tonight…tomorrow morning, I'll be back."

"If you don't get killed, you mean."

His father shot him a look. "Michael—I'll be back. I promise."

But neither of them quite believed it.

And nothing was left to say. The boy stumbled off to his bed, and the man took one last look at the machine gun before moving on to his Colt .45 automatic, which could use a cleaning.

When he was done, O'Sullivan made his phone call.

For several hours that rainy evening, at the small restaurant in downtown Rock Island, not far from his newspaper office on Second Avenue, John Looney met with certain key associates. Looney was handling his own legal matters now, since the demise of Frank Kelly, and he needed to make sure the wheels would move smoothly while he had his little rest out at the ranch.

His bags and a trunk were already waiting at the train station, where they would head now—a ten a.m. night coach west awaited. Seven bodyguards—Sean and Jimmy among them, all the boyos armed to the teeth—would be at his side, throughout his travels, just in case Mike O'Sullivan hadn't taken their little church talk to heart.

Even the boss got chased out at closing time, and as the restaurant staff piled chairs on tables, and lights winked off, the old man and his six young bodyguards (the seventh, Jimmy, had stayed with the Pierce Arrow) shrugged into topcoats, Sean plucking his umbrella from where it leaned against the wall, and prepared to head out into the storm. Out the restaurant windows, the night was as dark as it was wet, raindrops streaming down in glimmering ribbons, the street black and shiny, as if freshly painted.

Thunder growled, as Looney stepped onto the sidewalk, rain pelting the umbrella Sean held for him. Sean and the other watchdogs had no umbrellas of their own—the rain had at them, assailing them as they flanked their boss, their eyes searching the darkness, the downpour, for anything suspicious, any moving shape, any sign of life on streets where reasonable men had long since been driven indoors by the weather.

The two automobiles were parked down the street a bit—Looney's Pierce Arrow touring car, and the Velie sedan, for the bodyguard overflow—and the old man walked quickly, not anxious to get wet, his shoes and spats taking a shellacking as he strode through puddles. He paused at the car—did he hear something? Something other than the relentless raindrops?

He looked around, and so did Sean, and so did the others. Nothing. Just ovals of streetlamp light and pools of water making strange designs on the pavement as rain slanted down like a watery ambush. How welcome the dry heat of New Mexico would be after this sodden godforsaken night...

Looney waited for Jimmy to open the door; he could see his driver, behind the wheel, but not clearly, the rain-streaked window clouding the issue. Annoyed, Looney tromped around to the driver's side, the bodyguards following, Sean keeping the old man covered with the umbrella—and shook the driver's door handle, saying, "Hey, Jimmy! Open the door, boy—Jim!"

His shaking of the locked door handle was just enough to prompt a reaction from Jimmy—who slumped forward onto the steering wheel, face tilted toward the side window. Even through the smear of rain, the dark-red hole in Jimmy's forehead could be seen, as could the man's open, empty-staring eyes.

"Christ," Looney said, stepping away from the grisly, ghostly sight, "Mike's killed him... *Jimmy's been shot!*"

And all around him his bodyguards drew their weapons, spreading out along the traffic-free street, eyes fanning the rain-swept darkness.

Looney did not carry a gun—he left that to his men. And a small army of his soldiers were all around him. O'Sullivan would know what he'd be up against—so he'd killed Jimmy, as a warning, to spook Looney, and fled into the night. The old man just about had himself convinced of that when thunder shook the night.

Not God's thunder: a Thompson submachine gun's.

All around Looney, in rapid succession, his bodyguards—few of them even getting their weapons unholstered, to fire off shots of their own—were cut to pieces by a rain of lead, the chopper blazing orangely in the dark, sending his soldiers tumbling, stumbling, flopping, dancing, shaken like naughty children, blood mist puffing in the night. One by one these fierce men with guns splashed whimpering to the wet pavement, blood flowing into rain puddles, turning the street a glistening pink.

Looney could not watch. Unarmed, he could not act. Trapped, he could not run. So he just stood there and stared at the pavement and listened to the ungodly roar of gunfire until it had stopped, only to echo through the empty streets of Rock Island.

And now, scattered all around him, his loyal boyos, this one on his belly, that one on his back, this man in the gutter, that man rolled into a ball, another with brains leaching out of his shattered skull like jelly...and Sean on his side, the umbrella just out of his grasp, as if he were reaching for it, the gun in his limp hand only half-raised. Rain pounded the blood and the gore, diluting, then obliterating it; and lightning flashed and thunder clapped, and in a momentary flash of white, there stood O'Sullivan— down the street—with the Thompson in his hands.

Then, without moving, he disappeared into darkness. Looney waited. Why run? Mike had figured it, hadn't he? The only way to get Capone to give up Connor was if John Looney were dead.

The old man could hear the footsteps on the wet pavement, growing closer, closer, and then Mike O'Sullivan—the machine gun in his left hand now, the .45 Colt in his right—was standing before him, the two almost close enough to reach out to each other...but not quite.

"You would kill your father," Looney said, "to avenge your son?"

"You're not my father."

Looney's chin jutted—trembled. "I was as much a father to you as to my own boy."

"Only I wasn't blood."

The old man swallowed. "And now you need mine, don't you?...Well, those of us who take this path, we *know* don't we, son? Someday...some night...we all may come to an end like this."

O'Sullivan kept the .45 trained. "Spare me your blarney, old man."

But there was truth in his voice when Looney said, "If this way it must be...I'm glad it's you."

O'Sullivan shot him anyway.

Looney, a bullet in the brain, stumbled back into the Pierce Arrow and slid down the side of the car, sat for a moment, then fell on his side. A stream of blood from his forehead made its way toward the gutter.

O'Sullivan stood for several long moments, staring at the corpse of a man he had loved; he had wept over his dead wife and son, and for Michael too, and he might have been weeping now, but the rain streaming down his face concealed it, even from himself.

Around him, in buildings on all sides, lights were going on in windows, yellow squares glowing in the dark wet night—then faces appeared in those squares, indistinct, smeary bystanders looking down on the carnage in silence from the warmth of their lodgings.

Only one man in the street was standing—the rest were scattered in various postures of violent death. He must have looked so small to them, O'Sullivan thought, viewed from on high, a man standing alone in the rainy street.

He looked up at them, his face moving from blurred face to blurred face, explaining himself...no, warning them of where life could take them.

"*Go back inside!*" he called, voice echoing like the earlier gunfire. "*And pray—pray that God never puts you on my road!*"

But the lights stayed on, the faces continued to watch...to judge. Police would be called; sirens would wail.

And Mike O'Sullivan—knowing he hadn't made his point to these witnesses, but confident he'd made an impression on John Looney—walked back into the rainy darkness, which swallowed him, leaving the empty street behind.

The almost empty street.

Though Frank Nitti's office was in the Lexington Hotel, he—unlike Capone—did not live on the premises; he'd come over from his home on the near West Side to be available when O'Sullivan called back.

Right now, with most of the lights off, he sat at his desk, in his shirtsleeves and suspenders and no tie, taking his second call tonight from the remarkable Mr. O'Sullivan.

"It's done?" Nitti asked.

"John Looney is dead," O'Sullivan's voice said over the scratchy line, as cold and matter of fact as a nurse saying the doctor will see you now; the sound of clatter and chatter in the background indicated the man was calling from a restaurant or diner.

Nitti asked, "You expect any retaliation?"

"No—I took down his seven best men, too. Best, after me, that is."

"Seven," Nitti said, impressed. "You've tied the St. Valentine's Day record."

"I wasn't keeping score. You want Rance's records returned to you, Mr. Nitti, or should I send them to the feds?"

"Send them back addressed to me here at the hotel," Nitti said. "What do you want in return?"

"The money I've taken from you...and a permanent truce between us."

"Done...How long will it take you to get here?"

"I'm two hours from the city. I'll have no opposition?"

"Those were your terms," Nitti said, putting his shrug into his voice, "and I agreed to them."

"Mr. Nitti, if this is a trap, pray I don't survive it."

Nitti sighed. "Mr. O'Sullivan, I have been sympathetic to your cause from the start. It was only due to business concerns that I couldn't aid you, before."

"Where does Capone stand on this?"

"With the old man dead, Al won't give a damn about Connor Looney...in fact, with both of them gone, it opens the door wide for us in the Tri-Cities. But then, you've already figured that out, haven't you, Mr. O'Sullivan?"

"Yes."

"Are you still interested in working for us?"

"No."

Nitti twitched a smile, but that he kept out of his voice. "If you change your mind, I'm sure we'd have a position for you. You're the best at your trade I've ever encountered...Mr. Capone agrees. But in any event, he will want your assurance that, after this...it's over."

"You both have that assurance...My son and I will disappear."

"Good...You remember where the Lexington Hotel is, I assume? Well, you're looking for room 1032."

"…You sure you want this done on your premises? Won't that attract undue attention?"

"Oh, Mr. O'Sullivan—you of all people should not be so naive. Here we control things. Do you really think every dead body that turns up in a ditch died there?"

"…Remember what I said, Mr. Nitti—if this is a trap…"

"Don't lower yourself with a threat, Mr. O'Sullivan. Have a little dignity. Retain your aura of mystery."

And Nitti hung up.

Then the Chicago mob's top business executive—the real spider at the web's center—considered going home; it was, after all, late on a Sunday night, though his wife Anna would be asleep by now. Perhaps he should stay until O'Sullivan arrived at the hotel, and this nasty business was over…

On reflection, this seemed to Nitti the prudent course of action, and he selected a file from a stack on the desk and, in a pool of yellow light from a desk lamp, went to work.

It had rained in Chicago, too, but on the drive from Rock Island, the downpour had faded to a drizzle and now it was a memory, the streets in the Loop taking on a slick, glisteny black sheen reflecting streetlamp glow and the neon of sleeping businesses, as if the pavement had caught occasional fire.

O'Sullivan parked down the block on 22nd, glad to be alone, pleased not to be making his boy part of this. The Thompson was in the car, in the backseat, still assembled; all he was carrying was a .45 in his shoulder holster and a .38 in his topcoat pocket. The wind picked up scraps of paper, which seemed to race across South Michigan Avenue, scrambling across toward the Lexington Hotel. O'Sullivan took his time. He was in no hurry.

This endless night had been long coming.

No doorman was on duty, not in the wee hours of early Monday morning. And the lobby was nearly deserted—a hotel man at the front desk; and by the elevators, skinny, edgy, snappily dressed Marco—who'd been his armed elevator operator on O'Sullivan's last visit to the Lexington—seemed to be the only watchdog.

"Marco," O'Sullivan said.

"Angel," Marco said, with a respectful nod.

And the watchdog reached over and pressed the UP button for him; the grillwork doors opened, Marco stepped aside, and O'Sullivan stepped inside. The doors closed, leaving an unconcerned Marco behind.

On the tenth floor, O'Sullivan exited the elevator, taking the corridor at left, following Nitti's instructions. His gloved hand was in his topcoat pocket clenching the .38 revolver. He moved down the empty corridor, glancing at doors, ready to react—trusting Nitti, but not trusting him.

At room 1032, with his left hand, O'Sullivan knocked twice—softly. Almost at once, the other brawny watchdog from his previous visit—Harry—answered the door.

The two men nodded at each other, Harry standing aside as O'Sullivan entered the comfortably plush, well-appointed suite. In the adjacent room, a radio—turned up perhaps a shade too loud—played Paul Whiteman music, jazz for white people who hadn't heard colored people play it.

O'Sullivan gave Harry a look, and Harry nodded toward a door.

"Bathroom," Harry mouthed, and pointed.

O'Sullivan nodded, and Harry moved back nearer to the entry, as the Angel of Death made his way deeper into the suite, approaching the door the watchdog had indicated.

He took a breath, and pushed open the door, a bright white-tiled bathroom, larger than some whole apartments; the mirrors were fogged, the air thick with steam.

Lolling back in the hot, soapy bath, a whiskey flask near his reach on the edge of the tub, Connor Looney—his eyes closed, dark hair plastered down—said, "Harry—take your piss down the hall, for Christ's sake! A little privacy, please."

O'Sullivan stood looking down at the pale figure—a scrawny-looking naked man, such a pitiful creature to have caused such a fuss.

Then Connor sensed something and his eyes popped open and his sallow complexion paled even further, his mouth open as if frozen in midbreath.

"I should take my time killing you," O'Sullivan said, "but I can't bear your company."

Connor's eyes narrowed, flaring in defiance, and he was coming up out of the tub when he said, "I'll see you in hell!"

O'Sullivan shot him once in the chest, and again in the stomach, the naked man smacking against the tile wall, making a bloody trail as he slid back down sloshingly into the tub, not dead yet.

"Hell will be heaven," O'Sullivan said, "if I can spend eternity making you pay for what you did to them."

And O'Sullivan shot Connor in the head—just as he had the man's father.

The corpse dropped down into the soapy, blood-frothy water, the white tiles surrounding spattered and smeared with crimson.

When O'Sullivan emerged, Harry said, "That was quick," and the Angel said nothing, not waiting even for the watchdog to open the door for him. He walked down the corridor, staying alert, and at the end of the hall—as Nitti had requested—he dropped the murder weapon to the carpeted floor.

He would still have his .45 if the little gangster crossed him.

But Nitti was true to his word, and O'Sullivan's exit through the Lexington lobby was as uneventful as his arrival. Within minutes he was in the maroon Ford, heading back to his son.

Michael had slept very little. He never did put on his pajamas. He tried to read the Big Little Book, but the Lone Ranger just seemed...silly, now. From time to time, he would kneel by his bed and pray for his father's welfare.

But he was confused—because he wasn't sure if God could protect Papa, if what Papa was doing was a sin. After all, his father wasn't Mr. Looney's soldier, anymore. Maybe he was God's soldier, now—administering justice to sinful men like Mr. Looney and his son.

And Michael had never sorted out his feelings about his godfather. The man had been like a grandpa to Peter and him, and in these long weeks, in the boy's mind, Mr. Looney had become a sort of boogeyman...and yet the good images of his godfather remained in his memory. Papa had said all men—and that included boys like him—were sinners. Could a sinner seem kind, like Mr. Looney, and really be a monster?

When he heard the footsteps at the hall, he'd been sitting on the edge of the bed, eyes shut tight, praying for his father—at this point, just that his father would return. Never mind any of the rest of it.

And then he opened his eyes, the footsteps very near, surprised to see light coming in the window—dawn—and the key turned in the lock...the boy's hand moved toward the small revolver on the nightstand...and the door opened.

Papa.

The man shut the door behind him and rushed to the boy, dropping to his knees, and Michael threw himself into his father's arms. Had their embrace been any tighter, it would have hurt.

Then Papa held him by the arms and looked into the boy's face. "The man who killed your mother and your brother," he whispered, "is dead."

"Good...Did he suffer?"

"Not enough," Papa admitted. "But the world is rid of him."

"And...Mr. Looney?"

"He's gone, too. It had to be, son. Don't ever ask me of it."

"I…I won't, Papa."

His father sighed, smiled tightly. "…And now we can finally go on with our lives."

"To Perdition, Papa?"

"Yes…but together."

They hugged again. Michael closed his eyes, blinking away tears—and the brightness of the dawn. The way the sun was pouring in the window, you would never know how hard it had rained last night.

EIGHTEEN

My memories of the drive to Perdition may be less than trust-worthy. Everything I remember prior to that day is a winter memory—largely in black and white, like old movie footage, or some people's dreams.

But the drive to Perdition, in my mind's eye, is in full color, dominated by the clear blue of the sky and the green of a world that had had been bleak winter yesterday and was glorious spring today.

Surely these recollections are influenced by emotions and time—the last day of winter is not a dead thing, with the first day of spring an explosion of life.

Yet that is how I remember it. And while I have endeavored in these pages to provide the reader with factual background material, the most valuable commodity I have to offer is my memories—however accurate or inaccurate they may, at this late stage of my life, be.

I am, after all, the only one left. I'm in my winter now, recalling the spring day we drove to Perdition.

They had spoken little, on the first day of the trip to Perdition, but a new warmth seemed to bind them. Smiling like the child he still was, the boy was enjoying the spring day, drinking in the sun, hanging his head out the window, letting the wind skim over him and roar in his ears. That his son had retained a certain innocence after this ordeal was a small miracle—that the little revolver O'Sullivan had given Michael had never been used gave O'Sullivan strength, and hope.

The man did not want to spoil the boy's joyful disposition with what he knew would be disappointing news. He intended to leave Michael with Bob and Sarah—just for a while—until he had started a new life, perhaps in the old country. He wanted to make sure this was really over—that Capone's people indeed weren't after them...and that Frank Nitti could be trusted.

Michael would be disappointed, but O'Sullivan would make him understand that this was only a temporary state of affairs. In six months, a year at the most, he would send for his son; and they would start over—clean, fresh...a second chance.

They stayed at a motel in Missouri, knowing they would be at the farm on the lake by the next afternoon, evening at the latest. And now, gliding down paved roads—the sun reflecting off the green leaves so brightly, the man had to stop and buy sunglasses—they began to talk. For the first time, the father and son seemed to share something beyond blood—they liked each other. They were comrades who had shared hardship and weathered adversity, who had helped each other through a difficult, even tragic time.

But there was nothing serious about their conversation, with only a few passing references to Annie or Peter. Michael asked him what it was like growing up as a boy in Ireland, for example; and O'Sullivan was only too glad to tell him. And somehow his son seemed instinctively to know not to ask about his combat experiences in the Great War. They both had had enough of their own war, in recent days.

Then O'Sullivan—feeling more than an occasional twinge of guilt over how little he really knew about the boy—would question his son about his likes and dislikes. He heard the entire story of how the Lone Ranger was the last of a band of Texas Rangers who had been "betrayed and bushwhacked by the Cavendish gang." He heard about Tom Mix, and Mickey Mouse, and Little Orphan Annie.

And that the boy, it turned out, was really interested in sports—an enthusiasm of Michael's that O'Sullivan had only been vaguely aware of.

"I'm a good shortstop, you know," Michael said.

"I bet you are. Are you fast?"

"You couldn't beat me."

"Ha. Care to wager?"

"Save your money, Pop."

"Did you play at the Villa?"

"No...the diamond's over at Longview Park."

That cast a slight pall—Longview Park was on 20th Street, across from the Looney mansion.

"Well, maybe I'll take you to a big-league ballgame," O'Sullivan said, shifting the subject slightly. "We could see the Cubs play."

"But we're going to Kansas."

"We'll have our car...Anyway, Kansas is still America, last time I looked."

The boy was shaking his head. "They don't have a team."

"They have a minor league team."

"What're they called?"

O'Sullivan shrugged. "I don't remember."

"See what I mean? They don't have a team."

"I'll take you to see the Cardinals in St. Louis."

That excited the boy. "Really? They could take the pennant this year—they're really good!"

Later, Michael asked his father about music. The boy approached this delicately, and finally O'Sullivan figured out why: Michael only knew his papa could play piano because of the duet O'Sullivan and Looney had played at the McGovern wake.

"Did you take lessons?" the boy asked.

"No...I just picked it up. By ear, they call it."

"Really? You could hear the notes?"

O'Sullivan, driving casually, one hand on the wheel, shrugged. "Well, you just sort of hit keys and listen and remember...It takes time. My grandmother had a piano."

Michael's eyes were wide with interest. "I never met her."

"No you didn't. But she died on this side of the ocean."

"The Atlantic."

"That's right, son."

Somehow it bound them further, this sudden realization that they both had lived lives filled with incident and interests; O'Sullivan looked forward to getting to know his son even better. And he could tell, from the boy's questions, that Michael felt the same.

By late afternoon of the second day they were on a rural gravel road, surrounded by startling foliage.

"How can Kansas be so green?" Michael asked, as his father pulled up alongside the road, near a dirt trail through high grass leading to lush woods.

"It's always green, near any lake, this time of year," his father said.

"...Why are we stopping?"

"Because we're here." O'Sullivan considered taking this moment—alone together—to tell his son about his need to leave; but he couldn't bring himself. Anyway, maybe he could stay on at Perdition. Open a shop in the little town. Or find a farm of his own...

"We'll walk the rest of the way," O'Sullivan said, getting out.

Michael closed his door, and was half-standing on the road, half in the ditch. "Why don't you drive right up to the house?"

O'Sullivan was locking the car. "Son, we still need to be careful."

His wheelman thought that over. "Sneaking up to check and see if cars are there, huh?"

"We're not sneaking up—just trying not to be stupid."

O'Sullivan still had his .45 holstered under his left arm, beneath his brown suitcoat.

The boy shrugged, said, "Okay," and soon they were angling down a hillside—no topcoat for the father, no jacket for the son, in this inviting weather—emerging from the woods, where a beautiful if oddly desolate landscape awaited.

Dusk was dispensing shadows to soften the view, touching the stretch of beach along the lake with cool blue; a light breeze blew in off the lightly whitecapped water. The cabin-like farmhouse had no barn next to it; the farm was across the road, out of view. No sign of any car except a battered pick-up truck that belonged to Uncle Bob.

Looking toward the house on the beach, Michael asked, "Is that it?"

"That's it. Ring any bells?"

"Sort of…I'm not sure."

"Here comes somebody that'll jog your memory."

From around the house a big mutt came loping, floppy ears and lolling tongue, a friendly conglomeration of breeds whose tail was wagging at the sign of company. Michael ran to meet the dog, and immediately they began to play, running toward the beach.

O'Sullivan did not join them. He merely stood and watched his son behaving like the boy he was.

"Forgive me, Annie," O'Sullivan said softly, "for the dangerous road I've taken him down."

Then he loped on toward the house, allowing his son to caper on the beach with the hound. Up the porch and through the open screen door O'Sullivan went, following light at the end of a hallway to the kitchen. He called to Sarah and Bob, announcing himself, but received no immediate answer.

And the kitchen was empty. He looked around—the evening dishes had been put away, the room clean and white. Over the sink, sheer curtains billowing, was an open window onto the lake, where he could see Michael on the beach, bending to pet the dog.

"Hey!" someone said, and O'Sullivan whirled, already sensing something, but his hand hadn't reached his holstered weapon when the first shot punched him in the chest.

Three more followed—single claps, echoing a bit in the kitchen, ironic applause—and it took the fourth one to knock him back into the windowed wall. He slid to the floor, leaving a smear of red, fighting to retain his consciousness, hoping to summon strength to go for the gun…

The man in the bowler—only he wasn't wearing one now—stood before him, a nine-millimeter automatic pistol in one hand, his camera in the other. His eyes were unblinking and crazed in a face whose boyish handsomeness had been replaced with a ravaged welter of scars, the aftermath of that shattered crystal lamp in Rance's suite.

"You disappointment me, Mr. O'Sullivan," the photographer said, and he put his gun on the kitchen table.

Good, O'Sullivan thought, only he was fading…could he even move his arm…?

Harlen Maguire—who had stowed the bodies of Bob and Sarah McGinnis in the pantry nearby, just about an hour before—moved in closer, positioning his camera, and began to focus it. He had paid an awful price for this picture—his face would never be right, even with plastic surgery—but this would be the crowning portrait for his gallery of death.

O'Sullivan—lying on the kitchen floor, life oozing out of him—would make an excellent subject, a special study in death, since a succession of photos would record the stages of dying… one photo would have the glimmer of life in those eyes, the next would show the blankness of death.

The photographer—studying the upside down image of the slumped, bleeding man—framed his subject carefully…no rush…

He took his first shot and a bright, hard flash filled the room.

"Try not to blink next time," Maguire advised his subject, who seemed barely conscious now.

A tiny noise behind made Maguire spin toward the doorway...

...And just behind him stood O'Sullivan's son—who had taken Maguire's own gun off the kitchen table, and now pointed it right at him.

Maguire had been in tight situations before—in the Rance suite, among others—but in those instances he'd been armed. Now he stood helpless, and a nausea-like wave of fear such as he'd never known rose up inside him. And Harlen Maguire suddenly understood that his fascination with death did not extend to experiencing his own...

Michael had known there was trouble when that dog ran up to him on the beach, and the boy had seen orange-red-brown dirt or something, streaked and caked on the animal's paws... *blood.*

He'd already been running toward the house when he heard the shots...

...and now the boy stood pointing the pistol, shaking not with fear for himself but for his father—his wounded father, bleeding on the floor, defenseless, barely awake...a fallen soldier. That this could happen to Papa, the boy of course had contemplated; and yet seeing this terrible tableau before him, he wondered how it could be possible...*was this another nightmare?*

Whatever it was, he was in it, and his father was in trouble, and Michael cocked the automatic and the sound was just a click...but it made the man, whose face was all scarred up now, jump.

And Michael almost pulled the trigger.

For once, the man blinked. "Hey!...Easy, son."

"I'm not your son."

"No...you're Michael, aren't you?" The scarred man had his hands up, and he was smiling a sick sort of smile. "This isn't about you, Michael...Your father's gone. This is over."

Michael aimed the gun. "It's not over yet."

The man was really, really afraid. "Don't...don't do this...It's Frank Nitti you want...he hired me...I'll help you get him..."

Michael shifted his gaze to his father, for guidance. *Should I shoot him, Papa?* his eyes asked, but Papa's response, a sort of weave of his head, didn't tell him anything.

"Kid...," the scared, scarred man said. "Please...it's a human life...it's a sin...don't...*please!*"

So many feelings pulsed through the boy—rage, determination, fear, desperation...Then his finger tightened on the trigger.

Two shots rang in the small room—tiny cracks louder than any thunder.

The scarred man looked at Michael, his eyes still pleading; then, like a light had switched off, the eyes were empty, and the man dropped to the floor, a puppet with its strings snipped, landing on top of his camera, making a crunch. A corpse now, the scarred man lay in an awkward, artless sprawl.

Michael, who had not fired, ran to his fallen father, who had. Smoke spiraled out of the snout of the .45 in Papa's hand, making a question-mark curl.

"I could have done it," the boy said, kneeling next to his father. "I could have!"

"But...you didn't," Papa managed, with a trace of a smile.

Michael took his father in his arms and held him, held him close but not tight, not wanting to hurt him, cradling Papa's head against his chest, getting blood all over himself, not caring.

The boy looked around them, dead body on the floor, smell of cordite in the air, his father bleeding. "What should I do, Papa?"

"For..."

"Yes, Papa?"

"Forgive me."

And his father died there, in the boy's arms; yet the boy kept rocking him, for a long time, as if the dead man were a baby he was soothing to sleep.

Out the window, where the wind whispered through, making ghosts of the sheer curtains, the vast, peaceful expanse of blue that was Fall River Lake glistened in the dying sun.

But by the time Michael moved from his late father's side, easing the man gently to the linoleum floor, the moon was bathing the gently rippling lake in ivory. Michael removed his father's coat, bundled it up into a makeshift pillow, and placed it under Papa's head, so he could rest better.

A scratching sound caught Michael's attention—the dog at the front door; and when he let the animal in, it led the boy back into the kitchen, and the pantry, where he found the bodies of his uncle and aunt, on the floor between walls of shelved canned goods. He was surprised to see them, but he didn't look at them close, or touch their bodies—just shut them back in, almost apologetically, as if he'd opened the wrong door and disturbed somebody. The dog positioned itself at the pantry door and whined.

Then Michael took stock of the situation, thinking it through as best he could. Finally, he took the car keys from his father's right-hand trouser pocket, and lifted the gun from Papa's stiffening fingers, and stuck it in his waistband. After kissing his father on the forehead, Michael left the kitchen, not even glancing at the sprawled scarred dead assassin in the center of the floor.

The dog scampered after him, and followed him through the woods to the car. From the back, Michael gathered what he needed, putting the stack of newspapers on the seat behind the steering wheel and affixing the blocks to the pedals. As the boy drove off, he was not thinking about where he was going; nor was he crying. He was worried, deeply worried…

…about his father. Papa had asked Michael's forgiveness, and Michael would gladly have forgiven his father anything, even though the boy didn't feel there was anything that needed forgiving.

But Michael O'Sullivan, Jr.—like his late father—was a good Catholic; and he knew that he couldn't give his father forgiveness...only a priest could do that. If a priest had been there, Papa would have been forgiven, that was certain. Last rites...absolution of his sins. And with no priest present, did that mean his father was in hell?

The boy and the dog slept in the car that night, in a park called Indian Foothills outside Marshall, Kansas; and in the morning Michael remembered the sealed envelope with his name on it, which Papa had put in the glove box, saying, "That's for you...in an emergency."

Seeing his father's handwriting made the boy simultaneously happy and sad, but—along with a fat wad of money and some keys—the sheet inside was not a letter, not even a note, just a list of banks with some numbers...*wait!* There were also instructions; Papa had even drawn a little map for him...

Hammer in hand, nails in his teeth, Bill Baum was working on the new roof for his farmhouse when their visitor came calling. Taking advantage of the generosity of that outlaw father and son, the Baums were rebuilding their farm. But life here remained hard, and Bill was sweating in his overalls, up on his ladder; and so was his wife Virginia, out working in the field.

The sound of the approaching car raised the attention of both Baums, and they turned from their work to watch as the maroon car drew nearer, kicking up dust in its wake. The car pulled up alongside the barn, and the boy got out. A big overeager mutt clambered out of the Ford after him and followed the young man, who—suitcase in hand, bareheaded, neatly dressed in white shirt and suspenders and new trousers—moved across the field toward Sarah.

Bill climbed down his ladder to go join them. Judging by the youngster's somber expression—and the absence of his father—bullets had finally made an orphan of him. Much as the farmer hated the thought of that, he was pleased to have this boy once and for all out of harm's way.

And Bill already knew he would repay the generosity of the lad's father by taking in the son—not just putting a roof over the boy's head; but giving young Michael a decent Christian upbringing, and heading him in the right direction, down life's rocky old road.

When he reached the boy, and tousled his hair, Bill found the boy hugging Sarah, desperately; but Michael O'Sullivan, Jr., held back his tears.

He was older now, and his father's son.

NINETEEN

The story of the soldier who was my father ends here.

Over the decades, I read what was written about Michael O'Sullivan, Sr. (and Michael O'Sullivan, Jr.)—newspaper stories, magazine articles, sections of books, even whole volumes dedicated to our weeks on the road. Some have called Michael O'Sullivan a fiend; others an avenging angel. He was described as a modern Robin Hood; and he was termed a cold-blooded hitman.

In 1960, the Robert Stack TV show "The Untouchables" did an absurdly inaccurate episode about us; and there were three movies, one starring Preston Foster and Jimmy Lydon in the 1940s, another in the mid-'60s with James Coburn and Billy Mumy, and (as I mentioned earlier) a big-budget version with an Oscar-laden cast is in production as I write this.

Since everyone else has had their say about our story, I have finally broken my silence and spoken my piece. For years I rebuffed the advances of editors and would-be coauthors; still, I guess I always knew I'd write the story of the man who was neither fiend nor angel…just my father.

The Baums were Baptists, but—in my young adulthood—I returned to the Catholic church. In recent years, as other, later events of my life have come to light, more questions have arisen. As I've reported, my father's last act was to spare me from killing Harlen Maguire; but I fully expect to be accused of manipulating the facts in this narrative—some will no doubt insist that I indeed did pull that trigger…that, there being no statute of limitations on murder, I have fobbed that deed off upon my father.

Believe what you will. Whatever happened in that kitchen in that house along Fall Rivers Lake, I did walk away with my father's .45 Colt, inheriting the weapon he brought home from the Great War; and I was my father's son, after all, with a family tradition of vengeance. That, however, is my story; and this has been my father's.

Two things may help explain why I eventually chose yet another road for my life. Like my father...like so many of us...I finally came to understand my need for redemption. At the same time, throughout the life I've led since Papa's death, I have been haunted by his dying request for my forgiveness, in absence of a priest.

These are high among the reasons why today I wear a backward collar, and sit on the listening side of the confessional booth. To date, however, I must admit I have not yet heard any sins to compare to those that turned a country priest ghost-white one winter afternoon.

There can be little doubt of what my father exclaimed that rainy night in Rock Island, when he stood against Looney and his army of bodyguards: "Pray that God never puts you on my road!"

If you will allow a preacher his sermon, what Papa failed to understand was that he had chosen his road; so take it from an old outlaw hiding out in priestly garb...God has nothing to do with the bad choices men make of their own free will.

Though I would make one simple request of you, in exchange for this wisdom: pray, would you, for the soul of Michael O'Sullivan?

Both of them.

A TIP OF THE FEDORA

NOTE: This is a slightly revised version of the original acknowledgements essay that appeared with the radically shortened 2002 edition.

As the author of the original graphic novel *Road to Perdition* (1998), I am in the unusual position of basing a novel on another writer's screenplay...based on my own work.

Having written numerous movie tie-in novels—including one for a previous Tom Hanks/DreamWorks production, *Saving Private Ryan* (1998)—I felt a prose version of that three-hundred-page comic-book novel was called for. I feared the original illustrated book would not reach readers who do not regularly partake of the comics medium...which is unfortunate, as that medium is as vital and compelling as motion pictures themselves.

I have done my best to honor David Self's fine and faithful screenplay, and am particularly grateful to him for heightening the Mike O'Sullivan/John Looney father-and-son relationship; at the same time, I've expanded his fundamentally condensed version of my narrative with material culled from the graphic novel, as well as adding new elements designed to bridge those two sources.

Both John and Connor Looney existed, the latter truly nicknamed Crazy Connor, and a loosely factual basis underlies this tale. Much of the background the narrator provides at the start of each chapter is true.

I stumbled across the story of the Looneys in researching *True Detective* (1983), the first of my Nathan Heller novels, one of three books comprising the *Frank Nitti Trilogy*. My research associate on those books, George Hagenauer, offered information and insights during the writing of this work, as well.

The time frame of this novel is consistent with history where Al Capone and Frank Nitti are concerned; however, much of the Looney material is moved up in time from the 1920s (though Looney's organization and the Capone mob were indeed connected). A few other liberties have been taken; the screenplay's use of the Lone Ranger (I had used Tom Mix exclusively in the graphic novel) had a nice resonance for me, and I retained it—though that character did not make its radio debut until January 1933.

My late friend Bj Elsner's *Rock Island: Yesterday, Today and Tomorrow* (1988) was a key reference work for both this novel and the original graphic novel. Elsner also provided further background material and came through like a champ at a difficult time (our mutual friend, author David Collins, died during the writing of this book).

Thanks also to Bill Wundrum of the *Quad City Times*. Bill got me interested in John Looney in the first place, when I approached him while doing Nathan Heller research; for this novel, I drew upon articles of Bill's as well as several of his locally produced books about the Quad Cities (the Tri-Cities, in John Looney's day). Bill and I met, incidentally, at the Lexington Hotel, the night Geraldo opened Al Capone's vault.

Among many gangland reference works consulted were *Capone* (1971), John Kobler; *Capone* (1994), Lawrence Bergreen; *The Legacy of Al Capone* (1975), George Murray; and *Mr. Capone* (1992), Robert J. Schoenberg. Various WPA Guides on the states through which the O'Sullivans travel were also used, as was the fine historical picture book *I Remember Distinctly: A Family Album of the American People in the Years of Peace: 1918 to Pearl Harbor* (1947) by Agnes Rogers and Frederick Lewis Allen. Also,

I used the article "Smashing Rock Island's Reign of Terror" by O. F. Claybaugh in the December 1930 issue of *Master Detective*.

Dean Zanuck and his late father, Richard—producers of the motion picture *Road to Perdition*—went out of their way to see that this novel came "home" to me. Kristy Cox of DreamWorks was generous with photographic materials and updated scripts; it might be of interest that this novel, like most movie "novelizations" (dreaded word), was by necessity written before I had access to the film. Writers of movie tie-in novels almost always are imagining what the film will be, working (like a director) with a screenplay and creating their own version.

I would also like to acknowledge the illustrator of the original graphic novel, Richard Piers Rayner, who so wonderfully brought this story to life; his artistry had much to do with attracting the attention of Hollywood to this material. Thanks, too, to Andrew Helfer, the graphic novel's editor, whose story sense was unerring; without Andy's dedication to this project, and his belief in it, none of this would have happened. Thank you Paul Levitz of DC Comics for publishing the graphic novel, and helping clear the bramble of rights to enable the writing of this prose version. I urge readers who enjoy this novel—and/or the Sam Mendes film version—to seek out our original work.

I would also like to thank my wife Barbara Collins and son Nathan, for their love, inspiration, and support; my friend and agent, Dominick Abel; and Steven Spielberg and Tom Hanks, for liking my story.

ABOUT THE AUTHOR

Max Allan Collins has earned an unprecedented twenty-two Private Eye Writers of America "Shamus" Award nominations, winning for his Nathan Heller novels *True Detective* (1983) and *Stolen Away* (1991), as well as the PWA "Eye" award for Life Achievement (2006). In 2012, his Nathan Heller saga was honored with the PWA "Hammer" award for making a major contribution to the private-eye genre.

His graphic novel *Road to Perdition* (1998) is the basis of the Academy Award-winning Tom Hanks film, followed by two acclaimed prose sequels (also published by Brash Books) and several graphic novels. He has created a number of innovative suspense series, including Mallory, Quarry, Eliot Ness, and the "Disaster" novels. He is completing a number of "Mike Hammer" novels begun by the late Mickey Spillane; his full-cast audio novel *Mike Hammer: The Little Death*, with Stacy Keach, won a 2011 Audie for best original work.

His comics credits include the syndicated strip *Dick Tracy*, his own *Ms. Tree*, and *Batman*.

For five years, he was the sole writer on the novel series based on the popular TV show *CSI: Crime Scene Investigation* (and its spin-offs), writing ten best-selling books, four graphic novels, and four award-winning video games. His tie-in books have appeared on the *USA Today* best-seller list nine times and the *New*

York Times list three times, including *Saving Private Ryan*, *Air Force One*, and *American Gangster*, which won the Best Novel "Scribe" Award in 2008 from the International Association of Media Tie-In Writers.

As an independent filmmaker in the Midwest, Collins has written and directed four features, including the Lifetime movie *Mommy* (1996); and he scripted *The Expert*, a 1995 HBO World Premiere, as well as the film-festival favorite *The Last Lullaby* (2009). His documentary *Caveman: V.T. Hamlin & Alley Oop* (2008) has appeared on PBS and on DVD, and his documentary *Mike Hammer's Mickey Spillane* (1998) appears on the Criterion Collection DVD and Blu-ray of *Kiss Me Deadly*. His innovative Quarry novels are the basis of a current Cinemax TV series, for which he is providing some of the scripts.

His play *Eliot Ness: An Untouchable Life* was nominated for an Edgar Award in 2004 by the Mystery Writers of America; a film version, written and directed by Collins, was released on DVD and appeared on PBS stations in 2009.

Collins lives in Iowa with his wife, writer Barbara Collins; as "Barbara Allan," they have collaborated on nine novels, including the successful "Trash 'n' Treasures" mysteries, with *Antiques Flee Market* (2008) winning the *Romantic Times* Best Humorous Mystery Novel award of 2009.

CPSIA information can be obtained
at www.ICGtesting.com
Printed in the USA
LVOW12s1545131216

517085LV00003B/709/P